This is the story of Eric "Rick" Richards: farm hand,
fighter pilot, gold prospector, businessman.

AF227799

JEFF MULLER

Printed in Australia

Cover by Liz McCracken @lizzacreative

Typeset by Book Burrow www.bookburrow.com.au

First printing: December 2024

Paperback ISBN 978-1-7638229-9-3

eBook ISBN 978-1-7638229-1-7

Distributed by Lightning Source

A catalogue record for this work is available from the National Library of Australia

DEDICATIONS

This book is dedicated to all the young men and women who've gone to war to protect our country.

ACKNOWLEDGEMENTS

Thanks to Judi Mulley, for her tireless editing, proof reading, and encouragement.

AN APOLOGY

My lead character refers to the Japanese as Japs and Nips in the text. No offence meant. From December 7th 1941 to September 2nd 1945, Australia and Japan were at war and both sides vilified the other. Terrible atrocities were committed. That was then. The Japan of today is a wonderful country, and the Japanese are our trusted and much valued allies.

AUTHOR'S NOTE

Kittyhawk is partly a historical novel, partly a fictional autobiography. I have based much of the World War Two part of the book on my father-in-law's RAAF WW2 logbook. Geoff Angus flew the Brewster Buffalo in Malaya with 453 Squadron, and the P-40 Kittyhawk in West Papua and the islands to the north with 86 and 75 Squadrons.

Other parts came from discussions with a number of RAAF servicemen from that era, including Bobby Gibbes, Jack Curtis, Ron Patterson, John Lessels, Gel Cumming, and my father, Ern Muller.

Geoff Angus's logbook provided an accurate template for my fictional character's air force career, right up to his Borpop attack. To my knowledge, no RAAF aircraft ever raided Borpop, as it was left for the RNZAF, USAAF, and USN.

101 Squadron is also fictional.

Borpop exists, and when I ventured there in the year 2000, was exactly as described, including the Japanese aircraft wrecks.

CHAPTER 1

April 2nd, 1945. Over Borpop airfield. New Ireland Province, New Guinea.

'Jesus, Tony, don't…' I plead under my breath when I see our leader bank steeply after pulling up from his strafing and bombing pass. Damn him! The targets we missed the first time are just too tempting for him, and he's now leading us around for a second run over the Jap airfield. Fear momentarily paralyses me. I feel like a giant fist is gripping and squeezing my throat, and I can barely suck in a breath. The first pass was exciting enough, and we've left three parked Nip aircraft burning fiercely, and several craters in their runway. It has also well and truly woken up the defenders. They are pissed off, and now every gun they have is furiously firing at us. I suddenly feel very exposed inside the thin aluminium skin and glasshouse canopy of my Kittyhawk

Before taking off at first light from Nadzab, the large RAAF base on the north coast of the New Guinea mainland, we'd been briefed to make just one pass on the enemy's strip at Borpop, on the island of New Ireland, hoping to catch them by surprise, then to hightail it for home before their defences woke up. We are also operating at the very limit of our range, and burning extra fuel in a second pass could make the difference between us making it home across the Bismarck Sea, or ditching in it.

I'm tail-end Charlie in the flight of four Curtis P-40 Kittyhawks. As such, I have no choice but to follow the three others around in the racetrack pattern.

'Shit.' A black puff of smoke blossoms just off my nose. I can't hear the explosion over the roar of my engine, but I know that the innocent looking puff is full of deadly shrapnel, red hot steel shards that could slice through my aeroplane as if it were made of butter. Any one of those shards could take off my arm, leg, or head. Seconds later, the sky seems to be full of black puffs from the defending 127mm cannons. Hyphenated streaks of tracer from smaller guns, probably 13mm machine guns, look to be rising slowly at first, then they zip past. The gap between each tracer round is filled with nine invisible rounds. One such stream wavers then begins to home in on my tiny cockpit. It passes so closely that I involuntarily duck my head. Against the odds, none of us have taken a hit. Not yet anyway.

I can see Tony and his numbers two and three swoop down in turn to make their second passes. I begin my roll in as they wreak further devastation upon the rows of enemy aircraft lined up along the eastern side of the strip. Two fueled-up G4M "Betty" bombers and a Ki-61 "Tony" fighter become instant fireballs, and another Ki-61 simply collapses into a shredded pile of aluminium.

My stomach-knotting fear gives way to exhilaration as I concentrate on lining up for my second attack run. The wind howling around the cockpit rises to a shriek, discernible even above the roar of the big engine in front of me, and the controls stiffen as my speed builds up in the dive: I glance at the ASI and see the needle going way past 400 mph, so I ease the throttle back a touch. Some potential targets are now obscured by clouds of black smoke rising from burning aircraft, and white smoke from the defending guns that wafts across the strip like fog, but I can pick out a G4M "Betty" bomber that was taxiing for take-off when we began our initial attack. I can see its crew scrambling out and running from it, leaving the props turning. It is growing rapidly in my gunsight, and I make a tiny adjustment with stick and rudder to aim at the wing centre section. The stick is trembling from the high airspeed, and when I squeeze the trigger under my forefinger, the whole aircraft shudders as its six .50 calibre machine guns spit a deadly stream of heavy lead into the big enemy twin. Within seconds it explodes like an immense firework display. It must have been heavily loaded for a bombing mission. Pieces of burning metal trailing white smoke arc high into the early morning sky, many directly into my path. They are followed by a roiling red ball.

I haul on the stick to avoid it, and ram the throttle forward. I must escape the maelstrom we've created. For a moment it sounds like I am flying through hail, and I feel a blast of heat. One thud resounds through the entire airframe. Then I am past, and the big, reliable Alison twelve-cylinder engine continues to roar without missing a beat.

Now climbing okay and breathing again, and I'm looking for the others. The euphoria of having survived the risky mission lasts all of five seconds. A glance in the small mirror mounted inside my armoured windscreen shows that my P-40 is leaving behind a dense white stream of oil or glycol coolant, or both. The P-40 has a big chin radiator that makes the aircraft vulnerable to even small arms fire in the low-level attack role, and a holed oil or coolant radiator could see a perfectly good engine overheat and seize very quickly.

A falling needle on the oil pressure gauge, and a rising needle on the engine temperature gauge confirm my worst fears.

Jesus, I'm done. I am about to go down into a hornet's nest, one that I have been partially responsible for poking. We all know what the Japs do to captured pilots. They might think execution by beheading was an honour, but it didn't appeal to me. Dread, bordering on panic, swamps me for an instant.

Then the effects of two years of intensive training kick in, and, as the engine begins to wind down and my airspeed decays, I shrug off the paralysing fear that momentarily threatened to overcome me. The words of my instructors are imbedded in my memory. '*Fly the aeroplane, trim for best glide speed, cinch-up your harness, slide the canopy open, look for a place to crash-land.*'

Can I make the beach? Unlikely, as the engine will seize at any moment, and I'm too far inland. Is that a clearing ahead? Yes. It's small. Just a grassy patch in the forest, scattered trees within it. Please please please, Mister Alison, I can hear you growling in pain because your coolant and oil are running out, but please keep running for a few more seconds.

I'm down to less than fifty feet above the tree tops. The large three-bladed prop jerks to a halt and the P-40 is now no more than a big and heavy glider. The comforting bellow of the V-12 has gone, and is replaced by the decreasing roar of wind past the open canopy. I push the pitch knob into the feathering position and I ease the stick back as we begin brushing the dark green treetops. I push the selector for full flap, then curse myself when I realise that the flaps don't move because I have lost hydraulic pressure. I quickly pump the emergency hydraulic pump handle.

Just above the stall, my Kittyhawk brushes the tops of the trees bordering the clearing. In seconds, tall kunai grass whips the underside of wings and fuselage, and softens the thud as we hit the ground. The grass is so high I can see nothing until a lone but very solid-looking tree stump materialises out of the blur directly ahead. I stamp on the rudder pedal but it has no effect. We hit the stump with the right wing, just outboard of the propellor arc, still doing about 45mph.

My leather helmet does little to protect me when my forehead smacks the gunsight. I'm conscious long enough to register that we've come to a very sudden stop, and that I should evacuate the aircraft quickly in case of fire. But my arms are heavy, and it is just too much effort to unbuckle my harness. Then my vision blurs, and the last image I recall is a bright white light narrowing into a pinpoint, then disappearing altogether.

CHAPTER 2

Pre WW2, a farm near Molong, Central Tablelands, NSW.

My first clear childhood memories revolved around my father, and my dog. My mother had died when I was a toddler, and I had only the fuzziest memory of her as a warm and protective aura that one day was not there anymore. For a long time, I used to look at Dad's old photos of her and try to conjure up something more out of the flat black and white images, but it never worked. Dad said I looked a lot like her. Whilst he was very tall and solidly built, I'm just above average height, and leaner. Always have been. Where he was dark haired and had a long face, with strong nose and chin, I'm brown haired and have softer features. Where he stood out in a crowd, I melted in.

My dog Spinner, a kelpie-German shepherd cross, came into this world in November 1928, when I was about to turn four years old. For some time Dad, Spinner, and our farm, made up my entire world.

It was only by chance that Spinner had become part of it.

Dad ran about 2500 sheep and grew some crops on our 2,000 acres. That was more than enough for any one man to handle, but the farm was not quite big enough to afford permanent employees. Until I was old enough to contribute, his only regular help came from his four kelpie dogs. The kelpie is a medium sized dog, short haired, long tailed, lean and athletic, that is born to work sheep and cattle. Herding is so deep in the kelpie genes that when not herding livestock, they'll try to round up anything that moves. Chickens, ducks, or even any kids that live on their farm are all subject to the working dog's attention.

Kelpies are smart, and loyal. They'll work all day, asking nothing more than an occasional pat, a good meal, and a rough bed at the end of a long day. As much as Dad loved our kelpies, they weren't pets. They were treated with affection, and lived in better conditions than any other farm dogs I ever saw, having spacious pens and warm kennels, and were always well fed, but they were there to work, and never came into the house.

A good kelpie can do the work of several men when rounding up and herding, and Dad's kelpies were said to be the best in the district. His reputation as a breeder and trainer was such that when his top bitch had pups, they were highly sought after. It was a sideline that added a very handy boost to the farm's annual income.

Dad drove around the paddocks in his old Ford utility, a T-model that had started life as a 4-door open tourer, but had had the rear half of the body cut off and replaced with a wood-panelled tray. The dogs all loved the ute, and would leap onto the back in great excitement. If Dad had to go into town for supplies, there would be space for just one dog behind the makeshift cabin, tethered with a short lead to prevent it falling off onto the road.

One day in September 1928, Dad and I did make such a journey, and he chose the bitch, Sally, to come for the ride. It wasn't a good choice for that particular day, as it turned out. He parked the Ford in front of our regular grocer, leaving Sally in charge of the ute.

When we returned an hour later, we found Sally and Gus, the grocer's old male German shepherd, in amorous embrace. Dad hadn't realized that Sally was just coming into season, but the local street-wise dog had been quick to spot an opportunity. Not as agile as the smaller and younger kelpie, Gus still found the height of the tray of a T-model was no obstacle to such a prize.

I'd never seen Dad so flummoxed, nor so angry. In fact, I'd never before seen him flummoxed or angry at all. There we were, in the middle of the busy street, with Dad trying to separate the canine pair, all three of them in a strange dance on the tiny tray of the ute. It got even worse when Sally's leash got wrapped around Dad's ankles, causing him to topple and land on top of the entwined dogs.

The numerous onlookers thought this was marvelous entertainment, until someone took pity on him and produced a bucket of cold water, which, aimed at Gus, did the trick, while unfortunately drenching Dad as well.

Although at the time I couldn't understand why, on the way home I could tell Dad was upset and worried. He was unusually silent all the way. Much later I realized that a successful mating meant that Sally would produce a litter of worthless mongrels, thus denying Dad of the bonus income that he relied on so much each year.

Just over two months later Dad's worst fears were confirmed. Instead of a half-dozen tiny black and tan beauties, Sally gave birth to just one big blue-grey pup.

Dad was a kind-hearted and well-meaning man, so he let Sally enjoy her new pup for several months. However, he always had the intention of offering the pup free to anyone wanting a pet. It was the middle of the great depression, and money was too tight to waste on a useless dog. That spring was very dry, and the summer hot. The creek all-but dried up, and Dad worked 16 hours a day putting out feed for the sheep, watching for flyblown animals, keeping the windmills working and the troughs clean. He also had to be both father and mother to me. How he did it I'll never know. One job that got put aside was the disposal of Sally's pup.

Meanwhile, the pup had grown and changed colour. His soft, blue-grey coat slowly changed to black, except for his head, where tan patches made him look just like an overgrown and muscular kelpie. Like any kid, I was fascinated with puppies, lambs, or any of the young wild animals we came across on the farm, and I'd played with the pup since he was about six weeks old. I had become quite attached to him, and he loved playing ball with me.

✱✱✱

When the un-named pup was about seven or eight months old, Dad decided, just for the hell of it, to try him as a trainee sheep dog. It was a hopeless task. The pup ran enthusiastically all day, easily keeping up with the adult kelpies, but had no clue on what he was meant to do. Just as the four working dogs would have the mob all bunched up and moving steadily in the right direction, he'd just as likely run through the middle of the flock, or in its path, panicking the sheep and causing them to flee in all directions.

It was soon obvious that the pup had not inherited one iota of the kelpie herding DNA. He had another problem too. While kelpies are hardy dogs that work all day running through burrs and thorns, this pup had sensitive feet. He'd go from full speed to a stop, and stand still with a paw raised in the air. Then he'd refuse to move an inch until Dad or I could brush off the offending burr from his pad, or pull the grass seed. Dad gave up trying to train him.

One night he sat me on his lap, and explained the problem. 'Ricky, that pup can find more prickles in a lucerne paddock than a dingo would find in a desert full of spinifex. He's useless!'

'What's spinifex, Dad?'

'It's a grass that grows in the centre of Australia. Every tussock is just a mass of spines, like a bloody hedgehog! You know, I think we should name that pup Spinifex.'

'That's a great name, Dad. I'll call him and see if he likes it.'

'Not now, Ricky. I'm sorry son, I know you have grown fond of the pup, but I can't afford to feed useless dogs. New name or not, he has to go.' That was awful news for me, as apart from Dad and weekly visits to friends at a neighbouring farm, Spinifex was my only regular companion. However, young as I was, I knew the harsh realities of farm life in the 1920's, and I could not bring myself to pressure Dad into changing his mind.

✳✳✳

Until I went to school when I was six, I was with Dad most of the day. However, there were tasks he had to do where he just couldn't watch me at the same time. One such task was the periodic slaughter of a sheep for the larder. That was something he did not want me to see until I was much older. He'd therefore carefully fenced off with chicken wire a grassy area in our lovely backyard, and made a sand pit for me to play in, so that he could leave me for an hour or so in safety. It was shaded by a tall and spreading peppercorn tree, and I could play happily with my toy tractor and truck.

On the very next day after accepting that Spinifex was to go, I asked if I could play with the pup in my little enclosure for the last time. Dad had lots to do, so he was happy for me to do this, and he headed off towards our machinery shed. Half an hour after leaving the pair of us, Dad heard the pup barking and yelping.

'That's unusual,' he thought to himself, 'I've never heard that pup bark before. The two of them must be having fun.' It was minutes later that Dad realized that the yelping had become quite frantic. With sudden unease, he decided to investigate. Dropping tools, he ran towards home. Rounding the corner of the machinery shed, Dad saw me backing into a corner of my wire pen. A few yards in front of me was the coiled, dull brown body of a very large eastern brown snake, one of the deadliest snakes in the world. In the days before antivenom was developed, a bite from this snake was a likely death sentence for an adult, and almost certainly for a child. Spinifex pranced back and forth in a defensive line between me and the reptile, making mock attacks on it before leaping back from each attempted strike.

Dad froze for a moment, then raced back to the shed, grabbed a long-handled shovel, and ran to the pen. He leapt the fence, and with one blow crushed the serpent's head. He dropped the shovel and swooped me up. I began bawling, and Spinifex, emboldened, rushed in and grabbed the still writhing reptile, shaking it furiously. Dad held me tightly to his chest with one strong arm, and grabbed Spinifex's collar with the other, pulling him away from the snake.

When I stopped sobbing long enough to speak, I said 'Dad, you always said that if I came across a snake, just leave it alone. You said that most likely it would be more scared of me, and it would go away. This one wanted to BITE me!'

'Ricky, I'm so sorry. It's getting close to winter, and I think that big snake was looking for a hole to bed down in. You were just in his way, but you're all right now. Spinifex was looking after you.' In a shaking voice, he hoarsely called 'Good boy Spinner.' I think I even saw a tear in his eye.

He carried me the few yards to our back step, and opened the screen door. Spinifex followed, sat down, and looked expectantly up at us, a grin on his face, his tongue lolling. Dad, hesitated before letting the door swing shut behind him. Then, to my amazement, he pushed it wide open and said 'come in, Spinifex. I guess you deserve a permanent home right here after all.'

From that day Spinner, as his named morphed into, slept every night in a corner of my bedroom, in a special woven-cane basket, with a soft mattress and, in winter, a warm blanket. He grew into a handsome dog. He was as smart as a regular kelpie, (apart from his inability to herd), and looked like one, but was bigger. Whereas some kelpies are nervous of strangers, he had a confident swagger, and all our friends were his friends too. He loved soft toys and rubber balls, and was the best soccer goalie outside the big league. At every opportunity he would present his ball, to be kicked towards his imaginary goal posts. Any ball outside those goal posts would be ignored, and left for someone else to fetch. Within the arc of the imaginary goal posts, he was deadly. No matter how hard the ball was kicked, from close in or from afar, he could pluck the ball out of the air faster than a human eye could follow.

✶✶✶

We had great neighbours on both sides. On our western boundary we had the McMillans, an older couple who had been in the district all their lives. Dad often dropped by their old house to have a chat to Fred, or give him a hand with heavier jobs. I was always made welcome there. On most Sundays, Dad and I called into the Hetheringtons, our neighbours on the eastern side. Our houses were just one mile apart. They managed their farm for a wealthy absentee land owner, and had been in the district about 10 years. Dad and Mr H would sit on the veranda, discussing in easy companionship the weather, the state of the crops, and the state of the world in general. It was the only time during daylight hours that Dad truly relaxed. Mrs H would fuss about in the kitchen, always producing something tasty for us all.

Max, their son, was the same age as me, and we quickly became best friends, a relationship that was to last our lifetimes. As we got older, we would roam in ever increasing circles. The first time we took Spinner with us, he immediately made himself known to the Hetheringtons, including their farm dogs. His easy and confident manner overcame the canine territorial instincts of the resident farm dogs, and so he was always welcome. Max, Spinner and me became a team in our expanding forays across the three farms.

✳✳✳

I was about to turn six when, as we sat in our large kitchen eating dinner one night, Dad announced that it was time for me to go school. I was horrified. As far as I was concerned there was plenty on the farm to keep me occupied forever.

'But Dad, I don't need to go to school. I can learn everything I need to know right here. You teach me now anyway.'

'Son, there is a big world out there, and one day you'll regret it if you are not equipped to go out into it. School is going to teach you much more than I can, and when you've finished high school, you might even decide to go to university.'

'But Dad, how are you going to manage without my help every day?'

He chuckled. 'Well, I'll just have to. You can still help me after school, and on weekends. And there are term and annual holidays.'

'ANNUAL holidays? You mean this schooling is going to take more than a year?' I think I may have started sobbing at that point. I can remember Spinner nuzzling up to me, as he hated seeing anyone upset. Only then it occurred to me that he and I were to be separated for whole days every week. That made me even sadder.

***

For the first few weeks of school, Dad walked me to the farm gate every morning, and of course Spinner came too. From there, Mrs Hetherington would pick me up in her battered Oldsmobile tourer, to take Max and myself to school in Molong. She'd go back later to pick us up, and Dad and Spinner would be waiting at our gate.

After a few weeks of that routine, Dad asked if I would mind if he didn't walk with me each day, as time to plough for our cereal crops was approaching, and he needed "all the daylight God will give me." That was okay with me. I knew Spinner would be with me on the morning walk to the gate. What surprised me was that he was also always there when I returned in the afternoon. Dad said that no matter what was happening on the farm, and no matter what the weather, come that time of day, Spinner quietly trotted off down the drive, to wait for Mrs H's car to return.

My mate Max took after his father, being fair-haired and solidly built, with broad features, big hands, blue eyes and a permanent cheerful grin. In contrast, his mother was slender, pretty, olive-skinned and dark-haired. She had long fingers that seemed inappropriate for her passion for baking bread, scones, and biscuits. At school, Max was smarter than me, grasping arithmetic with ease, and having no difficulty remembering historical dates. He was also better at ball games, though I was physically more powerful. Outside the classroom, however, he was a follower, not a leader. Somehow, we recognised each other's strengths and weaknesses, and that made our friendship all the stronger.

By the time I was eight we both had pushbikes. To get together we could walk along the creek in a more-or- less straight line, or cycle the slightly longer route on the road. Spinner would be ahead, or alongside, all the way. I began visiting their house more frequently, and Mrs H would always tell me that I needed fattening up, (Max was a bit fat, in my opinion), and produce some of her hot out-of-the-oven scones and cakes for the two of us.

Then Mrs H had a baby, a girl. It wasn't too much of a bother at first, except that Mrs H was often too busy to bake, and sometimes we had to make do with biscuits from a tin. One day, sitting at the table in the Hetherington's bright and airy kitchen, Mrs H suddenly thrust the baby in its shawl at me, saying 'Here Ricky, have a hold while I get you some fresh-squeezed orange juice.' I was dumbstruck. I tried to back off but the bundle was shoved into my hands. It smelled! Not a bad smell, I suppose, but not something I wanted to get involved with. From that day on I avoided getting close to that bundle, even at the expense of missing out on biscuits and orange juice.

One morning I was enticed back into Mrs H's kitchen, and I sat at the table. Then the baby appeared, actually walking! Well, waddling, stumbling, occasionally plopping on its bottom onto the polished lino, but mobile. It came straight at me, and though I cringed away, it grasped my knee, and gave me a big wet smile. Mrs H and Max both laughed. 'She obviously likes you, Ricky. Normally she is reticent with people outside the family.'

It got worse as the years went by. Even when we were old enough to go to high school, Max's scrawny little sister tried to tag along when we went exploring. Thankfully, by then Max and I could ride our bikes from home to where our road met the main highway, and that's where we joined the new bus service to school. We would join the older kids near the back, while the little kids like Max's sister stayed up front.

On the bus one day some older boys began teasing her about the red tinge in her long dark hair. She kept smiling until the barbs got more personal. One bully, William McLaren, was in the year ahead of Max and me.

'Hey everybody,' he yelled. 'We've got a red Indian wog in the bus. I can smell her from back here.' He made a whoop, and pantomimed an Indian war dance in the isle. His thuggish mates all laughed. Max and I looked at each other. We both thought that it had gone too far. As McLaren sat, I stood up in the swaying bus and advanced on the loud mouth, who was now sitting in the centre of the rearmost full-width seat, just two rows behind. Max followed me.

'That's not very nice, McLaren.' I said. 'Quit hassling Max's sister.'

He stood and laughed in my face. Although only one year older, he was a good bit heavier than me, and built like a barn. A solid barn at that. His mates, sitting each side of him, giggled.

'How are you going to make me, squirt?' He asked. 'You and what army?' He then leaned forward and shoved my chest with his open hand. I stumbled, and would have fallen on my backside if Max hadn't been there to prop me up. I saw red. I made the first aggressive move of my life. I regained my feet, then my left fist shot out into his stomach. My right fist, also aimed at McLaren's stomach, followed a millisecond behind. I didn't allow for his reaction to the first punch. Nobody had ever stood up to him before, so he was caught totally off-guard. As my left fist drove into his solar plexus, both his back and knees folded. My right fist caught him as he went down, square on his right eyebrow.

With a whoosh of escaping breath, he collapsed back into his seat. His hands shot to cover his face. Not another word was spoken. There was no more giggling from his wide-eyed sycophants. I resumed my seat, half expecting an onslaught from the rear, but it never came.

In fact, nothing was ever said again about the incident. There was no more bullying of younger kids on the bus. I don't know how he explained the black shiner he sported for many weeks thereafter to his father, the biggest landowner in the district, or to teachers.

∗∗∗

The road that passed our farm gate only served half a dozen properties. Ours was the third along, then there was Max's. The road finished at the last farm, because the land beyond was hilly and covered with natural bush. These farms all lay in the valley that ran east-west. There were forest-covered hills both sides, but it wasn't a steep-sided valley. The undulating cleared slopes were dotted with big gum trees left to provide shade for stock, and were gentle enough to walk up without getting too puffed out until you reached the rocky ridges that topped each. Max and I explored every inch of the three farms over the years: we knew where the grey kangaroos hung out during the day, and where the wombats' burrows were. We had our secret cave hide-out on one hill, where a few giant granite boulders had been exposed by weathering. By climbing on top of the biggest boulder, we could see almost all of our two farms.

Both our houses had been built on flat land near the creek that ran through the valley. Long ago the creek must have been quite a river to have created such a wide alluvial flat of good farming loam alongside it. The creek was now just a gentle flow over smooth pebbles, and it filled only after very heavy rain. Sometimes in summer the flow almost stopped, but there was always a trickle feeding a few pools that remained clear and fresh enough for us to swim in. One pool had a tiny waterfall, just a couple of feet high, but enough to make the gin-clear water bubble like lemonade.

To protect the purity of the mountain water, Dad had fenced the creek off from stock access. He used the flat land alongside mainly for growing lucerne, which he'd bale for hay. Only occasionally would he allow sheep in to graze along the creek, and then only to mow down excess grass growth. That meant the strip along the creek remained unspoiled, and bush grew for about thirty or forty yards each side. This natural belt was a haven for all sorts of birds and reptiles.

The pools were each probably a hundred yards long. They were home to resident platypuses, ducks, tortoises, and the occasional red-bellied black snake. The red-bellies weren't deadly like the brown snakes, but we still avoided them, and they us. I particularly loved watching the platypuses. They are shy creatures, but they got used to us, and we got to recognise them individually. They have sleek brown fur, white eyebrows, a black duck's bill, webbed feet, and powerful claws. They lay eggs in long burrows with underwater entrances that they dig in the river banks, and they suckle their young. They swim along the muddy bottoms of the pools, using their bills as digging implements for whatever it is they eat.

Very few people ever saw Platypus, but we knew how to find them. We'd sit still and quiet on a bank above one of the pools during the early morning, or late in the afternoon. The first sign one was up and about would be a tell-tail trail of bubbles, then a small bow-wave, then a head would appear. After a few seconds it would dive again, showing the curve of its back as it went.

Sometimes we'd try to show our platys to other people, but no matter how quiet we were, they'd stay out of sight. Uncooperative little buggers!

The strip along the creek was also a jungle for Max and me, where we stalked imaginary lions and fought imaginary foes. We built a cubby house from some scrap timber in a small clearing, and Dad gave us an old sheet of corrugated iron for a roof. We even had a couple of wobbly old chairs and a tiny table. It was our secret headquarters for several years. One day it would be a medieval castle, on another a soldiers' fort. A few times we slept overnight in it, with Dad's permission of course. We called it "the secret fortress."

Dad was what we'd later call, "a bit of a greeny." He was before his time, in that he believed that "all the native animals and birds have a right to make a living." Even when wombats pushed like mini bulldozers through the fences separating us from the bush on our hillside boundaries, and were followed by grey kangaroos that enlarged the holes, he took it stoically. He made sure that the native animals always had access to water.

So, most mornings we awoke to the sound of currawongs, rosellas, galahs, cockatoos, corellas, whip-birds, magpies, kookaburras, and smaller birds, and to the sight of kangaroos taking a last nibble of our pasture or cereal crop before retreating to the tree-covered ridge tops for the day.

Dad was a nature lover, a good stockman and farmer, and a great dog handler and trainer. What he wasn't so good at was understanding machinery. When we had a good year, some money would be left over to update or renew our farm equipment, but he was frequently in trouble figuring out how to use new things, or how to fix inevitable breakdowns on older stuff. By the time I was ten years old, we had acquired an old Fordson tractor, an equally old Sunshine harvester, a hay baler, a large four-wheel trailer, and a small (two-stand) shearing shed. The Ford T-model ute had been relegated to farm use only, and he now luxuriated in a four-year-old Oldsmobile 30E sedan. It had a six-cylinder engine, mechanical brakes on all wheels, a roof, and windows you could wind closed. Truly a wonderful machine!

Dad grew up at a time when farms had been run with horses, not vehicles, and he seemed to regard the new contraptions as some sort of man-made but wondrous life-form, and so steadfastly evaded any of my attempts to explain to him how things actually worked. More than once I tried.

'Dad, most things break down only if you don't maintain them properly, or if they are just plain worn out. When they are getting that way, they usually give some sort of warning. So, we've just got to make sure we oil and grease things, keep them clean, and if a part wears out, replace it.'

Dad believed that given the opportunity, sick mechanical devices could heal themselves just like people and animals do. When the battery in the Oldsmobile was so flat that we'd have to push-start the car, Dad would expect that with a few days break it would regain its full power. When the rubberised canvas discs that served as universal joints on driveshafts of several machines (including the Oldsmobile) began to shudder, Dad would give the machine a rest, fully expecting the cracked and hardened discs to be healed, pliant and smooth-running for the next time it was needed. When bearings or brake shoes wore out and were replaced by new parts, Dad wouldn't hear of disposing of the old parts: he'd carefully store them away. No matter how often he was ultimately disappointed, he retained his faith in the powers of the "healing shed".

I quickly learned to operate all our equipment. That is, except for the Olds. I wasn't allowed to drive on the road, so the new car was out of bounds until I was in my early teens. I knew every nut and bolt of the old Ford T-model, and it wasn't long before the ancient ute replaced my pushbike. That suited

Spinner, as for him there was nothing better that riding on the tray, head in the breeze, tongue lolling, eyes as sharp as tacks. I don't think any animal enjoyed life more than did Spinner.

I loved working on any sort of machine, far more than I enjoyed regular farm work. After school, and on weekends, I'd be roaming the bush with Max, or up to my armpits in greasy farm machinery. It just naturally worked out that I kept all the machines repaired and maintained, freeing Dad for what he did best. Dad told his friends that I "had a way with machines," likening my understanding of their workings to some sort of spiritual connection with them.

CHAPTER 3

Herman and the mutt.

My reputation for having expertise with machinery was reinforced in an unexpected way. Dad had told me that he had one living relative, a distant cousin named Herman. Herman was, I was told, an educated and wealthy man who lived in the city. One day, out of the blue, Herman turned up at our door. That wasn't the only surprise. Herman's threadbare clothing and worn heels clearly showed that he had fallen on hard times.

Herman was a big man, easily six foot and six inches, and no lightweight in build. He had big features too: bulbous nose, a wide mouth, prominent ears, and dark hair overdue for a trim. He was amiable, and he enjoyed talking. He spoke often about his wide experience and distant travels. His stories were fascinating to begin with, but after the third or fourth telling, sometimes varying in small but critical detail, they became a little less credible.

Herman was a big eater, and a big drinker. Dad never touched wine or spirits, but after a particularly hot day in the sun, would savour a glass or two of beer. Herman would match that every night, hot or cold, and then some. Dad had to give up his simple pleasure, because to ensure there was a bottle of beer available when he wanted one, he'd have to buy a dozen for every one left for him to drink.

In the six months he lived with us, Herman never once contributed to the grocery bill, nor anything else, which put Dad under some financial pressure. Dad took me aside a few days into Herman's stay, and confided that at least Herman could help out with work on the farm. "Don't worry, he'll pay his way," he said, somewhat hopefully.

Not only did Herman share our table, accompanying him was a small and obnoxious silky terrier. Its name was Roland. Herman brought Roland into the house as if nothing else could be expected. I never understood why Herman was so besotted with the mutt, as it showed no affection to anyone, Herman included. It trotted around the house as if it owned it. Dad was annoyed, but did his best to hide it. Spinner was flummoxed, never before having seen a dog smaller than a kelpie. I think he would have considered it vermin, but for stern warnings that the guest was to be treated as such. Roland quickly recognised his immunity, and sensed the opportunity to rule over the much larger dog. He assumed right-of-way whenever the two crossed paths, and Spinner didn't argue.

It was near the end of school summer holidays when Herman arrived, and we were in the middle of a fencing job. This was hard work at the best of times. Posts had to be cut and dressed, holes had to be dug, and the posts hammered in. Wire had to be run out and stretched. In the 1930s, there were few mechanical aids for this kind of work. After a couple of days convalescing from his arduous journey from Sydney to Molong, Herman was expected to join us. Dad got him out of bed before first light, and he grumbled as we ate breakfast. He became amused when he saw Dad and me prepare our drink bottles for the day. We would take cool water from the Coolgardie safe and pour it into gallon jugs that were wrapped in hessian. During the day, a periodic splash of water on the hessian would help keep the contents cool by evaporation. Dad offered Herman a spare bottle.

'Gee, you fellows must be soft. I can go all day without a drink, no matter how hot it gets.'

Well, January in Molong does get hot. It must have been close to a century on the old scale by mid-morning break. Herman was red-faced and looked about ready to collapse. He had already drunk all of Dad's water bottle; and was eying mine.

'Herman,' Dad said, taking pity on him, 'why don't you go back to the house and get your own water bottle. It is rather hot today.' Herman complied with alacrity, taking the ute, and we didn't see him until we had to walk home as the sun was going down.

The next morning, we were to continue with fencing. Herman cleared his throat, and announced his intentions as if he ran the farm.

'I noticed a bit of a noise in that old ute of yours yesterday. As you know, I'm a bit of a whizz with machinery, so I think I'll work in the shed today. I'll find that errant noise, and I'll give the poor old thing a proper once-over.'

I had not detected any unusual noise in the Ford, and I bristled at the suggestion that our equipment was somehow lacking in maintenance, but Dad frowned as I began to object.

Dad and I took the "new" sedan out that day, the first time it had been used in the paddocks. At the end of the day, we found Herman lounging on the back porch, beer in hand. Before Dad had a chance to say a word, Herman began.

'I flushed the radiator of the old ute, and the noise in the water pump has gone away. I also did a thorough check over the whole thing, and gave it some overdue oil and grease.'

'Did you put some oil in the radiator water?' I asked.

'I most certainly did not. Oil belongs in the engine, not in the radiator,' Herman replied.

'Not engine oil, just a bit of soluble oil. Cutting oil is what I use. If you don't, the water pump will seize within a few months'

'Rubbish, never heard of such a thing,' Herman huffed. Even Dad knew I was right. Later, I quietly added the required oil.

A few days later we had some very heavy rain overnight, and as Dad and I had urgent sheep work to do, he asked Herman if he'd take the Fordson tractor and check the stock in the far paddock. Off Herman went, and returned two hours later on foot.

'That blasted tractor of yours got bogged. I went down near the creek, and coming back up the slope the wheels just kept spinning until they dug a hole. I've had to leave it there and walk a bloody mile to get here.'

'Did you try the diff lock?' Dad asked.

'What's a diff lock?' said Herman. Dad gave me a look of exasperation.

'Don't worry Dad, I'll go and get it out.' I said.

After that, Dad gave up any idea of getting Herman to contribute to farm work. He just became another mouth to feed. Well, two actually, if you include Roland.

✳✳✳

The Herman problem looked like it might be permanent, as he seemed to be very settled in his adopted life of leisure. He showed no sign of embarrassment in being a drain on our limited resources, and Dad became increasingly agitated. As it eventuated, Herman and Roland stayed only until mid-winter. It was Spinner who solved the problem for us.

By late April the nights were getting cold, and we began

lighting a fire in the living room every night. Dad and I each had our comfy chairs in an arc around it. Spinner loved the fire too, and would lay on the carpet between us and the fire, stretch his legs out, exposing his hairless belly to the glow. It was a precious and peaceful end to each long day.

On the first cold night, Herman added his chair, and we sat comfortably around the glowing fire. Then came Roland. He strutted to where Spinner lay, sound asleep. He bared his tiny teeth, then pounced on Spinner's neck. Dad, Herman, and I were too shocked to respond quickly. With a yelp of pain Spinner bolted upright, with Roland still gripping him below the ear. Spinner whirled quickly, shaking the little brute off, and snarled as he prepared to pounce. Then he must have remembered that he wasn't allowed to react to the guest's provocation, and he slowly backed off.

For the next month it was the same every night. Ugly Roland, nothing more than an overgrown and hairy rat, his mean little eyes almost hidden under a fringe of silvery hair, would strut to the prime spot in front of the fire. Any attempt by Spinner to come within the warm zone provoked a low growl. Dad and I seethed, but Dad avoided any sort of confrontation with either Herman or his abominable pet.

It was the first night in June, and the night was clear, still, and bitterly cold. We were all sleepy, except for Roland who must have been eyeing Spinner as he edged towards the warmth from the back of the room. Suddenly the furball leapt at Spinner, who reacted as quickly as he did when we played soccer. There was an almighty flurry of teeth, legs, and tails, a few spots of blood too, before Spinner had Roland pinned to the floor, jaws around his throat. The little dog squealed like a child, then went still, the whites of his eyes showing his terror. Spinner abruptly let the little tyrant go, and casually strolled to his old place in front of the fire, plopped down and instantly went to sleep.

Herman was frantic, but when he realised that no significant injury had been sustained, he put Roland down. Whimpering, the mutt retreated to the far corner of the living room to lick his imagined wounds. Dad whispered "Well done, Spinner". Spinner didn't move a muscle except for his tail, which flopped against the carpet twice. I think that was responding with "my pleasure."

On the two subsequent nights the same pattern was repeated. Spinner basked in the warmth, totally relaxed, while Roland shivered in the furthest corner. On the third day after the fight, we came home from twelve hours of hard work to find that Herman and Roland had gone, never to be seen again. That night Dad gave Spinner an extra helping of dinner, and said quietly, "Good boy, Spinner."

✳✳✳

A new shadow crept over our lives with the retirement of our neighbours on the western boundary of our farm. Fred and Beryl McMillan decided to retire to a cottage in town, and Bert McLaren, father of the school bully and the biggest landowner in the district, snapped up their 2,000 acres to add to the 6,000 he already owned. Not long after, Bert rolled up at our farm on a Sunday morning, just as we were about to visit the Hetheringtons. He was driving a brand-new black Chevrolet.

'Gooday Joe,' he called to my dad. 'Thought I'd catch you before you went off partying with your neighbours. Can I have a quiet word?'

Dad took the visitor into the kitchen, and motioned for me to follow. After a few pleasantries, Bert got down to business.

'Joe, you and your son are struggling on 2,000 acres. To make money these days you've got to get big. If you can't, you should get out. I want to buy your farm.'

We knew why McLaren wanted our farm. His (now) 8,000

acres relied mainly on bore water and some small dams, whereas our farm and the Hetheringtons had permanent creek water.

Dad assured McLaren that our farm wasn't for sale, and the visitor left after saying 'I'll get it one day, and the one next to you further up the valley.'

After this unexpected meeting, we began having problems with the fencing on our western boundary. We'd often be called to collect our stock that had "wandered" into McLaren's new property, and were frequently warned that next time, the McLarens would just keep our trespassing animals. So, for the first time ever, we had tension with a neighbour.

✳✳✳

That tension racked up a notch when Bert McLaren bought one of Dad's kelpie pups, a black and tan named Barney. He said that "young William" would be training it.

'Don't sell it to him Dad,' I insisted. 'If he treats his dogs like he treated the kids at school, that pup will be in for a hard time.'

'I can't refuse him, Ricky,' Dad replied. 'I've got no reason to suspect he'll be tough on animals. Maybe the responsibility of looking after the dog will do him some good.'

Bert came and picked Barney up. At a year old, Dad had already given it some rudimentary training with our own dogs, and he was prepared to help William and Barney develop into a team. Although dates were set aside for them to come over, not once did William keep the appointment. With all the other things on his mind, Dad eventually forgot about that pup.

It was a about a year later that a young guy rolled up at our place on a battered pushbike. He'd just been sacked by the McLarens, and was looking for a job. His name was Nick Salomon.

'Sorry Nick,' Dad said, 'I can't afford to pay wages for a

permanent man, but to help you out, I can give you a fortnight's work whilst we are carting hay.'

'That'd be really appreciated, Mr Richards,' Nick replied. 'I'm skint. That young bastard William sacked me because I objected to the way he treated his dog. When I complained to old Bert, he refused to pay me the wages I was owed and my accumulated holiday pay.'

While working alongside Nick as we baled and carted hay over the following fortnight, the story slowly emerged. William had reluctantly taken on training of the kelpie pup that Bert bought from Dad, but was too impatient to do the job properly.

'That little kelpie worked it's heart out for William,' Nick exclaimed, 'and it was doing a pretty good job for a youngster. But nothing satisfied William. No matter what the dog did, and no matter how hard it tried to please William, he would be yelling abuse at it. One day, after a really long and hot day's work, Barney stopped for a quick drink from a trough. William screamed at him to get back. The dog stood for a moment, hung its head, and just slunk away. It headed away from the stockyards, and we never saw it again. I think he broke its heart.'

Dad's face was ashen. Nobody around the district had picked up a stray kelpie, as far as we knew, so the chances were that poor Barney had gone away into the bush and died.

'I should have listened to you Ricky,' Dad said that night. 'I'll never deal with those bastards next door again.'

Knowing Dad like I did, he'd have thought about that missing pup for years to come.

✦✦✦

Max's dad, Peter Hetherington, was as friendly as he was big. Because of his fair complexion he was often sunburnt from being outdoors every day. He was always willing to lend a hand when Dad needed it. They'd become best friends long before I was born, and I know Dad looked forward to those Sundays, when they'd catch up to enjoy a beer and a chin-wag. I suppose Dad and Max must have told Mr H about my mechanical bent, because he began asking me for advice about his various mechanical problems. That meant that during my teenage years, I spent many a Saturday or Sunday at the Hetherington farm, fixing or adjusting things. Max was my offsider whenever more than two hands were needed. He didn't necessarily understand what we were doing or why we were doing it, but he was always there when I needed him.

All that was fine by me, except for being sometimes pestered by Max's little sister. Ellie would sometimes hang around watching what I was doing. She even tried to help periodically, but would really just get in the way. She was a nice little kid, so I did my best to discourage her without being rude.

Ellie might have been interested in mechanical things, but her real love was horses. She was still quite young when given her first horse, and over the years she became quite expert. More than once she encouraged Max and me to try riding. Max was okay, but I never got the hang of it. It seemed a lot of bother to catch and bridle a horse when you could just crank a handle to start the farm ute.

When both Max and I turned twelve, we were each given a .22 rifle by our respective parents. They were simple bolt action, single shot types. It was illegal for anyone under eighteen to operate a firearm, but the reality is that kids in the bush grow up with guns, and guns are a necessity on the land. Most farming fathers reason that early training is the best training, so country kids drove cars and used guns long before they legally could.

We shot tin cans off fence posts, then graduated to shooting rabbits. While city folk thought of rabbits as cuddly pets, anybody on the land saw them as rodents to be rid of. If they'd stuck to chewing a bit of grass like kangaroos did, they wouldn't have been so disliked, but they didn't. They dug burrows that triggered erosion, they ring-barked trees, they decimated some native plants to extinction, and they pock-marked smooth paddocks with their diggings. They also 'bred like rabbits.' We hated them.

Foxes too would be shot on sight, despite their attractive red coats and bushy tails. They preyed on native mammals and ground-nesting birds that had no defences against them. Dingoes were another matter. We rarely saw them, because a bounty had seen them all but wiped out. Dad's attitude was that they were native animals, and we were occupying their territory, not the other way around. He argued that it was up to us farmers to protect our sheep at lambing time, and to leave the dingoes be. He tolerated the occasional loss to them, but few in the district were of that mind.

Max was soon a crack shot. He had a steady hand and perfect vision, and he could spot a hiding rodent long before I could. I was good at moving targets, being a better judge of the lead required in aiming at a running rabbit, no matter its speed or angle from me. Spinner could sniff out a concealed bunny in any thicket, and in his prime could run a few down. The three of us made a pretty efficient team. and we kept the rabbit population in check on both farms.

The years went by so quickly. By high school I'd accepted the fact that school was a necessity for modern life, but I still couldn't wait to get home every day. Holidays were a dream. Overall, life was great for Dad and me except for the niggling neighbour, and Dad's growing concern about the potential for war in Europe. On a very exciting visit to a big store in Orange, he bought an AWA radio and gramophone combination, a big piece of furniture in highly polished dark wood, with a large dial that showed the callsigns of dozens of radio stations in every state of Australia. Except on the occasional very clear night, we could only receive one station, the new ABC radio network. Dad would also read the Sydney newspaper, but it was a few days old by the time we got it.

I turned fourteen late in 1938, and I could tell that Dad was worried that war would come just as I reached the right age to be swept up in it. There was one conversation that was repeated every few months.

Dad would say 'I've put enough aside for you to go to Sydney University and study mechanical engineering. It's an important profession, and Australia needs more engineers, so no matter what happens, don't think of volunteering for the armed services. You've got a bigger role to play.'

For me, the thought of leaving the Molong district, for any reason, was out of the question, so I reassured Dad about volunteering, and side-stepped the issue about going to uni. Max was in a different situation. Despite his obvious ability with words and numbers, he had no aspirations beyond farming, and no ambition even to explore new rural avenues. He and his parents were content with the prospect of him living his entire life on a farm somewhere in the Molong-Orange district.

'Just think, Ricky, before we settle down, we could join the army and get to see places we've never even heard of. We'd probably go to England first, then maybe France. What an adventure, eh?' Like so many farm boys that had gone before him, Max thought himself as being bullet-proof, so nothing bad could possibly come of it.

CHAPTER 4

Declaration of war.

On Sunday September 3rd 1939 British Prime Minister, Neville Chamberlain, declared war on Germany in response to the invasion of Poland by Hitler's forces. Immediately we began to hear of young men leaving the farms around us to help defend the mother country. I felt no such pull. Europe was half a world away, and events there seemed so unreal that they may as well have been on another planet. By then I'd accepted that I was to go to university to become an engineer, a profession in great demand, and meanwhile was helping Dad to feed the nation by working on the farm every hour I could.

Dad and I listened to the ABC radio news at breakfast and after dinner every day, and Dad avidly read the already-old newspaper that arrived in our letterbox each day. We heard that within a week of the British declaration, the Australian and New Zealand governments had rallied behind Britain, and declared war on Germany. Canada followed a few days later, as did many countries throughout the Middle East and Africa. It began to sound more serious when Britain sent four army divisions, totalling 158,000 men and 25,000 vehicles, across the channel to France, where they were deployed along the French-German border. More were soon to follow. Germany responded by transferring six divisions from Poland to their side of the border, as Polish resistance had all but collapsed. Minor skirmishes began in the air and at sea, but the first really bad news came on September 17th.

'My God,' Dad said, 'a German U-boat has sunk three British tankers and the aircraft carrier *Courageous*.' That jolted me. I began to pay some attention to what I heard and read, and for many months, little of that was encouraging. The Germans seemed to be taking all the initiative. Another U-boat sailed through a narrow gap in the defences at Scapa Flow, the base of Britain's home fleet, and sank the battleship *Royal Oak*, with the loss of 810 lives. The battle of the Atlantic had begun. By the end of December, Britain had lost 422,000 tons of shipping, and Germany had lost 224,000 tons.

I tried to visualise what it would be like to be thrown into the sea after your ship was sunk, probably at night, possibly into blazing oil. Fortunately, I couldn't. Despite the carnage, these first eight months came to be known as the "phoney war."

RAAF 10 Squadron was the first air force unit in the British Dominion to be committed to the war. Its Sunderland Flying Boats left Australia, and arrived at Pembroke Harbour, Wales, on December 26 to join the RAF's Coastal Command.

✷✷✷

In 1940, fighting quickly escalated on land, in the air, and on the sea. On April 1st, German troops invaded Denmark and Norway, and on May 9th it was the turn of Holland and Belgium. France braced itself for an attack. On paper, the Germans and the British and French armies they challenged were evenly matched, but the German tanks were superior, and they had air cover. A multi-pronged attack sent the unprepared French reeling, and poor communications between the Allies meant that the British failed to appreciate the scale and speed of the invasion until it was too late to reinforce the French in the front line.

In a brilliantly planned offensive, which advanced at up to 50 miles per day, the Germans quickly opened a breach 80 miles wide in the French front, while the British sent reinforcements to the wrong places. Some successful counterattacks by individual British units shook the Germans into believing that the Allies were much stronger than they were, and so Hitler and his high command ordered a halt. They wanted the troops to catch up with the Panzer spearheads. It was a huge lucky break for the Allies.

While the Germans dithered and delayed, the British Expeditionary Force escaped. On May 22nd the withdrawal into the Dunkirk perimeter began, and boats of all sizes, military and privately owned, shuttled back and forth across the Channel to evacuate British and French troops, under constant attack by the Luftwaffe. By June 4th, 338,000 men had been evacuated back to England from the Dunkirk beaches, and another 160,000 from Boulogne, Le Havre, Cherbourg, Nazaire, and Bordeaux.

Operation Dynamo, as the evacuation was called, was a miracle for the Allies, but they left vast quantities of guns, vehicles, and other equipment behind for the Germans to utilize. In their lightning campaign to occupy France, Holland and Belgium, the Germans had suffered 60,000 casualties but had taken over a million prisoners.

On June 10th, Mussolini, the Fascist Italian leader, jumped on the Nazi bandwagon by declaring war on the Allies.

Britain then prepared for invasion. Fighter aircraft production and pilot training were accelerated. Coastal defences were manned around the clock. On the other side of the English Channel, the German Army loaded their invasion craft in readiness, and awaited the word from Hitler.

Prior to operation Sealion, this planned invasion of Britain, the German Luftwaffe had first to destroy the Royal Air Force, and it began by attacking RAF airfields, and progressed to bombing London and other cities and ports. The RAF Hurricanes and Spitfires defended valiantly. Known as the Battle of Britain, it lasted through July until the end of October, and if the RAF hadn't won it, the Nazis would have invaded.

The air battles that raged over London and the pretty Kent countryside were watched by millions. Our radio news and newspapers were full of heroic stories, and the Spitfire and Hurricane fighters became symbols of Britain's defiance. The clean lines and distinctive elliptical wings of the Spitfire caught our imagination, and to the man or woman in the street, whether it be in London or Sydney, soon every aircraft that flew past was incorrectly labelled "a Spitfire."

We schoolboys, having no concept of the realities of the desperate and deadly aerial battles being fought on the other side of the world, found it exciting. As our own air force stepped up its activity, aircraft on cross-country training flights began to appear over Molong, and in time we could all recognise Tiger Moths, Wirraways, Brewster Buffalos, Fairy Battles, and the occasional Lockheed Hudson.

In December, Australian troops took the heavily defended North African port of Bardia from the Italians, and aided British troops in capturing Tobruk a month later, severely denting Mussolini's vision of spreading Italian influence on the African continent. Hitler then sent to Libya the first elements of the Afrika Korps, under General Erwin Rommel, which heralded an enormous and costly campaign. Rommel was soon giving Allied forces a lesson in desert warfare, and the U-boats were winning in the Atlantic, sinking up to 200,000 tons of shipping every month.

In Europe, German forces invaded Greece and Yugoslavia. Belgrade was reduced to smoking ruins by waves of bombers, day after day.

In May 1941, British shipping losses were almost half a million tons, some convoys losing half their ships. Liverpool was heavily bombed one night, killing 4,000 civilians. In London, 2,200 uncontrolled fires raged. The Royal Navy lost its newest and largest battleship, *HMS Hood*, taking 1,413 sailors with it. In return, RN torpedo bombers sank the German *Bismarck*, killing 2,200 sailors.

In June, Crete was lost to the Germans, and Rommel's tanks advanced from Libya into Egypt. Three million German soldiers, along an 1800 -mile front, attacked Russia. In Japan, one million men were conscripted into the armed forces. In July, France's Petain puppet government relinquished its bases in Indochina to Japan, the Germans were approaching Leningrad, and aerial battles between the RAF and Luftwaffe raged over France.

In August, Petain introduced a new fascist constitution for France, and the Germans advanced to within 150 miles of Moscow. The Australian garrison at the key port of Tobruk continued to beat off German assaults and withstood up to 21 air raids per day. German radio called them "rats caught in a trap," so the Aussies then called themselves the "Rats of Tobruk."

In September, the Germans began the siege of Leningrad, and Kiev fell. An SS-trained Ukrainian squad killed 28,000 Jewish civilians. In rare good news, US Navy destroyers were now escorting convoys part way across the Atlantic, reducing losses from up to 1,600,000 tons to "just" 500,000 tons per month. The individual human tragedies didn't bear thinking about.

In October, we had a change of government. John Curtin became our new PM. In Japan, strongman General Hideki Tojo was elected PM. The Russians claimed to have killed 3 million Germans for the loss of 1.1 million of their own. In Poland, 17,000 Jews were executed by the SS, and in Yugoslavia, 2,300 Serb civilians were shot in reprisal for partisan attacks on German soldiers. In November, the German army was approaching the outskirts of Moscow, while Australian, New Zealand, and South African forces battled Rommel in the desert. The RN lost the carrier *Ark Royal* to U-boats.

✳✳✳

I was 18 years old, and I was finishing my last year at high school. I read how Britain suffered under nightly bomber raids, and how it was besieged by U-boats in the Atlantic. War raged in North Africa, Russia, North Africa, Greece, and the Balkans

The war overtook the weather as the most discussed topic whenever we met someone. It went from being something terrible that was happening on the other side of the world, to a contagion that threatened us directly when, in December, the Japs bombed Pearl Harbour, bringing the USA into the war, and the war into the Pacific.

CHAPTER 5

1942

Disaster followed disaster in early 1942. Within weeks of the new year, the Japanese had swept down the Malay Peninsula, ultimately taking Singapore and the Dutch East Indies, and landing on the north coast of New Guinea. Many Australian soldiers and airmen were captured or killed. A massive air raid on Darwin killed 240 people, and sank ships in the Harbour. We weren't to know then that Darwin would be bombed 64 times over the following 21 months.

The RAAF had fighter aircraft in England, North Africa, and the Dutch East Indies, but we did not have a single fighter on home soil. The British refused to supply us, being hard pressed on the home front. Our prime minister, John Curtain, then pressured the Americans for new P-40 Kittyhawks, but was rebuffed until a number of crated aircraft that were destined for Dutch forces were diverted to Australia when Java fell to the invaders.

A new squadron, number 75, was hastily formed under

Squadron Leader John Jackson, a veteran of the fighting in the desert of North Africa, and quickly sent to Port Moresby. At the time of their departure in March, most of the pilots had only 5 to 7 hours on their new aircraft. So began what became known as the crucial 44 days, when John Jackson's inexperienced pilots met the cream of Japan's Zero pilots over the skies of Port Moresby, and were a major factor in Japan's failure to take it.

In those 44 days, the squadron lost 22 aircraft and 12 pilots, but destroyed 86 enemy aircraft. They held off the Japanese until the Americans arrived, which was just in time to meet a Japanese invasion force that had set out from Rabaul

This force was to tasked to take Port Moresby and Tulagi (in the Solomons). It included three aircraft carriers, ten cruisers, thirteen destroyers, and eleven transports, but was intercepted by an Allied force consisting of two USN carriers, eight cruisers, (including two Australian), and eleven destroyers. In what became known as the Battle of the Coral Sea, each side lost a carrier and a destroyer, but the Japanese loss of aircraft was so great the invasion of Port Moresby was postponed. They did, however, succeed in landing at the undefended Tulagi.

In June, the RAF made the first 1,000 bomber raid into Germany, the US Navy sank four Japanese carriers for the loss of one at Midway, Rommel finally captured Tobruk, (taking 35,000 prisoners), the battle for Malta intensified, and Japanese midget submarines entered Sydney Harbour. The mothership sub shelled Sydney and Newcastle, and a Japanese reconnaissance plane flew over Sydney. We all wondered if they intended to invade Australia next. My presumption of a stint at university, then a long, innocent and carefree life on the farm suddenly seemed a naïve and unlikely proposition.

✳✳✳

The world changed very quickly in that year of 1942, as these battles raged across much of the globe. My personal world changed quite dramatically too. The first upheaval began when Max dragged me along to a dance at the Molong Community Centre, I didn't want to go, because I had never really spoken to a REAL girl, and I didn't know how to dance. I visualized an embarrassing evening being a wallflower until able to escape. For the first half hour it was all that I'd expected, and I dreaded the next couple of hours. I made small talk with a few mates that felt much the same as I did, and I watched with envy more confident boys like Max whirling and laughing with their pretty dance partners. Then I spotted someone I thought I should know, but couldn't quite place.

She was sitting, chatting to another girl. I could see that she was petite, but curvy. Her curly hair was fair, and shone in the dance hall lights. She had a slim face, and a strong nose. Her dress was simple but elegant. She turned and caught me looking at her. She smiled, not a wide smile, but an inviting one, framed with dark red lipstick. I was like a rabbit in the headlights, and I didn't know what to do.

She broke my spell. She walked up to me and said 'Hello Eric, I've never seen you at a dance before.' Then I recognised her. It was Lyn Chappel, one year behind me at school. My god, how different she looked out of the school uniform of plain tunic covering a checked shirt, and bobby socks.

'Er, ah, well, I'm not much of a dancer, so I haven't come here before,' I stammered.

'Oh, that's okay, dancing is easy. Let me show you.'

She took my hand and led me, actually more accurately dragged me, to the dance floor. I liked music well enough, and I could hear the beat, but no matter how hard I tried, I couldn't synchronise my feet with it. Our feet collided, and once I stepped on her toes, and I expected her to politely disappear as soon as the bracket was over. Instead, she stood before me, hands clasped together, and looked into my eyes. I could tell that she was amused by my quandary, but I had no idea on how to react.

After a few attempts, at last I plucked up the courage to speak. 'Would you like a lemonade?' That was all I could think of.

I drove her home that night. Max was exhausted from his energetic dancing, and he slumped into the back seat of my Dad's Olds, quickly falling asleep. Lyn lived with her parents in town, so it was a short detour for me. When I switched off the engine, we both sat awkwardly for a minute, listening to Max's snoring. Then she leaned over and brushed my cheek with her lips, opened the door, and almost ran to her front door.

It took me two weeks to pluck up the courage to seek her out. I found out that she had a holiday job at a local store, and I phoned her there. I fully expected her to politely decline, but to my surprise, Lyn agreed to "catching up". We met for a milkshake at a café on the main street, then I took her for a picnic on the following Sunday. It was to one of my favourite places in my "secret" forest.

Over a few weeks it all developed so naturally. I now had a girlfriend, and I was a little bewildered by how quickly and easily it had all come about. We saw each other at least twice a week. I'd take her out on Saturday night, and on Sundays she would come to our farm. Dad liked Lyn, and she soon became comfortable in our house. She'd often insist on helping in the kitchen to prepare lunch, and to do the washing up. Spinner took to her, and slowly it dawned on me that here was my future, a comfortable future, just spreading out in front of me. I still visited the Hetheringtons regularly, but as close as Max and I remained, I realized that my life had now turned a corner.

✳✳✳

The second upheaval in 1942 occurred when Max left to join the army. My best pal was no university candidate, and as the Hetheringtons did not own their farm, he was always going to find a job elsewhere after finishing high school. Volunteering to join the army was his plan for a quick bit of adventure before settling down. I joined his parents in trying to reason with him, but there was no dissuading him.

He was called up in June. I drove him to the rail station at Molong, and he gripped my hand fiercely as we stood on the platform. 'Rick,' he said, 'don't worry about me, I'll be fine. Just keep helping Mum and Dad, and little Sis, just like you've always done. I'll miss you, brother, but I'll be back in a few months, as soon as we've whipped the Japs, and it will be just like old times.'

Little did we know that it would be much more than a few months before we would reunite, and how different our circumstances would then be. One thing I did know for certain was that it was never going to be 'just like old times' again. Our age of innocence was over, and joining the real world was the only option. I turned to walk away as the train disappeared from sight. A large poster on the ticket office wall caught my eye: a picture of a magnificent machine, a flying machine. The legend said "the RAAF needs you!" That was the moment I began thinking seriously about aeroplanes.

✳✳✳

The third personal upheaval that year, though I did not immediately recognise it as that, came when Dad became friendly with Mrs Mavis Doak, who worked part time as a secretary for Reg Wilson. Reg was a prominent businessman in town. He was a lawyer who handled legal matters like wills and conveyancing, and he also owned a real estate agency. He was a councillor on the Molong Council, and although not widely liked, he was respected. Mrs Doak had been a widow for a decade or more, and lived with her son in a small cottage behind the main street in town.

I had noticed that Dad's weekly visits to town seemed to be taking longer, and I then discovered that he was having lunch with Mrs Doak. Not long after Lyn had become a regular Sunday visitor, Dad invited Mavis to join us too. Sometimes her son Phillip, who was three years younger than me and still at school, came too.

Mavis fitted right in. She would have been a pretty girl once, but had put on a touch more weight than was ideal for her average height. She was fussy about her hair, and was always well dressed, but she was a typical country lady, always willing to pitch in, nothing worried her, and so she and Lyn soon paired up to kick Dad and me out of the kitchen on Sundays while they chatted away happily together. We men would retreat to the veranda, often with a beer, and wait for the inevitable feast. Sometimes the Hetheringtons would come too. For the first time in many years, our house was full of noise and bustle.

Spinner knew when it was Sunday, because Dad and I didn't get out of bed at or before first light that morning. He'd wait anxiously for the visitors to arrive, as he knew that more people meant more scraps dropped surreptitiously under the table for him. After lunch, he'd shiver with excitement at the prospect of more people to play soccer goalie with.

I noticed how Mavis looked at Dad, and after this routine became established, how he was enjoying being fussed over by a woman. The only cloud over us was the desperate war being fought to the north. I was beginning to feel guilty that I was living comfortably and leaving the important work to others.

✶✶✶

The second half of 1942 was a tough time for Australia and the rest of the free world. July began with the Japanese almost making it to Port Moresby via the Kokoda Trail, only being halted by our under-equipped, underfed, and untrained militia. Air battles between the RAAF, USAAF, and the Japanese continued over Port Moresby and the beachheads on the north coast of New Guinea. In July, Australian coast watchers alerted our military that the enemy was building an airfield on Guadalcanal, obviously as part of a barrier to our north. The Japanese wanted to at least isolate Australia, if not to occupy it, to prevent it being used by the US as a base for operations. In England people continued to hang on grimly.

On August 7th US Marines landed on Guadalcanal, thus beginning a round of fierce battles around the Solomon Islands that lasted more than six months on land, sea, and in the air. Two days later we were staggered to hear that the Japanese navy had sunk three US and one Australian cruiser, the HMAS Canberra, in a night battle at Savo island that lasted barely forty-five minutes. The Japanese escaped virtually unscathed.

The Germans reached Stalingrad, and a Canadian raid on Dieppe failed, with the loss of over 4,000 men. There was some good news. Malta was saved, the Japs lost a carrier and many aircraft in the eastern Solomons, and Rommel's latest advance had been halted.

In August we learned that an attempted landing by 2,400 Japanese marines at Milne Bay had been thwarted by Australian militia and AIF soldiers, and in September that the Jap campaign on Kokoda Trail had also finished with their defeat. The war was see-sawing on many fronts. The battles raged over Guadalcanal and in the waters around the island, with US Marines grimly holding on to Henderson Field against a determined enemy. Allied troops landed in Africa and Italy that month, Russians were holding out in Stalingrad, and the RAF bombing campaign across France and Germany continued despite high losses of aircraft and crew. At last, the U-boat menace had been blunted, with losses of ships being cut dramatically and more German subs sunk with the use of radar, long range aircraft, and escort aircraft carriers. Thirty-seven of Germany's subs were sunk in one week.

✳✳✳

Dad was reading the morning paper. He shook his head sadly.

'What is it, Dad?' I asked

'So many young men in our district are leaving to join the armed forces. Some are going to England to join RAF and RAAF units there. At this rate, Australian farms are going to only have women and old men to run them.'

What remained unspoken was that many Australian airmen had been killed over England and occupied Europe. What we didn't know then was that around half who left Australian shores would be lost in action. An RAF Bomber Command posting was almost a death sentence at one time.

I continued to be tormented by the image of my contemporaries in the district putting their lives on the line, while I continued to live a relatively comfortable life. I knew that it was only a matter of time before I'd have to tell Dad that I intended to volunteer. Ever since I saw that poster, I knew where my destiny lay. One night I told Dad I was going to sign up to join the RAAF.

There was no argument. He knew nothing would change my mind. The next day I drove to the recruitment office in Orange. I passed the basic medical test that day, papers were signed, and all I had to do was wait. The following Sunday, I told Lyn. To my surprise she accepted my decision.

'I don't want you to go, Ricky, but I know you have to follow your conscience. You'll never forgive me if I stop you. So go, and I'll wait. Don't forget that. I'll wait as long as it takes.' As of that moment, we considered ourselves engaged to be married.

That Sunday afternoon I took Lyn home to her parents' house, as usual. When I got out of the car, she took my hand and led me to the front door. She whispered 'Mum and Dad are away tonight. They won't be back till tomorrow.'

✲✲✲

Now that I'd enlisted, I wanted to get on with it. I waited every day for a telegram from the RAAF. The year came to an end and I'd still heard nothing from them. I thought that perhaps they didn't need me after all. I wasn't sure whether I was relieved or disappointed, but I knew what both Dad and Lyn were thinking. I finished high school in December, and enrolled at the School of Mechanical Engineering at Sydney University. The first year of my course began in early March 1943.

I was excited at the prospect of going to the big city, but at the same time dreaded any break with my life on the farm. In the last few years, we'd improved many things. All the equipment we had was in top shape, fences were mended, crops sown and sheep drenched and shorn. I knew Dad would be okay, for this year at least. It was Spinner who I worried about. He was now fifteen, which is old for a dog of his breeding. He'd slowed over the last few years, but only in recent weeks had declined to go on long walks with me. He seemed happy to find a nice spot in the sun during the day, and when we played soccer goalie, the game would last only a minute or two before he'd walk away, signalling "game over". I feared how he'd cope when I left home.

On the day before I was to leave for university, I did a round of visits to friends. My last call was on the Hetheringtons. Both Mr and Mrs H hugged me tightly.

'Keep in touch, Ricky.' They both said. 'Don't forget us when you get to the big city.' Mrs H added that Ellie had just gone on an urgent errand, and she'd be upset that she'd missed me.

March 1st 1943 and the fateful day had come that I had to leave the farm for the first time. Dad and I were up long before dawn to drive into Orange. To my surprise, Spinner dragged himself out of his cane basket, and insisted on coming with us, despite normally accepting that he wasn't allowed in Dad's "good" car.

We picked up Lyn on the way. We all shivered in the early morning cold on the bleak platform whilst waiting for the train. None of us knew quite what to say, and it was a relief when the train pulled away from the station.

After the emotional goodbye, Dad dropped Lyn off home, then drove straight to the farm. He told me in a letter that Spinner went straight to his bed, settled into a deep sleep, and simply never woke up.

✳✳✳

There was some good news. The Japanese Solomon Island campaign was over. It had cost them 24,000 of the 36,000 troops they'd landed there, plus about 1830 combat aircraft, an aircraft carrier, two battleships, four cruisers, twelve destroyers, six submarines, and numerous transport ships. US losses had been very nearly as bad, including 16,000 troops, (mainly marines), but the barrier between Australia and our northern allies had been broken. It was the turning point in the Pacific war. Although we didn't realise it at the time, it was the beginning of the end for Japan's hopes of dominance in the Pacific. I even had the thought that if the RAAF didn't hurry up, I might miss out altogether on any action. Little did I know what the war would cost us all during the next two and a half years.

I found a vacancy in a shared terrace house in Camperdown, within walking distance of the university, and spent the following seven months studying hard. I caught the train back home for every second or third weekend, and during the two term breaks, so life on the farm, with Dad and Lyn, went on as close to normal as we could make it. Disappearing so regularly from Sydney meant that I didn't get involved with any sports clubs, and my loyalty to Lyn kept me from some parties I was invited to. Not being a big drinker, I avoided the customary Friday night binge, so I was then regarded as one of the "serious students," and never became "one of the crowd."

While I studied, Allied troops pushed the Germans back in North Africa, the Russian Army began to push the Germans westward, the Allied bombing campaign over occupied France and Germany intensified, the U-boat menace see-sawed in the Atlantic, and Australian and US forces slugged it out with the Japanese in New Guinea.

On the home front, we did have one disquieting incident. Ploughing for the winter cereal crops was an important operation. We had to wait for late autumn rain, then plough and sew the new crop before the soil temperature fell too low. Timing was critical. When I was home, Dad and I would work in shifts, driving our old but still reliable Fordson tractor, usually quitting around midnight, only to be back at work at daybreak.

We were half way though the operation when, one early morning, we drove the ute back to where we'd left the old Fordson. We smelt burning rubber before cresting the low rise in the half-ploughed paddock.

'Jesus,' Dad cried, 'some bastard has tried to burn our tractor!'

Petrol had been splashed over the blue bonnet and

mudguards, and both big back tyres. An empty drum lay beside the back wheel. Incredibly, because we'd always kept the old girl clean of excess grease and oil leak-free, only the rear tyres and one engine hose had caught fire. The tyres were both reduced to wire coils around the rims, and bits of rubber that clung to them still smouldered. The paintwork had blistered, but not burned.

New tyres had to be shipped from Sydney, and we were back in operation in two days. We were lucky. In the busy season, tractors were in short supply, even if you had the money to buy one. Had the arsonists succeeded, we'd have been unable to grow the cereal crop that year, and the bank manager would have been hovering.

'Who the hell would have done that to us, Ricky?'

'Who else, Dad? The only people who'd have known where our tractor was that night were our neighbours just over the fence.' That fence was our western boundary, the one we shared with the McLarens.

✳✳✳

In the September term break, Lyn and I saw each other most days. On one, we climbed the hill to the lookout rock where Max and I used to play. 'Rick,' she began. 'I'm not letting you go back to Sydney alone next year. I'll be finished with high school in December, we can have the summer here at Molong, then I'm coming to Sydney with you.'

'That would be fantastic, Lyn, but I can just pay my share of the rent in a shared house plus feed myself as it is. There's no way we can have our own place!'

'Don't be silly. I'll get a job, of course. We can live on my salary.'

I thought about it for a few seconds. The idea began to

appeal enormously. I grinned and was about to speak when she interrupted.

'But Rick, I'm not going to live in sin with you. We'll have to get married first.'

And so it was agreed. We'd have a Christmas wedding. I'd be 19 years old, and Lyn 18. We planned to announce our engagement in a few days.

***

We walked back home to find a telegram under the door. Straight away I knew what it meant. There would be no December wedding, nor second year studies at the school of engineering. I was to report to RAAF Bradfield Park on October 2nd 1943, just seven days away. Lyn burst into tears, Dad looked disconsolate, and I couldn't fathom my own mixed emotions. One thing I knew for certain, my destiny was in other hands now.

This time my departure was more finite. I had no idea when I would get any leave long enough to come back home. In the predawn darkness I threw a couple of last-minute items into my suitcase, and had a sombre breakfast with Dad. Before getting into the car, I did a silent round of the yard, past the sleeping kelpies, the shearing shed, and the machinery shed. Most of my world was right here. Dad and I hardly spoke as he warmed up the car, or when we drove out onto the road as the first rays of the sun lit up the trees around us. As Dad accelerated away from the farm gate, I was astonished to hear thundering hooves alongside me. I turned to see Max's little sister, Ellie, on her pretty chestnut mare, galloping alongside us, and waving wildly. Her long dark hair streamed behind her, and her face was lit by a wide grin. I hung out the window, and shouted and waved enthusiastically, until she was lost in our dust. The mood in the car changed instantly. Dad and I laughed until tears came to our eyes, and our leave-taking at the station was with a hug and a grin.

When I sat back on the hard seat in the train, I found myself smiling at the image of Ellie on her flying horse. I knew that no matter what sacrifices we had to make to preserve our land and its people, people like little Ellie, Dad, and the H's, it was worth it.

I then noticed that a boy, aged about 12 and sitting opposite, was looking at me quizzically. He said 'What's the joke, Mister?'

'It's a long story, young fella. Maybe I'll write about it one day and you can read it yourself.'

***

After clearing my few belongings from the shared terrace in Camperdown, I caught the suburban train that crossed the iconic harbour bridge and took me up the North Shore line to Bradfield Park. From there I walked to the RAAF Barracks. My dormitory was in one of the numerous Nissan huts lined up in rows. My hut contained two rows of beds, twenty in all. The interior was cold, draughty, and gloomy. It was painted in a dull yellowy cream, and the linoleum on the floor was grey. I was the first of the new intake to arrive, and I sat alone, somewhat bewildered, on my allotted bed. I wondered what I'd let myself in for, and wished I was back home in familiar surroundings.

Other equally bewildered men of about my age began to drift in, and some tentative introductions were made. It was still unnerving to bunk in with nineteen strangers, after a lifetime with only Dad and me on the farm. Little did I know then that in this hut, and the others around me, were some of the finest men I'd ever meet.

CHAPTER 6

Entering the RAAF.

If I thought entering the RAAF to become an airman was going to be glamourous, I was soon to be disabused of the notion. Eating mass-prepared food with a hundred others was one thing, but communal showers and toilets were just horrible until I got accustomed to them. Worse was to come.

In the first morning, we were made to form four lines in a frigid and draughty hall, and told to strip naked. Doctors sat at desks at the head of each queue. I was used to cold weather, as Molong can even see snow in the dead of winter, and then we'd dress accordingly, but this was humiliating as well as freezing. We all shivered. One by one we were interviewed by a medico, who poked and prodded us. He even asked us to bend right over and touch our toes with legs apart. The joke later was that if the doctor could see daylight up your arse, you were out.

I passed, and was handed on to the eye doctor. At least I had some clothes on by then. He tested my eyesight, and my ability to distinguish numbers in a field of dots. I think it was called the Ishihara colour blindness test, and I passed that too. Minus a few who didn't, we were then led to the section that issued out uniforms and other basic kit. The clothes sizes handed out bore little resemblance to our actual measurements, but by swapping with others later, we were able to get reasonably close fits. The following day, we assembled for our first class.

For what seemed forever, but was really just weeks, we learned how to be RAAF airmen. Nothing to do with flying aeroplanes mind you, but everything to do with organising your kit, parades, inspections, recognising different ranks, the RAAF command structure, how and when to salute, and a myriad of other things that seemed boring to me, but which the RAAF considered essential to winning the war. Then there was marching, "square bashing" we called it. Lots and lots of marching.

As in any group of young men, there were loud ones and quiet ones. Some were outgoing, others not. They came from all areas and all backgrounds: there were farm boys and city boys. Some came from wealthy backgrounds, others not. One was the heir to a well-known retail store chain, but many others were sons of labourers or bank clerks. Most farm boys were well used to driving tractors and operating all sorts of farm machinery, though a few grazier's sons had never been on anything faster than a horse. Most of the city boys had never operated anything more complicated than a bicycle, yet we all had one thing in common: we all aspired to fly 400 mph fighters.

Bradfield Park was tiresome, but we endured it, or at least most of us did. Then it was off to elementary flying school. I was posted to 5 EFTS at Tamworth, one of twelve elementary flying schools the RAAF ran. This looked much more promising. A group of us travelled by train, second class of course, to Tamworth. When we arrived, the big grass field outside the town was buzzing with activity. Yellow-painted aeroplanes were everywhere, some in a constant whorl of take offs and landings, "circuits and bumps" we would later call this stage of training, while others buzzed around high overhead. We couldn't wait to get our hands on a real aeroplane.

First though, we had more lectures, but at least the subjects were interesting because they were about actually learning to fly. There were lectures on the principles of flight, weather, and navigation. Most of the following two months consisted of lectures for half the day, and two flights each in the other half.

My very first ride in an aeroplane was with Flying Officer James Corlette. I became so nervous as my turn drew near that my knees were shaking. To go so high into the air in a flimsy contraption now seemed to be a foolish idea. The aeroplane creaked under my weight when I climbed in, and I was all fingers and thumbs when strapping myself in and tightening the harness. I wasn't comfortable. I'd never had a strap of any kind restraining me. An aircraftsman swung the prop, and with a cough, a bang, and a cloud of smoke, the engine stuttered into life. The whole aeroplane shook and shivered, and I had a sudden attack of claustrophobia. I was close to unbuckling and jumping out when with a burst of the engine, we began to move.

To get off the ground was a revelation. We climbed up to cloud base on that first flight, darting through the trailing whisps of a pure white cumulus cloud, and I knew then I'd been born to fly. The Tiger Moth itself was something of a disappointment to me. I'd imagined all aircraft to be complicated, roaring, powerful beasts that took a firm and manly hand to control: something like a thoroughbred race horse would be. The De Havilland DH82 Tiger Moth was anything but that. It was a plywood and fabric biplane, with the two open cockpits in tandem, and it was light and simple. There were a few dials on the instrument panel, a large compass, a control stick, and a few other knobs. There was no electrical system at all. To speak to the instructor, one had to shout down a pipe called the Gosport tube. There were no brakes, so to turn involved a burst of power and a boot full of rudder. The engine didn't roar much either: more of a clatter, really. It developed all of 130 horsepower.

The Tiger Moth had been designed to be simple to fly, and it certainly was that. There had been instances where pilots had swung the prop with the throttle too wide open, with the result that they had to leap out of the way of the propellor as the biplane proceeded to take off all by itself.

Once off the ground the climb rate was pedestrian, and the top speed not much more that of a family car. The controls were very light, but the roll rate was sloppy. It seemed to just want to wallow along, more or less straight and level, unless upset by a gust or a thermal.

You'd think that such a slow and stable aircraft would be very safe, but still people managed to kill themselves in it. While I was at 5EFTS, an instructor and pupil spiralled into the ground, and one early solo pupil attempted a slow go-round and ended up rolling into the ground. All three died.

Some pilots loved the dainty Tiger Moth, but in all the time I flew the type, I never really developed any great affection for it. It did its job, however, as in two short months I went from a novice to a pilot, (receiving a "good average" grading), with fifty hours in my logbook, and having learned the principles of flight, steep turns, emergency procedures such as forced landings, and basic instrument and aerobatic flying.

✳✳✳

The next big move was to the Intermediate Training Squadron, at Amberley air base, west of Brisbane. Here we were to transition to the twin-engine Avro Anson. That promised to be much more challenging. The Anson looked like a modern aircraft. It had a low wing, a fully enclosed fuselage, and you climbed in from a door behind the trailing edge of the wing to climb forward to the side by side cockpit. The Anson felt like a real aeroplane. It had a retractable undercarriage, brakes, and an electrical system that powered starter motors, intercom, radio, and navigation equipment. The two Cheetah seven-cylinder radial engines each produced 350 horsepower. This, I thought, was more like it. I spent another two months with the ITS, under the watchful eyes of Flying Officer Keith Scandrett, learning night and instrument flying, and cross-country navigation. It took my total flying hours to one hundred, and I passed with an "average plus" rating.

∗∗∗

The Advanced Training Squadron was also based at Amberley, and there we flew both Ansons and Wirraways. The first part of the course, still on Ansons, consolidated instrument and cross-country flying to a new level. We could now, theoretically at least, fly in all weathers. With 167 hours under my belt, I passed with an "above average" rating, but perhaps I would not have but for a very lucky break. Flight Lieutenant Gavin King took me for my final test: a three-hour navigational exercise, all under a hood over my head to simulate zero visibility. I had done a number of these flights already, and I had no trouble maintaining a heading, and tracking progress across a chart with ruler and timepiece. I never once got lost, until this day. This time, I really messed up.

The first leg was to Brisbane City, followed by legs to Kingaroy, Dalby, Toowoomba, and finally Amberley. Stupidly, I forgot to note the time I'd changed course over Brisbane, so I had no idea at what time I'd reach Kingaroy, where I'd make my next course change. We were in cloud all the way, and I was underneath the hood, I could see under it and outside the aeroplane only through a tiny gap at the corner of the left side window. By pure luck and just at the right time, out of the corner of my eye, a hole in the cloud appeared in that sliver of visibility. I saw a wheat silo for a split second. I recognised it, I'd seen it before, it was the silo we used as the turning point at Kingaroy. I announced that I was changing course to Dalby. 'Very good. Well done, Richards,' said F/L King. The rest of the exercise was uneventful.

***

On Tuesday June 6th 1944, the invasion of Europe was launched. On D-Day more than 125,000 men landed in Normandy by sea or air. By the end of the day, 2,500 had been killed, and that was just the opening. By the end of June, almost a million men had landed. There was a long, long way to go, but it had to be the beginning of the end for Hitler.

In the Pacific, The US Navy and Marines stormed the Marianas, only 12,000 miles from Tokyo. We all wanted the war to end, but privately hoped we'd get through training and into action before it did.

For the second part of the advanced course, we had to convert to the Commonwealth Aircraft Corporation (CAC) Wirraway. The Wirraway was built in Australia under licence from North American Aviation. It was basically an early version of the American AT-6, otherwise known as the T-6 Texan in the USAAF, SNJ in the US Navy, and Harvard in Canada, UK, New Zealand, and South Africa. The AT-6 first flew in 1935, and after some development, became a very successful advanced trainer for these and other air forces. A lot of them got bent by ham-fisted pilots, and quite a few pilots died in them, but it was a very honest aircraft in that it was demanding to fly, and you had to fly it right, but if you did, it would always respond accordingly. If you didn't, it would bite. It was the perfect trainer for the fighter aircraft of the era. If you could fly the T-6 well, you could fly a fighter. The CAC Wirraway wasn't quite so good to fly, because it kept all the less desirable features of the earliest version of the AT-6, and added a couple of its own. Nevertheless, it made real pilots of those who mastered it.

The first thing that struck me as I strapped myself in for my first flight, was that I could see bugger all out front over the big engine cowling. The second was that on starting, the 600 horsepower Pratt & Whitney 9-cylinder radial engine shook the airframe so much it felt like riding a runaway bull. The third thing was that CAC had placed the controls in such a haphazard fashion, that on take-off I was switching left and right hands from the control stick to other knobs and levers as I sought to manage undercarriage gear, flaps, throttle, manifold pressure, trim, and the strong tendency to swing initially left then right, then left again as take-off speed built up.

Few of the trainees on my course liked the Wirraway all that much, but those of us who came to terms with it did come to respect it. It demanded undivided attention. For those who lacked a firm hand it could ground loop even on take-off, and frequently did on landing. It had an indifferent roll rate, and could stall a wing at low airspeed without much provocation. Over the two months on this part of the course, I did another fifty hours flying time, dual and solo, learning the basics of fighter tactics, dive bombing, and formation flying.

In that two months, half of the pilots on the course failed, and were relegated to other flying duties, such as air gunnery or navigation. Those that had passed the course were asked if they had a preference on what they'd like to fly. I wanted to be a fighter pilot.

'So what's it to be, Richards,' the CO asked. 'Fighters?'

'Of course, Sir, what else?' I answered. Some others chose bombers, but I couldn't understand that. Of course, what we desired had little influence on where Postings would actually send us, so we waited anxiously. A day later I received my posting: I was to report to 1 Operational Training Unit, (1 OTU), East Sale. My heart sank, because that meant I was to fly bombers, most likely the Bristol Beaufort.

As a schoolboy I had visualized that the daring fighter pilot was the elite, and at the forefront of the attack against the enemy, duelling one-on-one against them. I guess I still had that view. By comparison, bombing from way above didn't seem nearly as glamorous. It was of course a view born of ignorance, as I learned in time that the low and medium level bombing by the Beaufort boys was as daring as anything done by the fighters. The losses over Europe with the heavy bombers was the worst of all.

***

Before I was to report at Sale, I was granted some leave. Three days and a few trains later I made it back to Molong. Both Lyn and Dad consoled me on my bomber posting. Dad said 'I imagine that the bombers would be a lot safer than fighters, Son, and I really would like to have you back home when this war is over.'

Little did we know that you didn't have to go to war to die in a Beaufort. Many were lost in both training and in action. By the end of the war, 1 OTU suffered 147 training accidents, killing 131 airmen. Of the 700 Beauforts that the RAAF had, 93 crashed in training accidents. It was eventually discovered that there was a fault in the elevator linkage, but by then the war was over.

The day before I had to board the train for Victoria, I received a telegram from RAAF postings. I had been reassigned. I was to go to 2 OTU, RAAF Mildura.

'Two OTU!' I shouted to Dad. 'That means fighters. Kittyhawks or Spitfires. Whoopeee!'

Lyn and Dad were not quite so pleased, but Dad tried to

hide his dismay. It was just as well he didn't know the facts. By war's end, 2 OTU would suffer 43 accidents with Kittyhawks, killing 26 pilots. Altogether, 47 pilots died in training on the various types flown there.

∗∗∗

Even if I'd been aware of those statistics, it wouldn't have bothered me. Like most young pilots, I felt that I was "bullet proof", and I arrived at 2 OTU Mildura with unshakable confidence. The sight of rows of front-line fighter aircraft and bustling activity thrilled me. I knew that the base had been nothing but a dry and dusty field in March of 1942, but in the 15 months since, proper runways had been constructed, plus buildings for the instructors, officers, sergeants, airmen and WAAFs, plus their messes, and classrooms. There were also seven huge maintenance hangars, transport and stores buildings, flight huts, and a rifle range, library, and theatre. Even a substantial concrete building for squash courts was under construction.

The base was neat and tidy, with watered lawns around most buildings. I was soon told that the base commander, Group Captain Reginald Garrett, was known as "Rock Garden Reggie," due to his fastidious attention to how the base looked. Probably the only thing one might legitimately complain about was the dust. Mildura lay in a very dry area, and so if the wind blew from the east, west, or south we got brown dust, and if it blew from the north, it was red. It was all fine dust, and it got into everything. I sympathised with the engine mechanics and instrument fitters, who had a tough job keeping so many aircraft operating under harsh conditions, and didn't need the abrasive Mildura dust that made their jobs so much more difficult.

∗∗∗

I quickly found that although the purpose of the base was deadly serious, the flying training hard and dangerous with consequent frequent accidents, it was generally a good place to be. Hard mattresses and thin blankets aside, the RAAF did as much as it could to make us comfortable. The locals supported the air force personnel, and did much to mollify the strain on both instructors and pupils. Quite a few local families regularly took airmen into their own homes on weekends, giving them the taste of the home life they no doubt missed. Some of the local young ladies took it upon themselves to extend that welcome beyond the call of duty. I guess we had an aura about us. We were young and fit, wearing smart new uniforms, flying iconic fighters, and about to sally forth to teach our enemies a lesson. As I was engaged to be married, I resisted such temptation, but it wasn't easy. Not many of my colleagues had such self-discipline.

There were two hotels in town, the Grand, and the Murray. On weekends, the demand for accommodation was so great that several guest houses had sprung up to cater for the excess. Personally, I preferred to stay on base, or occasionally volunteer for some unpaid farm work around the district.

One day a duty sergeant called out above the babble of voices in the mess. 'Anyone here who can play the piano?' I volunteered, knowing the duty would most likely have nothing to do with music. 'Right then, pick an extra hand, get a truck, and move the dead cow on the road outside the base.' Some people quickly learned never to volunteer for anything.

Also impressive at 2 OTU was the list of famous pilots who came through the base as commanders or instructors. All were combat veterans, from fighting the Germans over England in the Battle of Britain, the Germans and Italians in the Middle East and Africa, and / or the Japanese in Malaya and New Guinea. Wing Commander Jeffrey, Squadron Leader Truscott, Squadron Leader Rawlinson, Group Captain Arthur, Wing Commander

Caldwell, Wing Commander Gibbes and many others were household names.

Whilst the base resounded to the roars, snarls, and rumbles of Kittyhawks, Spitfires, CAC Boomerangs, and sometimes a visiting Beaufort, Beaufighter, Vultee Vengeance, Republic Lancer, or Consolidated B-24 Liberator, it was back to the Wirraway for us. Crammed into just twenty days was a 31-hour course, plus supporting lectures. It was an introduction to combat flying, including gunnery and bombing.

Our previous cautious relationship with the Wirraway didn't improve, because the examples at Mildura were very tired. These machines were used daily for extreme combat manoeuvres, and often suffered mis-handling by over-zealous students. Despite the best efforts of the maintenance men, they often burned or leaked oil and/or hydraulic fluid, ran roughly, or over-heated. Radio failures were a daily occurrence, and faulty navigational instruments led many of the unwary astray.

The Wirraway was particularly contemptuous of any pilot who couldn't land it properly. The RAAF insisted that we do three-point landings most of the time. That meant that the pilot had to judge the exact height to cut the power and round out, lifting the nose into the correct attitude for all three wheels to touch down at the same time, then dance on the rudder pedals to keep the beast straight as it slowed down. Rounding out too high meant that you stalled the aircraft, and it would drop and hit the ground with an almighty bang, or worse if a wing dropped. Leave it too late and you hit mainwheels first, the tail would drop, and the aircraft would bounce back into the air at the point of the stall. If a wing did drop, you risked a bent wingtip, or even a bent wing.

Far more sensible to me was the wheel landing, where the pilot kept on a trickle of power, rounded out enough to touch down with mainwheels first, then kept the tail up in the breeze as long as possible to maintain rudder control. By the time the tail dropped of its own accord, the aeroplane would be going too slowly to seriously misbehave. In fact, there were some tail-wheel types of aircraft that couldn't be landed any other way, but the RAAF persisted with three-pointers. The result was that we had so many ground-loops that we were eventually threatened with instant dismissal for the next offender. Thankfully, though I was never any good on the dance floor, I could dance on those rudder pedals and never had a problem keeping any aeroplane straight.

The Wirraway might have been a bit of a bitch, but boy, did we learn fast, and there were no fatal accidents on this part of my course. There very well could have been. The course ahead of us were now flying P-40 Kittyhawks, and one of their exercises was to dive head-on towards a Wirraway in a mock attack. One of the instructors called to me.

'Hey Richards. We're going to practise head-on attacks. Want to come along as an observer?'

Of course, I did. Within weeks I'd be doing these practise attacks, so to see how it was done from the "victims" angle seemed a good idea.

We flew at a steady airspeed at a constant 5000' altitude. I had nothing to do but watch as one by one distant dots thousands of feet above grew in size as they dropped on us. I could see that it wasn't easy for the Kittyhawk pilots to judge just when to start their dives, as our combined speeds meant we were closing at well over 500 mph. Five of the "attackers" got it fairly close, and were able to draw a bead on our Wirraway for a few seconds before rolling away and continuing the dive past us. The sixth and last pilot left his dive too late. He tried to compensate by diving more steeply, and in a desperate effort to bring his gunsight to bear on us, he left the roll away too late also.

The P-40 pilot, my pilot, and me all realized that we had a

problem at the same time. The P-40 pilot tried to push forward even further, to dive below the Wirraway. At the same instant, my pilot tried to pull up and roll out of the way. The Kittyhawk's tail fin struck our left wing, severing both. While our broken wing fluttered down, our right wing kept flying, with the result that our doomed Wirraway snapped into a violent, nose-down rotation. All this happened in the blink of an eye.

I'd never used a parachute, but we'd had plenty of instruction on emergency procedures. The world was in a whirl, and I think I froze for a few seconds. Then the training cut in. I reached up and slid the canopy forward, unplugged my earphones, then unbuckled the seat harness. I pushed with my legs and in the next second I was sliding past the open front cockpit. I looked down into it and saw it was empty. My instructor pilot had already gone. For a few seconds I seemed to fall at the same rate as the Wirraway did. I feared the rotating right wing was going to come around and clobber me, but I outpaced the aircraft, and found myself alone in mid-air. I don't remember reaching the D-ring on my chest, but I must have pulled it. I do remember the wrench on my crotch straps as the chute opened.

I gripped the shrouds tightly, caught my breath, and slowly scanned around me. The Wirraway was now well below, still spinning. The diving Kittyhawk had already hit the ground, a cloud of dust marking its final destination. Two parachutes were floating below and behind me.

CHAPTER 7

Kittyhawks!

We hadn't joined the air force to fly trainers, and we all longed to fly frontline fighters. Sleek, deadly, beautiful Kittyhawks and Spitfires awaited us. We all wanted the Spitfire, but the choice wasn't ours. My day came on August 1, 1944. I'd flown three types so far, the Tiger Moth, The Avro Anson, and the CAC Wirraway, and I'd had an instructor train me for each, flying dual for hours, before I went solo. The Kittyhawk had just one seat. There was not going to be a soft introduction.

I strapped in to Kittyhawk A29-45 and listened to the instructor run through the start procedure, the critical numbers and settings for take-off, cruise, descent, and landing. It didn't sound like a big jump to make, and everything the instructor said made sense. I nodded confidently, and Flight Lieutenant Lloyd Boardman gave me the thumbs up, patted me on the shoulder, and jumped off the wing. My stomach did begin to churn when I pressed the starter for the big Alison V12 engine. The prop turned slowly for several revolutions before a cough and a puff of white smoke, then the engine caught. The airframe shook before the engine settled into a steady 1200 rpm idle.

The nose of the Kittyhawk is long, but narrower than the Wirraway's, so forward visibility was better. I felt perfectly at home as I slowly opened the throttle for take-off. That was a revelation: those other aircraft seemed feeble by comparison to this 1200 horsepower thoroughbred.

Over the following six weeks I flew 42 hours in the P-40, practising formation flying, combat manoeuvres, dive bombing and strafing. It was demanding, but I loved it all. I really did feel like a fighter pilot now.

There were some close calls. Two of the pilots on my course had undercarriage failures, and their Kittyhawks ended up on their bellies. Near misses in practice dogfighting was an occupational hazard, as was ground-looping on landing. Twice we had all six guns of a kittyhawk fire whilst it was parked, scaring the living daylights out of anyone in front of the offending machine. Several trainees were hauled over the coals for parking aircraft and leaving guns armed.

Towards the end of this part of the course we were taken on a gunnery exercise by a well-known squadron leader. He was a household name, as his exploits flying Kittyhawks in Africa with 3 Squadron had been well publicised. He had a number of aerial victories against the Italians and Germans, including against the clearly superior Messerschmitt 109. He was just five feet four inches tall, but a hard flier, hard prankster, and a hard drinker. He was very popular, but sometimes his apparent disdain for what he called "sprog" pilots irritated us.

On this day he led us out to the gunnery range at Yalta, where a white sheet approximately 2 yards square was set up as a target. The sheet was changed after every run. Before we took off, he concluded his briefing with a challenge.

'Anybody who gets more bullets on target than me, I'll buy

them a case of beer. Anybody who gets less, buys me just a bottle of beer!'

I was the second to dive on the target. It was a blustery day, with probably a 35 mph wind across the range, which means that to counter drift, you're angling the aircraft a little. That of course interferes with your gun sighting. I made what I thought might be a suitable correction, aiming a few yards to the left of the target. My guns jammed after only a half-second burst, but the few puffs of dust well to the right of target were enough to see that I'd underestimated just how much drift to allow for.

I flew back to Mildura, the armourers quickly cleared the stoppage, and I was instructed to complete the exercise. This time I got the allowance for drift just right. I didn't make holes in the white sheet, I obliterated it.

I'm not sure if our esteemed squadron leader was aware of my sighting shot, but nothing was said. I wasn't going to tell him, either. A few days later a case of beer was delivered to me, without comment. Not being a big drinker, I shared it with my fellow "sprogs", and for a few days at least was the most popular guy around for two reasons. The beer was one, getting one over "himself" being the other.

I finished the course with an 'above average' rating. Two of my colleagues didn't finish. One spun in from high altitude, probably after a failure of his oxygen system. The other left his pullout too late on the gunnery range. They were both buried in the military cemetery.

It was September 7th and our time at 2 OTU was over. The new base captain, Group Captain Wilfred Arthur, came to address us. "Woof" Arthur, at just 24, was not much older than we were, but was already a legend. He was tall, thin, square-jawed, and good looking. He'd flown with 3 Squadron in Africa, and 75 Squadron in New Guinea. He was credited with ten aerial victories, before being injured when his P-40 caught fire. He knew what he was talking about, and we hung on every word. He spoke quietly but sincerely.

'Congratulations, Gentlemen, you have passed this arduous course, and you are now fully-fledged fighter pilots. You will soon be joining squadrons on the front line. As you must be well aware, and perhaps to your disappointment, at this stage of the war the Japanese are well and truly on the run. Most of their remaining fighters have been held back for defence of their home islands, and it could be that you will never encounter an enemy aircraft in the air. But, if you do, I want to give some advice. Advice that could save your life.

'Before the war began, we were told that the Nips had poor eyesight, were poorly trained, and their aircraft were obsolete. Nothing could be further from the truth. The fact is that the Zero can outfly your Kittyhawk in almost every aspect. It is faster, has a higher rate of climb, a higher ceiling, a much longer range, and is far more manoeuvrable. This discrepancy between the types increases with height, as your Allison engine has only a low-boost supercharger.

'Fortunately, that is not the end of the story. To achieve that kind of performance advantage, the Japanese designers made the Zero extremely light. The airframe is not very strong, and has been known to break up in combat manoeuvres. They have no armour plating to protect the pilot. They have no self-sealing in their fuel tanks, so they burn easily, and they have relatively light armament.

'In contrast, your Kittyhawk is beautifully built. Overly built, in fact, so it is heavy. It will stand battle damage that would destroy most other aircraft. That heaviness means that you can dive away much faster than the Zero. The Allison engine is good and honest. It is much more reliable than the Spitfire's intricate Merlin. The Kittyhawk will do its utmost to bring you home.

'In the event that you do find yourself in aerial combat with a Zero, you must use your advantages to counter theirs. Never try to out-turn the Zero. Turn into an attack: you outgun the Zero, so the enemy will avoid a head-on pass. Then dive away, outrun the Zero, and live to fight another day.'

Privately, Woof Arthur told a group of us about the death of Squadron Leader John Jackson of 75 Squadron. Melbourne-based brass had called him a coward for refusing to dogfight the Zero. Insulted, on his last mission he tried to do it their way, and paid the ultimate price.

✳✳✳

It was time for our postings. Rumours were that we would go to 77 Squadron, 82 Squadron, or the now-forming 101 Squadron. 77 Squadron was the plum, because it was already in action in New Guinea. 82 was the next choice, as it was being readied to go. 101 Squadron was the last choice we all made, because it could take forever to amalgamate all the requirements to form a fighting unit and move it overseas. We waited anxiously for several days.

A WAAF officer from Melbourne, F/O Vicky Keech, came to take us out of our misery. She was from postings. Although I was near the top of the course, I was posted to the bottom choice, 101 Squadron, which was forming at Bankstown Airfield, not far from Sydney city. Several of my colleagues did go to 77 Squadron, but most went to 82 Squadron. Sensing my dismay, Vicky, an attractive blond about my age, had a quiet word to me.

'Gods are said to move in mysterious ways, F/O Richards,' she admonished, 'and so does RAAF Postings. I'm sure the RAAF has plans for you, so it's best not to complain.'

Against all the "inside knowledge", and common sense, 82 Squadron was to spend the following 11 months in a never-ending series of practice missions all over NSW and Queensland.

One of the pilots I kept in touch with, George Morris, added 180 hours to his Kittyhawk total during this period. Surely these guys must have been the best trained fighter pilots anywhere in the world yet to see action. Defying logic, 101 Squadron was destined to leapfrog 82 Squadron, so I wasn't unlucky after all. But all that was ahead.

✳✳✳

On September 19th1944, just twelve days after I received my posting, I had to report to my new squadron. It took one day to return to Melbourne by train, then another day to get to Sydney. The third day got me to Orange, where Lyn and Dad awaited. It was so good to be home, and a whole week of normal living stretched ahead. I'd looked forward to this for so long, but strangely, by the time I had to return to Sydney, I was anxious to go. There was a war on, my new squadron was forming, with new aircraft, and I didn't want to miss out on the action.

It was at Bankstown Airport that we were introduced to our brand new P-40N Kittyhawks. Like every other P-40 I'd ever seen, they'd come out of the US factory painted in olive drab on the uppersides, and neutral grey underneath. But whereas the tired training aircraft at Mildura had been touched up with any paint available, (mostly jungle green and mid-grey), giving them a patchy and dishevelled look, the new mounts were pristine. We were even encouraged to personalize them a little, and some rather clever cartoons appeared on the engine cowlings. I left mine unadorned.

Frustratingly, just as I'd feared, more time went by while rumours of our imminent move circulated daily. We flew every day, on gunnery and dive-bombing practice, formation flying, and long cross-country nav exercises. There was no leave, but there were plenty of incidents to keep us occupied. I had a tyre burst on take-off one day, and an undercarriage leg fold at the end of night flying a week later. Problems with the P-40 undercarriage were not unusual. The most serious accident was with Pilot Officer Crasley, who had to bail out when his aircraft inexplicably caught fire.

I was lucky not to become 101 Squadron's first fatality. The exercise was to climb to 20,000 feet and run through normal manoeuvres to feel how differently the aircraft responded at altitude. I did that okay, noticing just how sluggish the P-40 became as I climbed past 15,000 feet, but then decided to complete the flight with a power dive. I nosed over into a dive of about sixty degrees and kept the power up high. The airspeed indicator wound up rapidly, and the wind over the canopy increased from the usual roar to a fierce howl. When the airframe began to tremble, I figured that I'd gone far enough with this, pulled the throttle back some and tried to do the same with the control stick. It wouldn't budge. The ASI needle jerked around even more: we were increasing our speed. I brought the throttle right back and heaved on the stick. There was no response, and the hundred foot needle on the altimeter was unwinding in a blur. I guessed that I'd already lost half my height, and I was fast running out of ideas.

The trim. I wound back on the trim, then gripping the stick with both hands, and almost standing on the rudder pedals, hauled with all my strength. Bit by bit the nose edged up, and the howling gale lessened ever so slightly. I glanced at the ASI and the needle was creeping back under 500mph. God knows what it had gone to. By the time I regained level flight, I was looking at trees sideways as much as from above. My knees were actually shaking.

One exercise was to fly out to Narromine on a Sunday morning to show off our Kittyhawks to the sprog pilots at the EFTS there, stay the night, then return to Bankstown. On

Saturday I sent a hasty telegram to Dad, asking him to be outside the Hetherington's house at 9 am the following morning. I led the flight of three, and it was only a small detour to Molong. We descended from 8,000 feet down to about 200 feet above the ground as we swept up the familiar valley in line astern. When the galvanised roof of our house came into view, we dropped another 100 feet, and were doing over 350mph as we approached the Hetherington's house.

They were standing together in the wheatfield alongside the house. Dad, Mr and Mrs H, and not-so-little Ellie. They all had their arms in the air. Ellie was furiously waving hers. We flashed over them, pulled up and one by one executed climbing slow rolls before turning right, and heading for the town. Two minutes later we blasted over the main street low enough to scatter pigeons and startle the churchgoers who were lining up for the morning service. It was a bustable offence in the RAAF, but I knew that no Molong resident was ever going to complain.

After climbing back to our cruise altitude and regaining our course to Narromine, a sudden thought jolted me. I should have asked Dad to arrange for Lyn to be there in the wheat paddock too.

CHAPTER 8

New Guinea.

Then everything happened, in a rush. We were going to New Guinea. Over five days we were to stage through Amberley, Townsville, Iron Range, Horn Island, Port Moresby, Nadjab, Tadji, Hollandia, and finally to Kamiri Airstrip on the island of Noemfoor, West Papua, where 77 Squadron was already in residence. It was a harrowing trip. The northern monsoons were in full swing, and the weather closed in on us as soon as we left Townsville for Iron Range, a distance of 400 nautical miles. The only way we could find Iron Range was to head well out to sea before we got there, descend slowly on instruments until we broke through the heavy rain clouds at about 500 feet, (hoping we wouldn't run into an island in the process), then turn west to find the coast, and follow it north until we found the strip. All very nerve wracking when you are low on fuel and there is nowhere else to go if you miss that strip. The last P-40 to land must have been running on fumes!

Heavy rain lashed the area during that night, and our tents

flapped in the near cyclonic wind. The airfield looked more like a lake in the morning, so we called a lay-over. Iron Range is the last vestige of true tropical rain forest left on Cape York, after millions of years of gradual drying out. None of us had ever been to the tropics before, so with a borrowed army jeep, some of us explored the lush coastal jungle and heath-covered mountains. We saw our first palm cockatoos, large black birds with red cheeks and a distinctive call, and our first salt water crocodiles.

The heavy cloud remained, but the rain eventually passed, so we took off from the muddy strip and scudded north, following the coast visually. At times we were down to 250 feet to avoid entering cloud, so the tension was high all the way along the wild and uninhabited cape. It was a relieved bunch of pilots who made it to Horn Island intact.

We were lucky. We learned that one entire squadron of USAAF P-39 Airacobras had been lost in fierce thunderstorms along the Cape. A pair of P-47 Thunderbolts had followed the coast north, under low cloud, had missed seeing Horn Island, and ran out of fuel half way down the western side.

✳✳✳

Not one of us had been outside Australia before, therefore it was with great excitement that we lifted off for the relatively short hop across the Torres Straight to the southern coast of New Guinea. We had scattered islands and coral cays below us along the way, and so having a single engine didn't seem a great disadvantage.

Port Moresby surprised us: we expected a tropical jungle like Iron Range, but we discovered that the coastal fringe in the Moresby area is in a rain shadow. There was more dust than mud. The primitive facilities that the RAAF and AIF had fought under in 1942 and 43 had long been replaced by quite reasonable digs. It was the last time we'd be living in comfort for a long period.

Crossing the mighty Owen Stanley Ranges required an early start, because heavy clouds would frequently obscure the mountains by late morning. We made it to Nadzab, the main RAAF base on the northern side, in time to refuel and do a coastal scud run all the way to Noemfoor Island, on the Dutch side of the border. It was Christmas Eve, 1944, and this was to be our base for some months.

Noemfoor was a low-lying island, covered with tropical jungle, and ringed by coral reefs. It had been a Japanese stronghold until US Marines landed the previous July.

Rather strangely, the maintenance people pounced on our aircraft immediately we arrived, and they worked all through Christmas day stripping the olive drab paint from the tails of our aircraft, and repainting with white. I asked Les, one of the armourers, why?

'You've heard the rule around here, haven't you Rick? When the Japs fly over, we take cover. When the RAAF flies over, the Japs take cover. When the Yanks fly over, everybody takes cover. The same applies to their AA gunners. The bastards are trigger happy, they shoot first and identify later!' I thought Les was pulling my leg, so I posed the same question to a senior Sergeant in Intel. He confirmed Les's story. The American AA gunners had peppered a number of USAAF and RAAF aircraft as they approached to land, more than once with fatal results. It was therefore deemed necessary to paint the tails of all RAAF aircraft in the theatre white, to assist identification and avoid being shot down by our allies.

✷✷✷

The accommodation was fairly rough: four men to each khaki-green tent, which would be red hot during the day, and heavy with humidity at night. It was monsoon season, and rain fell almost every day, converting dust to mud, so duckboards were laid between the tents and the basic facilities of meal tents and semi-open showers and latrines. Because of the heat, we quickly ditched wearing any part of our RAAF uniforms. Night and day we would wear just singlet and shorts, and for flying, unless we were going high, not much more. If we did plan on going high, donning warm clothing before jumping into an oven-like cockpit was murder until the big fan up front produced a blast of air.

I shared a tent with three other pilot officers. There was Harry, very tall and fair headed, with strong features and an RAAF moustache. He was authoritative, but softly spoken. Pat was average height, with dark complexion, a thin moustache, had impeccable manners that reflected the upper class schooling he'd received. Dave was from a working-class background. He was short, solidly built, fair, a real character, and constantly active. He was the one who was always in the know, and could ferret out extra rations, or an extra few bottles of beer. I got on well with them all, but Dave and I clicked. In no time at all we were great mates.

We spoke of our lives before the war, which helped us over the feeling of isolation most of us suffered. We decided that after the war, Dave would visit our farm, and I would travel to Melbourne to visit his girl and his parents.

After dark, and after what the cooks could scrape together as an evening meal, there was little to do. Boredom quickly became our greatest enemy. During the day the sun was so fierce that physical effort was unpleasant, though late in the afternoons we might have a desultory game of football or cricket. At night, it was always wet or even wetter, and any light drew countless insects, so mostly we lay on our bunks in the dark, talking for hours. Even then, moths would flutter in our faces, and wriggly flies would squirm on our skin.

We were all so different. I was the only country boy. We

had vastly different backgrounds and very different plans for the future. However, we were united in our love of flying our Kittyhawks, and the desire to inflict some damage on the enemy before the whole show drew to a close.

There were no missions on Christmas Day, but a volunteer was requested for a fishing expedition. Being a slow learner, I put my hand up. My task turned out to be dropping a bomb into the water just off the island, where a couple of boats were ready to pick up all the dead fish that then floated to the surface. We ate well that night. After the one-day break, we were sent into action.

Noemfoor lay barely 60 miles off the east coast of what was called Vogelkop, the bird's-head peninsula of West Papua. That's the bulbous land mass at the eastern end of the country, which was still occupied by the enemy. There were three Japanese airfields near the coast due west of us, and they and the enemy facilities around them were to be frequent targets for 101 Squadron over the next weeks.

On our first mission we couldn't find any worthwhile targets, but were fired upon by light AA. On our second, we dive bombed bridges near Ransiki and Anda. Joe Lyons left his pullout too late and hit a bridge there. He was 101 Squadron's first casualty. Others quickly followed. The very next day we were to bomb Sagan, but monsoon weather forced us to turn back. Bill Glendinning and Cliff Willis collided in cloud, and both were killed. Our fourth mission took us back to Moemi, where we strafed a few parked aircraft, and gun emplacements, but lost Vic Weymouth to AA fire.

The fifth mission was to Ransiki again. I was diving on a parked Nakajima Oscar fighter when I saw two white-overalled mechanics running from it. They dived into the bush on the edge of the strip, but their white overalls were still clearly visible. My first burst riddled the plane, and my second flattened the two

Nips, permanently. Les Bellert failed to return, so on the sixth day we combed the sea looking for a dinghy, but never found one.

On the seventh day we attacked Jap artillery positions and an ammunition dump. Fred Hewlett crashed on take-off, was badly burned, and killed three locals that happened to be foraging in the jungle at the end of the strip.

Our range of operations widened when the Americans took Middleburg Island, a couple of hundred miles north west, and just off the northern coast of the bird's-head peninsula. They quickly built a 5400-foot runway of crushed coral, which meant that by staging through there, we could attack Amboina, on the island of Seram, and Halmahera Island. 77 Squadron shared the same strip as us, and they began ranging even further west. We were soon to follow.

In February, we forayed as far as Halmahera Island, well past the western tip of New Guinea. Halmahera is mountainous, with stunning peaks and gorges. It is surrounded by white, sandy beaches, and is covered by unbroken and unspoilt forest. The Japanese had built up a huge base there, partly as southern defence for the Philippines. Davao was not far to the north. Even operating out of Middleburg, it was a nerve-wracking 3 hour and twenty-minute round trip over open ocean most of the way.

Day after day we bombed and strafed Halmahera's Galela and Lolabata airstrips, sank barges, destroyed bridges, and blew up fuel dumps. We bombed a convoy, and set some camouflaged barges alight. We lost more pilots to AA. Vin Palme spun in after being hit by AA, Bill Smithwick failed to return, as did Kerry Byrnes and John McLeod. Chris Brown crashed off Moemi. In all this action we were never confronted by Jap fighters, to our considerable disappointment.

One day I had engine trouble and had to abort the early morning mission. A coolant leak was diagnosed, but to get at the offending junction in the coolant pipe was awkward, and would take all day. Whilst I sat around swatting flies in the shade of a tree waiting for repairs, I heard a faint drone. Very high above, a lone aircraft passed over, so high it was almost invisible, and certainly far too high for me to identify. I walked over to where two maintenance men were toiling over my P-40's engine, their deeply bronzed backs glistening with sweat under the blistering sun.

'Hey Bluey, do you know what sort of aircraft that is?' I asked.

'Oh yeah, that's Charlie,' said Bluey. 'He comes over about this time every day. It's a Jap Dinah, probably out of Rabaul or Borpop. It's an unarmed reconnaissance aircraft. We just ignore him.'

I glanced at my watch: it was just a few minutes past midday. What I'd been told astounded me, so I wandered over to the intelligence officers' tent.

'Yes Richards, As I'm sure you know, the Mitsubishi Ki-46, has Allied code name Dinah. Sleek, light weight, long range, crew of three, two big Mitsubishi engines, around 1500 horsepower each. They're designed to operate at very high altitudes. Fast too. Forget about going after Charlie. He's too quick and too high for your P-40 to catch. He's cruising at around 265 mph, at about 35,000 feet. If you chased him, he'd put the foot down and run away at over 400 mph. Since the Japs probably don't have any planes left to attack us here, we just let him take a look, no harm done, and let him be. Don't bother to ask your squadron leader about him either. He'll tell you that you'd be wasting time and fuel.'

That incensed me. The very idea that this impudent bugger could fly over our base with impunity! A plan began to form, though I knew I would be playing with fire. Behind the active area stood a lone Spitfire. It looked a bit worn and unloved and apparently had been abandoned. I went back to Bluey and asked him about it.

'Yeah, it's a Spit mark five. It belongs to 79 Squadron, and months ago one of their blokes flew it here from Goodenough Island, then got malaria pretty badly. The whole squadron then got the word to move back to Australia for re-equipping with the new mark eight Spits. I think they've forgotten about this one.'

Comparing the Spitfire to the Kittyhawk was a bit akin to comparing a sports car to a truck. Even this old mark five would leave my P-40 bobbing in its wake. The Spit was at least 1500 pounds lighter, had an extra 300 horsepower, and was much more nimble. On the downside, the Spitfire was inclined to overheat in the tropics, and wear out fast in dusty conditions. With its narrow-track undercarriage, it wasn't well suited to New Guinea's rough airfields. Overall, the Spitfire hadn't been very successful in New Guinea. I'd never flown one, but that wasn't going to stop me, because with it, I reckoned I had a chance of catching that Dinah.

It took some pleading with Bluey, and a promise of some free beer, but by ten thirty the following morning, the Spit was ready for a "test flight", but I deliberately took my time to prepare. I asked the armourers to put in just enough ammunition for a five second burst. I calculated how much fuel I'd need for a twenty-minute full power climb to 35,000 feet, loiter for 15 minutes, go to full power for a couple of minutes, then glide home "on the fumes". I left my service pistol, flare gun, mae west, dinghy, and water bottle behind, and at exactly 11.25 am, started up for my quick sortie.

I'd never been above 26,000 feet before, as the Kittyhawk's climb rate above 15,000 feet was sluggish at best. In contrast, the Spit's altimeter just kept winding around. I loved the aircraft's snug cockpit. The bubble canopy wasn't much bigger than my head, and by stretching my neck and twisting around I could just see the outer tips of the tailplane. At 35,000 feet I levelled off, throttled back, and waited. It was freezing, and I shivered with cold or anticipation, or probably both. I'd worried that Charlie might be early that day, but my luck was in, and there'd been no sign of it yet. I settled back to wait. It looked a long way down from that little canopy. Knowing that the Dinah would be cruising at very nearly my maximum speed at this altitude, I figured that I had to see him first, and make a head-on pass. I'd arranged Bluey to make a short radio call if Charlie was sighted from the ground. I waited, orbiting over the field. Fifteen minutes came and went. Nothing. The fuel gauges were already ominously low.

'Just two more minutes,' I promised myself. Those minutes passed too, and I was about to pull the throttle back to glide home.

The radio crackled. 'Charlie sighted one mile east.'

Desperately I searched the sky. I was directly overhead the field, but where was he? I saw a flash of dark jungle green colour against the blue ocean to my left. There he was, almost abeam and about a hundred feet below me. A pretty aeroplane, with a glazed nose extending way back in a smooth curve, streamlined engine nacelles, and a steeply raked tail fin. Damn, am I too late? He was heading west, and I was heading east. I'd missed my opportunity for a head-on attack, and now, the question was, could I catch him before my fuel ran out?

I wracked the Spitfire into a steep left turn. The aircraft trembled, on the edge of a stall in the thin atmosphere. I levelled off directly behind the Dinah, but out of range. I rammed the throttle wide open, and held it there. At 370 mph, well above my Kittyhawk's top speed at this altitude, I was gaining, but painfully slowly. A minute later I was still out of effective range, and my fuel was disappearing at an alarming rate. I had to break off, as there'd be a court martial if I pranged the plane, out of fuel, on a fruitless chase. I had nothing to lose, so I raised the nose, aiming just above the Dinah, and pressed the gun button for a two-second burst. The Spit trembled under the recoil of the six guns: two 20mm cannons and four .303 machine guns. Nothing: the Dinah flew on oblivious to my presence. I had just one burst remaining. I raised the nose a fraction more, and my speed began to decay. It was now or never. I pressed the gun button again and instantly sparks flew off the Dinah's left wing-root and engine. My guns stopped, empty, and my quarry flew on without deviating, because the pilot hadn't realised that he was under attack. He was probably trying to deal with what he thought was a sudden engine problem.

His left prop began to windmill, and in seconds sparks grew into smoke, then there was a gout of fire. Bits began to break off, and the left wing dipped, exposing its sky-blue underside. I rolled away with minimum throttle, and dived for Noemfoor. Over my shoulder, I watched the curving smoke trail tighten into a steep death spiral. I lost sight of it when I had to concentrate on making it back to the field. I made a high gliding approach, and my engine quit, out of fuel, just as I rolled to a stop. I sat for a moment without unbuckling, contemplating the fact that I'd just killed three men.

I never admitted that I'd planned to attack the Dinah. I said that I just decided to test the Spitfire's ability at very high altitude. Bluey and his cobber kept their mouths shut. The Squadron leader had his suspicions, but could hardly bawl me out when the rest of the squadron was busy celebrating my aerial victory. It was to be the only one for 101 Squadron for the war.

✶✶✶

In March we continued to bomb and strafe Japanese airfields, jetties, fuel dumps, and army installations, losing three more pilots to AA. On the 5th, Bill Proudfoot ran up the arse of Len Gillam's Kittyhawk as we taxied for take-off. He destroyed the rear fuselage of Len's aircraft, the engine stalling only as the prop was shaving the back of Len's headrest.

On the 6th, we bombed a Jap convoy off Biak, in combination with some RAAF Beaufighters. One of these powerful twins was shot down by AA, and we spent the next day searching unsuccessfully for the crew.

Our next mission was to attack Babo airstrip, which was near the western edge of the peninsula, near Sorong. As the formation formed up after the attack, one of our pilots called up on the radio. He'd taken a hit from AA and his engine was overheating. Even with the static of a faulty radio, I had the horrible feeling it was Dave I heard make the call. Within a minute he called again.

'I'm going down. Engine's seized. I'll ditch just off that beach up ahead.' This time I heard Dave clearly, and I spotted him just as he made a perfect ditching, just half a mile off a white sandy beach a few miles west of our smoking target. Three of us orbited and watched him climb out of the sinking P-40, and swim towards the shore.

We stayed overhead for as long as we could, but we had to head back to Middleburg, the closest Allied strip, when fuel ran low. By the time we returned, escorting an amphibious US Navy Catalina, there was no sign of our pilot. Much later we learned that Dave had been captured and executed by sword, right there on that beach.

I wrote letters to Dave's parents, and his girl, but never heard back. I guess I should have been insulated by now after having lost a few colleagues, but this one hit me hard. I think often of Dave to this very day.

✳✳✳

Before we left Australia, we'd known that the tide of the war had swung very much in the Allies' favour. Now that we were in the theatre, it became very clear to us that the main thrust of the war had passed us by. The Americans had a two-pronged plan to defeat Japan. Australian forces had been at the fore-front of the western prong that had pushed the enemy from Kokoda back to Buna, then progressively back through West Papua into the Dutch East Indies, and now was heading towards the Philippines and Borneo. But, bit by bit, the Yanks had assumed the leading role. Only pockets of resistance were left along the way, including in Timor, Bougainville, New Britain and New Ireland, and a few outposts in West Papua. It was becoming more and more obvious that we were being left to mop up behind the main thrust.

Rumour was that Douglas MacArthur wanted to retake the Philippines no matter what the cost, and whether tactically it made sense or not. He also wanted all the glory of the victory, and didn't want to share it with Australia's General Blamey.

Instead of bypassing now-isolated Japanese outposts, leaving them to wither on the vine, Blamey was pushing us hard in what many considered useless actions to win some glory for himself before it was all over. We mere foot soldiers just paid the price with our own blood. I never heard a good word about Blamey from any of the guys doing the actual fighting.

In the big picture, the entire western prong was being outpaced by the one from the east. The US Navy and Marines, aided by our own navy, had pushed the Japanese out of the Solomon Islands and were island-hopping directly towards Japan. The fighting was fierce, and there were heavy losses on both sides, but in the frequent air battles, new US aircraft like the F6F Hellcat and F4U Corsair were proving to be vastly superior to the aging Zero. The Japanese were also running out of experienced pilots.

We continued to slog it out with the desperate remnants

left behind the front line. They fought hard because to them surrender was not an option. They fought to the death, despite diminishing, or even non-existent, supplies from the homeland.

✳✳✳

Although the pilots of 101 Squadron continued with normal ops of dive bombing and strafing, the initial mood of excitement and optimism slowly gave way to discontent. We questioned the value we were making to the war effort, and we complained about the living conditions, which cycled between dry and dusty, and soaking wet and muddy. It was almost always hot and humid, dysentery was a constant problem, and mosquitoes soon had many suffering from malaria and dengue fever. In many ways our maintenance guys had it worse than the pilots. They worked through blistering sun and steamy rain, and never had the respite from heat or boredom we had by going into action. No matter their herculean efforts, they could not keep our machinery up to the standard we sought. Spares, food, and drink were always in short supply. Strangely, we were never short of ammunition!

We still loved our Kittyhawks, but now saw the Americans being re-equipped with superior new types of aircraft. Even our cousins in the RNZAF were re-equipping, swapping their aging Kittyhawks for the Vought F4U Corsair. The RAAF Spitfires had not worked well in the tropics, and so we soldiered on with the P-40 as our frontline fighter all the way to the end. It was costing us lives, as our liquid-cooled engines were vulnerable to ground fire. Most of our losses came from damaged radiators. By contrast, the Americans had P-38s with twin engines, or air-cooled radial engined P-47s, F4Us, and F6Fs. We heard stories how the radial-engined fighters would sometimes come home even with a cylinder shot off.

I dreaded heavy rain that would scrub missions. Going

for days without flying meant intolerable boredom. Morale fell. Some took to drink, and got into trouble stealing from the limited supplies of alcohol available. Others gambled, and we all missed home. This continued right up to Easter, then a seven-day stand-down was announced. On Good Friday I was instructed to drop another bomb in the water off Noemfoor. We ate well that night.

Some of my squadron mates revelled in the prospect of seven days with little to do but rest. I dreaded sitting around, sweltering under the thin shade of coconut palms and drinking beer, followed by lying in extreme humidity in cloying canvas tents at night. So, I pricked up my ears when volunteers were called for a special mission. Despite now knowing that the first rule you should learn when joining the RAAF was "never volunteer for anything," and having suffered for forgetting it before, again I did. I later had cause to wish that I'd followed that unwritten rule.

In a short briefing, four of us learned that the Japanese garrison at Rabaul, although bypassed and largely ineffective, was a thorn in MacArthur's side, and he wanted it eliminated. Common sense said to let it be, as the 100,000 to 150,000 Japanese there were close to starving anyway. That didn't stop MacArthur. He said that they still represented the largest concentration of force the enemy had behind the moving front line, and he feared that the remnant force of G4M "Betty" bombers and Ki-61 "Tony" fighters on the satellite field at Borpop could make a nuisance of themselves by attacking the new US base on Green Island.

The New Zealanders had prime responsibility for maintaining constant harassment of the Rabaul garrison, and they used their Corsairs and Lockheed Venturas effectively, aided by periodic attacks by USAAF B-24s, P-38s, B-25s and B-26s, US Navy SBF and F6Fs from carriers, and RAAF Beaufighters.

A big raid was being planned, and the RNZAF asked our intel

people at Nadzab if we could mount a simultaneous supressing raid on Borpop, on the island of New Ireland, only a short flight from Rabaul itself. It was a stretch for our Kittyhawks, but we were the only aircraft available. Everyone else was intent on moving north west, and by now regarded Rabaul as a backwater that didn't justify the risk. No attack by ground-based forces was being planned for either Rabaul or Borpop: it was up to the allied air forces to eliminate the threat, such as it was.

✳✳✳

Four of us were to return to Nadzab, where we'd be further briefed for the mission.

'Should be fun,' I said to my mate Jim Austin. 'It'll beat sitting around here getting blotto!' I should have known better, but nobody ever accused fighter pilots of having any commonsense.

We took off in darkness, the field lit only by flares along the perimeter. Within minutes we were over the invisible ocean, still climbing to our cruising altitude of 15,000 feet. It was cold up there, and my feet were freezing. We had to go that high, because that's where our fuel economy was best. Our internal fuel and underbelly tank combined would only give us enough range to make the 500-mile overwater crossing and return with a reserve of a half hour's flying, if we were careful. Our initial heading was 090 degrees magnetic, to take us around the southern tip of New Britain. Then we would follow the coast (well offshore) heading 045 degrees, until abeam New Ireland's Cape St George. After that we'd cross the strait and follow New Ireland's east coast to Borpop.

First light came, the colourless world of the night rapidly giving way to a brilliantly clear morning. The sea below us quickly changed from black to deep blue. New Britain's low coastal jungle, separated from the sea by a narrow strip of white sand, appeared on the horizon right on schedule. We changed course, turning to 045 degrees, to take us to Cape St George, the southern tip of New Ireland. We began our descent as we swept up the east coast, ultimately to just a few hundred feet above a long offshore reef. It was now warm and humid, my feet were no longer frozen, and we knew it would soon be much warmer.

We'd studied the aerial photos to identify Borpop, so we knew to look for the bay's prominent northern headland. To avoid the AA guns on it, the plan was to angle in from the sea, sweep in over the southern edge of the bay, then make a single strafing pass along the enemy airfield. We'd be gone before the defenders woke up.

The headland was clear to see, so we cinched up our harnesses, pulled down our goggles, trimmed for speed, armed our guns, then, in line astern, pushed over for the attack. We hit the scattered Jap aircraft parked along the edge of the strip with all guns blazing. As we pulled up, we dropped our pairs of 250 pound bombs. We'd caught them napping alright, there was no sign of any defensive fire. I laughed aloud as a glance in my mirror showed several aircraft burning. We'd done it!

Euphoria lasted only until Tony began the turn for another pass. Call me psychic, but I knew immediately that this could end in tears, our tears. Or more specifically, as I was the last in the formation, most likely mine.

CHAPTER 9

Just north of Borpop Airfield, New Ireland Province, New Guinea, April 2nd, 1945.

The blackness and silence were total, but I became aware of a stabbing pain behind my eyes, and an urgent need to pee. That shouldn't happen, I thought. I'm dead. This feeling came and went a few times. Strange. The headache eased, but then my back began to ache. How could it, when I'd left my old body behind?

I sensed movement, and I strained to see. A face is hovering over me. White teeth. Strong white teeth, a contrast to dark skin. A wide smile. I slowly made out an outline. A strong, straight nose, dark eyes, a beehive of dense black and curly hair, then I heard her call, softly but urgently.

'Masta Jack, he awake. He awake. Come quick.'

I winced at the suddenness of the sound, and then the face was above me again. She giggled softly, then made soothing sounds. I became aware of my surroundings. I was in a hut, a small dark hut, not much bigger than the bed I was lying on. Well, not so much a bed as rough-sawn planks with some sort of matting. The only light came from the open doorway. I lifted my shoulders and swung my legs to try to sit up. I could see that the floor was hard-packed dirt. The girl stepped back into the doorway, still smiling. I suddenly realized that I was stark naked, and covered only in sweat. The hut was hot and the air stiflingly heavy with humidity.

I looked for something to cover myself, but there was no sheet, blanket, clothing or anything that would serve that purpose.

I heard a gruff voice, and another figure squeezed past the girl into the hut. A white man I thought, but so darkly tanned I was uncertain. He had an almost-white scruffy beard hiding most of his face. He wore a pair of tattered shorts and nothing else. He was wiry and slightly stooped, and I guessed he'd be well into his 70's.

'Awake at last, eh.'

I nodded, although the answer seemed pretty obvious, 'Where am I?' I winced at my own simplistic question. 'How did I get here?'

'Before I answer that, I'm Jack, and this here is Kala. She's from Huris village.'

I nodded again, still very conscious of my nakedness. I managed to mumble 'I'm Eric, Eric Richards. But call me Rick. Everybody does.'

'We figured that, since you've got a name tag that says Eric Ernest Richards. Since you crashed a plane from the RAAF, we guessed that you are a pilot in the RAAF too.'

I managed a lop-sided smile, threw a sloppy salute, which must have looked odd when I was sitting, and still stark naked. I responded 'Pilot Officer Richards at your service, Sir.'

We shook hands. Even in the poor light, I could see that the old man's hands were calloused and hard, with dirt ingrained into his skin. I could also tell that while his manner was gruff, his eyes were kindly.

'You've been asleep for two days. I reckon you must be hungry by now. Come over to my hut and I'll rustle up some grub.'

'I need a pee first, then that will go down well.' I glanced at Kala, registering that she was a very well-built girl, curvy, and pretty at that.

Jack laughed. 'Don't be bashful in front of Kala. Native girls grow up fast, and she must be nineteen, maybe twenty. She'll be married soon. She's been helping you with, ah, the necessities for the last two days.'

Kala brought me my clothes. They had been washed and dried in the sun. She watched as I pulled my undies and shorts on, rather self-consciously, and guided me as I stumbled out into the blazing sun. My eyes screwed up tight in the glare, and the world began to spin. In an instant Kala was holding my arm tight, and was helping me to a rough timber bench in the shade. Jack sat opposite, and I could feel his scrutiny. Kala handed me a bowl of creamy liquid. I tasted it hesitatingly. It was sweet pineapple juice, perhaps slightly fermented. My head felt light after I drank it all.

'How did I get here Jack? I thought I was dead until I woke up with Kala leaning over me. I thought she might be an angel for a minute.'

Jack smiled. At least I think he did. His beard was so bushy it was hard to tell. 'You are one lucky young fella,' he said. 'A couple of boys from the village were hunting wild pigs near where you crashed. When they plucked up the courage to take a close look, they found that you were still breathing. They pulled you out of the wreck and carried you to me. The Japs were not far behind, beating through the bush looking for your plane. They kept looking for you for a couple of days. Fortunately, they rarely get up into the hills here, so they have never found my camp. Not yet anyway, otherwise I'd be a goner.'

'Why are you here, Jack?'

'I've been in New Ireland for over a decade. I've lived in New Guinea for two. I came here and set up a small copra plantation, the only one this far down the coast from Kavieng. It was going well until the Japs came. All the plantation owners up north from here either got out in time, or got caught and shot. I'm the only one left, and I survived because I got away from the coast into this hide-out. Since I've always treated the locals fairly, paid them well and all that, they've been loyal and helped me hide. They bring me kau kau. Fresh fruit, yams, and the occasional bit of meat. Either pig or cuscus. Kala brings it. She was here when the boys brought you to me. Seems she took a shine to you and has stayed the last two days.'

I nodded, taking a bit of time to take this all in. 'Don't you worry that the Japs will find you one day?'

'Course I do. It's only a matter of time. The village kids have always been fascinated by my skin. Half of them think I'm a ghost and are too terrified to come near me, and the other half think I'm a curiosity and want to follow me around all day. It only takes one of them to make a slip and tell a Jap that I'm here, and they'll find me alright.'

'Does their searching for me increase the risk of them finding you?'

'Maybe. But the boys said that there was so much blood spattered all over the cockpit, they probably think you've just wandered into the scrub, collapsed and died.'

✳✳✳

For almost two weeks I lazed about Jack's camp, doing odd jobs where I could to help Jack and Kala. There were four rough huts, around a fire pit. Another smaller shelter had a rough plumbing system, consisting of a drum on the roof, and shower and basin inside. Alongside that was a long-drop toilet.

There was a post about five feet tall with a small table on top. Periodically each day brilliant red, blue, and yellow Eclectus parrots visited the table, and each time Jack or Kala would replenish the offerings that attracted them. A pair of kokomos strutted around the camp too. These large and inquisitive hornbills poked their bills into everything, and followed Jack everywhere like faithful puppies. They'd fly off sometimes, but would come back an hour or too later, their slow wing beats heralding their return.

The gash over my right eye was healing nicely, and I got stronger every day. I was actually feeling pretty fit, but then something weird happened. One afternoon I walked into "my" hut, and banged my left shoulder against the very stout left door post. It was a solid collision, and I stumbled back. Jack called me to sit down. 'Careless me,' I thought.

It happened again the next day. Unless I was extremely careful, I kept misjudging the doorway. Then the headaches began: throbbing headaches that made me feel that my head would explode. I felt giddy every time I stood up, and had to steady myself before moving. I noticed that Jack was watching me closely.

'Rick, when war broke out in 1914, I volunteered for the army. They said I was too old to be an infantry man, so I became a medic. A corpsman, I was called. I did some basic training, and off I went to France. I spent a year in the trenches, and I saw a lot of things one shouldn't have to see. I guess that's part of the reason I've hidden myself in this backwater for so long: I just don't want to be part of a world where men can do such horrible things to each other anymore. Anyway, the point is, I know what is wrong with you. I've seen it all before.'

I looked at Jack. I could tell by the way he avoided my eyes as he spoke, that this wasn't going to be good.

'I think you have bleeding on the brain, or at least, you did have after your crash. Now, your body is trying to disperse the blood clot by absorbing fluid into the cavity around your brain. It will continue to do that until it kills you. There's obviously more pressure on one side than the other, and your brain is being squeezed to one side. That's why you can't judge doorways.'

Jack hesitated. I was too dumbstruck to respond before he continued.

'There is a cure. A fairly simple one in most cases, and where there are proper facilities. That is to drill a hole in your skull to relieve the pressure. I think we have to do that. Of course, doing it here with what tools we have available is going to be unpleasant, and downright risky. Our facilities here aren't exactly sterile.'

I think my brain, even in its compromised state, refused to accept what I was hearing. I sat dumfounded for a minute. Even on the farm I was a bit squeamish with some of the things we had to do with our animals. The very idea of what Jack proposed appalled me.

'How the hell are you going to do that, Jack? You're not a doctor, you don't have antiseptics, antibiotics, surgical instruments, or anaesthetics. Hell, I'm going to die, aren't I?' My voice was surprisingly steady, not revealing the helplessness I felt.

Jack reached out and gripped my forearm. 'Not if I can help it, lad. I know it's risky, and believe me, it's the last thing I want to do, that is except for doing nothing but watch you die.'

Faced with two dreadful alternatives, I numbly nodded that I understood. Jack handed me a bottle of scotch whiskey. I shook my head. 'A beer or glass of wine is great once a while, but I've never touched that hard stuff, Jack.'

'Good for you, lad, but make this an exception. I've got two strong island boys coming shortly to hold you down while I operate, but believe me, it'll go better if you are drunk as a skunk. This is my very last bottle of the finest Scotch whiskey. I've been hoarding it for a couple of years for a special occasion. I guess this is it, so don't waste it by dying on me, ya hear?'

When the time came, I gulped the scotch and as I'd never been a big drinker, soon fell into a numb stupor. Jack used the last of his precious whiskey to clean the skin on my forehead. Then, with a cutthroat razor, shaved my hair almost to the top of my head. He then used the same razor to make an incision along the hair line above my right eye, and then down almost to my ear. He pulled the flap of skin back, and with an old carpenters' brace and bit that he'd last used in erecting his hut, drilled a hole into my skull.

I didn't feel the cut. I did feel my skin being peeled back. I felt and heard the grinding of the coarse drill bit, designed to bore holes through wood, and I heaved against the strong arms pinioning me to the hard bed. I heard a guttural scream, and realized it was coming from my throat. Not quickly enough, I passed out altogether.

When I awoke, Jack and Kala were sitting watching me. I groaned and tried to sit up. Jack immediately pushed me back down. While he held my shoulders, he spoke quietly.

'Rick, the operation went well. We've drained a lot of coagulated blood. We've done our best to prevent infection by boiling the tools I used, and the bandage on your head. I've stitched the cut, though my handiwork would look better on a scarecrow than on a human. Sorry about that. The thing is, you have now lost all the fluid around your brain. It's going to take a week or so for the hole to seal itself and the natural fluid to accumulate. In fact, we're going to elevate your bed at the foot end, to hasten the process. We'll leave it like that for three days. You have to lie on your back, without a pillow, for those three days. You can't sit up, not even to eat, drink, or pee. Then you must stay off your feet for another week after that. If you were to stand up and move around, you'd risk damaging your brain. You might then suffer seizures.'

***

Those first three days were the most miserable I could have imagined. My head throbbed, my back ached, and I was so, so, embarrassed when natural body functions couldn't be put off any longer. They weren't easy, lying on my back, but it must have been extremely unpleasant for Kala. Not that she even hinted at that. She was gentle but firm, and highly efficient. Drinking and eating were unpleasant chores. I struggled with swallowing anything, felt like throwing up, and ended up with a mess around my face and neck every time. My throat was parched, but when I drank, half of it went up my nose. On the fourth day Kala gave me a pillow made of coarse cloth and stuffed with dry grass. That made drinking and eating less of a chore for both of us.

On top of the pain and discomfort, I was bored, totally bored, I had nothing to look at but the dark thatched roof of the hut. Only Kala's constant attention kept me from going mental. She talked to me, but I could understand little. However, over that week I did pick up some basic words.

I was able to move around a little in the second week, and by the third felt moderately normal, just weak, washed out, and useless. I was beginning to believe that I was mending rapidly. At the end of the third week, the headaches returned. Again, I bumped into things, on my right side this time, and again my head began to feel like it would explode. I asked Jack if he knew what was happening to me.

'Rick, there was always a chance this might happen. I'd say that the bleed has been right across the front of your brain. I've drained one side, where the gash was, but the clot that's left on the other side is going to be a problem unless we drain it, too.'

'How much of a problem? Another one that will kill me?'

'I'm afraid so. The clot will continue to suck fluid in, squashing your brain. It won't be a nice way to go. The only alternative is to go through the same operation again, but on the left side. I've got to warn you that it may be that I just can't drain off enough of the clot, and even with a second go at it, I might not succeed.'

✳✳✳

I was utterly depressed when I went back onto the rough wooden plank that was Jack's makeshift operating table. Helplessness engulfed me and I shivered even in the heat as I resigned myself to another horrific operation, and another week of pure purgatory. This time it was worse, because the only anaesthetic Jack had left was some rotgut that he'd brewed from pineapples and other tropical fruit. It felt to me that the drilling was going on forever, because the rotgut wasn't nearly as effective as Jack's scotch had been.

Three weeks later I began to feel okay, but I feared another return of that pressure in my head. Every twinge, every ache, every slight misstep could have been the warning I dreaded, but my headaches gradually receded, and my strength slowly built up. After a month, Jack clapped me on the back.

'I think we're out of the woods, Lad. Well done! I think you are past the danger period. I was worried that the small holes I drilled weren't going to be large enough to let all the clot out, but by now I think we can say we've succeeded.

'You're not pretty anymore, with the scar from your crash plus my work with scissors, knife and needle, but now you've got an interesting face. And since I had to operate on both sides, you're now symmetrical!' He laughed, but I knew that the whole business had been a terrible strain on him too.

When I got to look in the mirror that Jack had hanging from a nail in his shower, I was horrified at the face that looked back at me. The part of my scalp that had been shaved was now covered with a new stubble. Angry scars ran from the hairline above each eye to the top of each ear. The stitching looked like the type you'd see on the top of a bag of wheat grain. My skin was dark from sitting in the sun, but it was lined like a man double my age. On my forehead there was the remnants of a large bruise, just to the left of centre

Jack saw me closely examining the damage.

'Don't worry son. When your hair grows back, you'll look almost human again.'

∗∗∗

I improved a little each day, and after a few more weeks I was quite active. Ever since I was a little kid, I'd had a list of jobs longer than there was time available to do them. Being idle was okay when physically I had no choice, and at one point I even wondered if I could come to enjoy idleness. I quickly admonished myself for feeling that way. Now I was bored just sitting around. I asked Jack to take me for the long walk back to my Kittyhawk. He reluctantly agreed.

I struggled in the heat, and when we got there, I was surprised to find that little was left of the P-40. The Japanese must have set fire to it, and only the tail and outer wing panels were recognisable, still exhibiting original paint. The rudder moved slightly in the light breeze, but otherwise there was silence. The kunai grass was burnt for a hundred yards around, and only a convenient late afternoon shower had likely saved the whole plain from burning.

On another day, Kala took me for the long hike to the coast. We were cautious crossing the coastal track, but saw no Japanese patrols. She took me to an idyllic V-shaped inlet, which had a narrow white sandy beach just 50 yards from end to end. It was bordered by thick jungle, and several tall coconut palms leant over the beach, so that their shadows reached the water's edge. The water was crystal clear, and shallow for 20 yards or more, going from turquoise to deep blue further out. You could see an occasional white cap as waves broke over the fringing reef some distance from shore.

We played in the warm sea like children, splashing and chasing each other, before lazing on the sun-dappled sand. I'd stripped to shorts, but Kala kept on her neck-to-knee, brightly coloured wrap. When wet, it did little to hide her athletic body. The gentlest of breezes swayed the coconut palms above us. We talked quite a bit, although neither of us understood much of what the other was saying. We were relaxed in each other's company, but then I sensed that Kala may be expecting more from me. Appealing as the thought might have been, I was committed already, and nothing was going to break me of that. I could see that in other circumstances it might have been easy to succumb to the rhythm of island life, and as they say, "go native."

Now it was obvious that the second operation had cleared my skull of the offending clot, I wanted to be even more active. So, when two of the village men wandered in and invited Jack and I on a fishing expedition, I jumped at the chance. Jack wasn't entirely happy.

'Look boy, you know what will happen if the Japs catch you. But if you must go, wear a pair of my old shorts, and a dirty shirt. The dirtier the better. Use some fat to smear your face and legs, and I'll rub some charcoal into it. Keep a bandanna over your hair.'

Duly anointed, I went off with the two boys in the early hours of the morning. I stumbled after them in the darkness as they followed narrow footpaths unerringly to the Borpop bay.

To my horror, we wended our way between the airstrip camp and the garrison on the northern headland that operated the anti-aircraft guns. At first light, almost under the guns, the boys pushed a dugout canoe into the still and warm water of the bay. From there we paddled towards the twin sandy islands just off the mouth of the bay.

Once past the islands, the boys anchored the dugout, (with a rope tied around a small rock), right on the edge of the reef that ran parallel to the coast. Within minutes, they were catching reef fish. Their technique was to stand in the canoe, with spear poised, make the thrust, then dive after the spear. They missed a few, but succeeded in spearing a variety of brightly coloured fish.

As the sun rose, the smell of fish did too. By mid morning I was frying, so I jumped overboard. The water was warm, and clear as crystal. The coral just below was stunning in its array of shapes and colours, as were the variety of small fish that darted in and out of the multitude of hidey-holes. I was fascinated. I doubted that any farm boy from Molong had ever seen anything like this. In my fascination, I completely lost track of time.

I'd drifted some distance from the canoe and the boys, and was beginning to tire. I wasn't used to swimming. I popped my head up and turned to find the canoe. What I saw frightened the living daylights out of me. A small Jap tender, probably one used to service their floatplanes, had come out of the harbour, and had pulled up alongside the canoe. A couple of Japs in uniform were talking to the native boys. I was a sitting duck.

I turned away, and pretended to look for reef fish. I bobbed up and down, as if diving with a spear. I was getting more and more tired, when I realized that the tide had turned, and I was drifting further out to sea. Was I evading the Japs only to drown? I was getting desperate, and I didn't have the strength to swim back to the canoe. It was hard enough to keep my head above water.

The tender parted from the canoe, Japs and boys waved to each other, and then the canoe was heading in my direction. They hauled me bodily out of the water, and I slumped, exhausted, into the bottom of the canoe with the fish catch. The boys looked concerned, then began to howl with laughter.

'White man' was all they could say. I then realized that the charcoal and fat disguise had been well and truly washed off by then, and if the Jap boatmen had taken more than a glance at me, they would have seen me for what I was. It was close call for all three of us.

***

Four weeks had gone by after the second operation, and I realized that it was the middle of July. I'd been with Jack for almost four months, I would have been posted 'missing believed killed' after our raid on Borpop, and it constantly worried me how Dad and Lyn would have taken the news. I began thinking of ways I might be able to get back to Allied lines, and I discussed these with Jack. He summed up the situation.

'The only way out of here is by boat or plane, obviously. Only the Japs have planes, so that leaves boats. Most boats on the island were used by plantation owners wanting to escape when the Japs arrived, or, apart from a few native canoes, were destroyed by them. Except for one: I've got this old whaleboat hidden in the mangroves, in an inlet about ten miles south of Borpop. It's a bit rotten, but I think it will hold together for one last voyage. I had planned to sail it to the mainland, but I have three problems.'

'Only three?' I asked. 'Is it a sail boat, or does it have an engine?'

'Yeah, well, there's the rub. It's got both, but you'd need the engine to get out of the inlet and far enough off the coast to pick up some wind. So, the first issue is that I can't get the engine started, and I have no idea what the problem is.'

'I'm fairly handy with mechanical things, Jack. Can I have a look at it?'

'Sure, Rick, but then what do we do for fuel? That's the second problem. I've got one four-gallon drum. We need more than that.'

'And what's the third problem?'

'I've had a heart problem for a long time, Rick. Before the Japs came, I sailed up to Namatanai and saw a doctor. He told me to retire and take it easy, otherwise I'd be dead within a year. Well, I didn't retire, or take it easy, and that year was up two years ago. He gave me some pills to take whenever I had heart pain, but I ran out of them a while back. I'm not feeling all that great at the moment, and I'm not going to be much help in sailing a boat for days on end. I've sailed these waters before, and I know the risks, and that was before the Japs came and complicated things.'

'Right, Jack, I understand. Wouldn't you be better off staying here? The Japs were well and truly on the run at the new year, so it can't be more than another year or so before they're kicked all the way back to Japan, and then you'll be able to get medical help.'

'Yeah, I know the options. I'm between the devil and the deep blue sea, literally. I've thought about it, and I'll take my chances with you. If you reckon you can handle the boat pretty much by yourself, then my best chance is to get to the mainland and get some new pills. There is one other issue too: Kala,'

I nodded, but wasn't quite sure what Jack was getting at. I said, 'What about her?'

'I'm worried that if I stay, there's a risk every day that the Japs will find me, or us. They'll snare Kala too. Very likely she'd be raped and then killed. She's a good girl, and I don't want that to happen. I think she either comes with us, or stays away from here altogether.'

'Come with us, Jack? Surely, she wouldn't want to do that?'

'I think she might. You can act dumb, but you must have realised that she's sweet on you?'

***

The following day we hiked, in single-file, the three miles or so through the jungle from Jack's hideout in the foot hills to the inlet. The narrow path was marked out of the dense forest by bare feet over the years Jack had lived there. We took with us the few appropriate tools he had. The nearer we got to the coast, the more careful we had to be to avoid running into Jap foot patrols that regularly used the coastal road.

That road had been widened by the German administration during the 1920s, from a footpath that had probably been used for centuries, to one suitable for light vehicles. Fortunately, Jack had found a perfect place to store his old boat: the upper reaches of a muddy tidal flat just a few yards wide, and surrounded by mangroves and thick scrub. It wasn't more than fifty yards from the coast road, but nobody would see it unless they accidently stumbled over it. Pushing aside spiny branches I clambered down a slippery bank and aboard the hulk. It wasn't an encouraging sight.

The bow was firmly anchored to a fallen log, but the stern of the open boat was barely floating, the gunnels being only an inch or two above the water. The boat had once been painted mid-blue, but most of that paint had long gone. What was left of it was chipped and faded. The wood of the transom looked like it had cracked. It was waterlogged and had partially rotted. A deep pool of black water filled the bilge, and it stank. Mosquitoes swarmed above it, and worse, the ancient and rusty Stuart Turner single-cylinder engine, mounted midships, was partially sitting in the foul smelling liquid.

'Jesus Jack, no wonder it wouldn't start. I hope the bilge water hasn't gotten into the sump, or the bore. The piston will be rusted solid to the bore if it has. Look at the electrics…all corroded.'

'Sorry Rick, but I've had a bit on my mind since the Japs arrived. I haven't been here for months. We're lucky it hasn't completely sunk.'

'Well, we've got to bail it dry first. Then I'll check the engine out.'

After several hours of kneeling in the slimy bilge, the whole time being plagued by resident mosquitos, I stood up, and wiped my oily hands on a dirty cloth.

'Jack, we may be lucky. There was water in the sump, but not enough to reach the bore. I've brushed all the corrosion off the wiring, gapped the points, and cleaned the spark plug. I've drained the dirty oil that looks like it has been in there for years. I hope you've got some new oil?'

'Yeah, plenty of oil. There's a drum of it under the log near the bow. It's petrol I'm short of.'

After topping up with new oil, I looked in the fuel drum that was attached by a hose to the carburettor. There was about a gallon in it.

'This fuel will be pretty stale, but let's give it a try.'

It took more than a dozen pulls on the frayed starting cord to produce a couple of coughs, and a cloud of white smoke. One more pull, and the motor burst into an uneven and noisy rattle.'

'Shit,' yelled Jack, 'turn it off before the Japs hear it!'

I did. The motor was long past its prime, but being of such a basic design, I was satisfied that I could keep it running. For a time anyway, if only we could locate some fuel.

✳✳✳

That night we had a conflab, and I explained my plan. 'Jack, there's only one place we'll get fuel, and that's from the Jap airfield. I'm going to sneak in at night and see if I can steal some. I'll use the couple of empty four-gallon drums you have, but I'll need two strong guys from the village to help me carry them. Can you organise that?'

Jack did. Two days later, two willing guides from Huris village arrived. They were happy to do anything in exchange for some of Jack's dwindling supply of sugar and tobacco. An opportunity to poke at the Japanese that had come uninvited to their land was a bonus to them. They were both lean and muscular, about five foot eight tall, and their dense curly hair added an inch or two to that. Their wide grins were spoiled only by the red stain of the betel nut they regularly chewed.

We set off at midday. What would have been an easy half day's walk on the coastal path, took much longer by the circuitous route, chosen to avoid Jap foot patrols. My two guides and I trekked through paths only the locals knew, foot paths worn by the women searching for yams and fruit, and the men for wild pig and cuscus. The going would have been easy enough to begin with, if it wasn't for having to be on constant alert. Alone, my companions would have had no fear of the Japs, but if caught with me, we'd all be for the chop, literally. By mid-afternoon I was wilting under the fierce sun, and longed for darkness.

When darkness finally came, so did the mosquitos. Soon I was itchy, sweating copiously in the still heat, and tiring. My guides unerringly followed paths that were almost invisible to me, and never missed a footing. I constantly slipped in mud, tripped over tree roots, scratched myself on thorns or collided with trees. The stifling humidity and whine of biting insects only let up an hour or two after sunset. Despite slowing the procession with my clumsiness, we arrived on the edge of the airfield plain at about midnight. I had to rest for a time, still itching, thirsty and now hungry.

There was a sliver of a moon, enough to make out the blackness of the forest on the other side of the airfield against the fractionally lighter sky, but it was too dark to make out anything of the Jap camp or its aircraft. I knew that they'd be on the eastern side of the strip, and at the far end. Whilst my companions waited, hidden in the tree line, I crept on, carrying the two empty drums.

I felt totally naked as I walked through mown grass along the edge of the strip. I assumed that there would be sentries: I just hoped they'd be at least half asleep at this isolated backwater of the war. As I got closer to where I expected the Jap camp to be, the unmistakable shape of a Kawasaki Ki-61 "Tony" fighter materialised out of the gloom. It sat, silent, well apart from the rest of the aircraft. I ducked beneath its wing, hid behind one undercarriage leg, and waited. I could just make out the upper outline of a Betty bomber about a hundred yards away. After about ten minutes, I heard a cough from that direction, so I froze. A minute later, a Jap soldier ambled out of the darkness and stopped, a bolt-action rifle over his shoulder. I was sure he looked in my direction, but he turned and slowly walked back the way he'd come.

I waited another few minutes, but the silence was uninterrupted. I searched for the wing fuel tank's drain cock, and found it is a recess just inboard the undercarriage. I pressed and rotated the cock, and was rewarded with a small but steady stream of aviation fuel. The cock was spring loaded, so I felt about at my feet and found a short twig to jam in the cock to keep it open. That worked. I set the drum under the stream, and it began to slowly fill. It was going to take a while.

My back was stiff from crouching under the wing, I had a sudden idea. How about I sit in the aeroplane? I quietly clambered up onto the wing, slowly slid the canopy back, and climbed into the cockpit. Without the cushion of the bottom-pack parachute Jap pilots wore, I sank low onto the bare metal seat. In the light of that sliver of moon, I could make out little of the knobs and switches, but we'd been trained to find such things by feel alone. I soon identified the basic switches and controls for everything from the undercarriage lever to engine temperature control.

An idea blossomed. Why bother with a leaky old boat? Why not steal this aeroplane? Jack would have to sit in first, and I'd have to sit on his lap. It wouldn't be very comfortable for either of us, but to fly the aeroplane, I had to be able to see out of the cockpit. Taking off in the darkness in an unfamiliar aeroplane would be a challenge, but I knew I could do it

The "Tony" is powered by a licence built German DB605 V-12 engine. It is not so vastly different to the Allison V-12 in the Kittyhawk. I fumbled about until I found what appeared to be the master switch. Holding my breath, I turned the big knob. The instrument lighting sprang on. A hasty glance showed, to my intense disappointment, that the fuel gauges indicated that both wing tanks were about one quarter full. Nowhere near enough to get us somewhere safe.

Reluctantly, I switched off the master, and carefully climbed out of the cockpit. It was back to square one: the boat. I slid down off the wing, squatted underneath, and checked the fuel draining under the wing. The stream had moved, and was now missing the open cap. I had to then hold each drum in turn close to the wing drain to avoid fuel running everywhere but into the drum. After about an hour, I was getting close to filling the second drum. My arms ached from holding the drums, and my back ached from the awkward squatting position.

I heard a noise, and was suddenly aware that I'd forgotten all about the sentry. It sounded like he was slowly walking my way.

I crouched behind the undercarriage leg and wheel, dragging both drums with me. I pulled at the stick in the drain tap, but the flimsy twig broke off. A steady stream of fuel continued to fall from the wing.

I made out the form of the sentry when he stopped about twenty yards away, and lit a cigarette. He stood for a minute, then began looking around, sniffing the air. He must have detected the leaking fuel. He walked slowly straight towards me, and peered under the wing. Being only a couple of yards away, he couldn't help but see me. He leapt back, his right arm reaching for the rifle on his shoulder. His mouth opened to yell, and the glowing cigarette fell out of his mouth. I jumped from under the wing and threw the second fuel can at him. It was heavy, and it landed short. It hit the ground on one corner half way between us, and a gout of fuel jetted from the open lid, all over the sentry, and the smouldering cigarette at his feet. The gasoline lit with a woosh. The sentry screamed. I leapt away from under the wing, because fuel was still falling from the wing drain. It was bound to ignite at any moment.

I grabbed the first can, the one with its lid firmly screwed on, and ran. I heard distant shouting, then a siren began to wail. Even a drum weighing close to forty pounds was no hindrance to my flight, as adrenalin made the drum feel light. I ran the near-mile to the tree line, and only then turned to see what was happening behind me. I saw an inferno, a flare when the fuel tanks blew up, and the twisted skeleton of the Tony collapsing.

I worried that the Japs might notice the burned four-gallon drum and piece together what had happened, but I hoped that the drum would be indistinguishable from the wreckage caused by the exploding fuel tanks.

The two boys and I carried our prize back to the inlet, and deposited the fuel into the boat tank. Only four gallons: not nearly enough, but it would have to do. I wasn't going to try that trick again. It was nearing midday when I collapsed onto the woven mat on my hard wooden bed. I was exhausted.

✳✳✳

I feared that the Japs would begin a hunt for a saboteur, but the grapevine via the village boys told us that they'd put it down to a stupid sentry lighting up a smoke directly under a leaking wing drain tap. Never-the-less, Jack appeared to be unusually agitated.

'Kala has told me that one of the Japs, a cook, is a quite nice older fellow, and he has taken a shine to the local kids. He hands out some nick-knacks in exchange for local fruit and vegies. He has learned to speak quite good Pidgin, apparently, and has been curious to know where the native kids had picked up their smattering of the language. It only takes one to say "from the old guy with the white beard who lives in the bush," and they'll search until they find me. And you. Also, more recently, Kala has hinted that one of the young village men has been pursuing her, and is jealous of the attention she's been giving you. The locals have been protective of me, but one good way to eliminate you as a rival would be to drop a word to the Japs. It would be tempting for him. Either way, dicky ticker or not, I think I should come with you, and we should make a break for it as soon as we can.'

CHAPTER 10

Escape from Borpop.

A week later our plan had to be pushed forward. It was mid afternoon when we heard a commotion from some birds just a few hundred yards away from Jack's camp. We melted into the jungle and waited. A Jap patrol hacked its way within a hundred yards, but didn't see our clearing. Nor did they notice the worn path they crossed. If they had, we'd have had to flee, leaving all our supplies behind. It was now only a matter of time before our luck ran out.

That night was going to be moonless, which would make navigating the offshore reef difficult, but we had to go. Jack explained to a tearful Kala that I had a sweetheart back in Australia, and the voyage was so dangerous we didn't want her to risk her life too. She cried, hugged me tightly, then turned to run. I stopped her, gave her my RAAF-issued wristwatch, hugged her, then let her go. I knew I would never see her again.

As we carefully crossed the coastal track, we heard voices.

Crouching in the thick bush we then saw torches, and a squad of Jap soldiers ambled past. It was high time we left Borpop.

It was very dark, and nearing full tide, when we pushed the old boat out of the mangroves. The mosquitoes were fierce, and I couldn't wait to get offshore. Jack, however, seemed to be immune to them.

We paddled quietly until the tide turned, which then helped carry us down the inlet and away from the deserted white sandy beach. The almost invisible palm trees lining the shore hung limply in the humid stillness. Luckily, the tide was still high so we crossed the coral reef with nothing worse than a few scrapes. When we were about a half-mile offshore, we started the old motor, and began chugging away. It sounded terribly loud. We had no compass, and I cursed myself for not thinking of that earlier. I might have salvaged the one out of my P-40s cockpit. Probably not, on reflection. If the Nips hadn't taken it as a souvenir, it would have been burned to a crisp.

As best we could, we maintained a course parallel to the coast, past Borpop's beautiful harbour. We'd keep a heading of roughly 050 degrees magnetic until we could round the southern tip of New Ireland. From there, we had two choices. The first was to aim for the eastern coast of New Britain, well south of Rabaul. The Australian AIF had landed at Jacquinot Bay a few months before our mission to Borpop. Would they still be there? It would take us only 24 hours in the leaky boat. The other alternative was to steer a course of about 190 degrees, guessing by the position of the sun, which would take us somewhere near the eastern tip of PNG. With luck we'd run into Goodenough Island before then, where there was a well-established Australian air and army base. With a fair breeze I figured it would take about 4 days.

Jack was adamant that we follow the latter course.

'We don't know what's left at Jacquinot Bay. The Aussies might have moved on, or moved out. Also, there's a much greater risk we'll run into a Jap barge, or even destroyer, along the coast around New Britain. I'll bet they're still running supplies from Rabaul to some of their isolated outposts to the south, and even across to the mainland. No, we're far better off heading well east, as far away from the bloody nips as we can get.'

✷✷✷

It was a blessed relief to escape the cloying humidity of the jungle and its mosquitoes and sand flies, and for some hours we revelled in the fresh sea air. I guessed that we were making about 4 knots, and in the near total blackness, our only concern was that we should keep far enough off the coast that we didn't ground on the reef. I felt safer than I had for months. Only a sudden thought by Jack upset my mood.

'Giving Kala that watch of yours probably wasn't the brightest idea. If they catch her carrying it, you know what they'll do to her.'

Our confidence that we were making good progress lasted until first light, which showed that we were barely a mile offshore. Now we were totally exposed to Jap air, sea, or beach patrols. It was the sea patrol that I feared the most. We might be ignored as just a native fishing boat if spotted from the air or beach, though, as far as I was aware, the locals used only dugout canoes. But a Jap boat would certainly investigate us, and our chances of surviving that sort of encounter were next to zero. We were both very anxious. I've been frightened whilst flying, but up there your fear is going to be over quickly, one way or another. We knew that we were going to be in dire danger all that day, and the days that followed, if we survived that long. It was a heavy strain on me, and must have been worse on Jack's weak heart.

Just as the new day came, the old motor coughed and died. It was out of fuel. For an hour or so we wallowed in a light swell, and for a time we feared the current was going to take us onto the beach. The sun was getting high enough to be uncomfortably hot, when a light east-nor-easterly sprang up. We hoisted the mildewed old sail, and tried to keep to the original heading. The whaleboat was never designed as a fast sailor, and with mainsail only and no jib, we couldn't point much into the wind. We eased off the mainsail sheet to pick up a semblance of forward progress, but that meant we were staying far closer to the coast than we'd wanted to.

I guessed our speed varied between two and three knots as gusts came and went, but I hoped the wind would steady once we left the island behind. At that rate we'd keep to my estimated three to four days to reach Goodenough Island or the Allied-occupied eastern tip of the mainland. We had enough water and food, but we were going to be totally exposed to the vagaries of the weather as well as detection by the enemy. We couldn't relax for a moment. Not during daylight hours, anyway.

Later in the day the breeze did pick up, but stayed obstinately from the same direction. Right on dusk we heard the rumble of a single radial engine. We strained to catch sight of it, but the aircraft was suddenly upon us before we could react. It was an Aichi 'Jake' seaplane. An observation aircraft, obviously patrolling the New Ireland coast. The pilot and his two observers must have seen us, as its wing dipped and altitude dropped as he flew past, but luck was with us. The lateness of the day, and the fact that darkness falls with little twilight in the tropics, must have deterred him from turning for closer investigation. No pilot would want to land in Borpop's small harbour after dark.

✳✳✳

As dawn broke, we could see Cape St. George off our right bow. The wind was now a gentle but steady nor-easterly, so we switched tack to a course of about 190 degrees. This broad reach meant that the old tub felt positively lively, and we guessed that we were then making close to four knots. Slowly but surely, we left New Ireland behind, and now had to sail on a heading that parallelled the coast of New Britain for at least a day. Although we were some miles offshore, we were still too close for comfort to the Jap fortress at Rabaul, and its second satellite field at Namatanai. Enemy air activity above us would likely be heavy. We knew that we did stick out, rather like a sore thumb.

As it turned out, though we heard and even saw a number of enemy aircraft on courses in and out of Rabaul , most went over quite high and none came near us. My real worry that day was Jack. He'd become very tired and sickly looking. Sometimes I saw him grimace and clutch his chest. It was all I could do to persuade him to lie still, but the hot sun and absence of shade made comfort an impossibility for either of us. Quite soon we were both sunburnt and dehydrated. I lashed the tiller and the boat ploughed on in the steady breeze, but I could only catch snatches of sleep.

By dawn on our third day, we'd left all sight of land behind. We felt that we could breathe a little easier, even though it was now obvious that our voyage would take five or even six days, not three or four as I'd originally imagined. I longed for it to be over, and swore that if we did survive, I'd never set foot on a boat again.

It was mid-afternoon on our fourth day when I spotted trouble. A dot on the horizon on our starboard stern quarter was gradually growing. Soon it became obvious that it was a warship.

Jack groaned, 'Oh shit. To come this far, then this. It's almost certainly a Jap destroyer. He'll be out of Rabaul Harbour, on his way to drop supplies to troops on the mainland during the night. We can only hope he thinks we are local fishermen, and ignores us.'

It looked promising for a while. Then the destroyer's course changed, to bring it right at us, and its decreasing bow wave indicated it was slowing. I have to admit that I groaned too, and said under my breath, 'Jesus, what more do we have to go through?'

It was a beautiful looking ship, low and rakish, with twin funnels, and formidable main armament of six five-inch guns in three turrets, plus 13mm machine guns and torpedo tubes. Its dark grey paint made it look as mean as it was. I recognised it as one of the Fubuki class, of about 2,000 tons. It began a late turn, to bring it within a hundred yards of us, and on a parallel course. I couldn't help noticing that several heavy machine guns on mounts on the midships deck were manned and trained on us. We tried to look nonchalant, but that wasn't easy.

Both Jack and I wore old khaki shirts that had been worn for a week without a wash. They were stained from sweat and the splashes of dirty bilgewater. Our faces and arms were deeply tanned, and Jack had shaved his white beard, so that only stubble remained. We both had wrapped dark bandannas around our heads to hide our light-coloured hair. It wouldn't fool anyone.

A voice boomed over the water. We could see an officer on the bridge with a loud hailer. We couldn't understand a word, but it was obvious that we were being commanded to stop. We quietly agreed that to pretend ignorance was our only chance. It didn't work.

A burst of heavy machine gun fire ripped across our bow, kicking up spray just yards away. It was no warning shot. Jack and I both dropped below the gunwale, not that the rotting planks offered an iota of protection against heavy calibre bullets. Seconds later another burst whizzed over our heads, and the third chewed off a chunk of our transom, spraying us both with splinters. It also blew apart the mainsail rope, and the boom swung parallel to the breeze as we lost way. The fourth burst began and ended suddenly. We heard shouting, even from a hundred yards away, and a sudden increase in the low throb of the destroyer's engines.

We both had our heads down below the gunwale, so it took a few seconds to register that the Japs had suddenly lost interest in us. Their forward 5-inch main guns went off with enormous bangs, and their machine guns began a continuous chatter. All guns were firing, and we could see, smell, and even taste burnt cordite. But they were not firing at us.

Then I heard the roar, the unmistakable staccato throbbing roar of twin Wright R-2600 engines. I could identify that aircraft even before I saw it. I looked up, still in disbelief. 'Jack look, it's an American B-25. It's attacking the Jap ship!'

We held our breath as the olive-drab B-25D medium bomber steadily grew in size. It was making a head-on diving attack on the ship. I saw the twin fixed 50 -calibre Browning machine guns each side of its nose twinkling. A fifth gun, aimed from the swivel on the centre of the glass nose, joined in. Bomb doors swung open.

Tracer leapt towards the swooping bomber, but nothing deterred it. Ricochets twanged off the deck of the Jap ship. As the bomber levelled out of its dive, probably no more than two hundred feet above the water, a stick of four bombs left the open bomb bay, and unerringly homed in on the ship.

The sleek warship accelerated and desperately began to turn away from us, but it was too late. The first bomb hit just off the bow, right where the ship would have been but for the turn. The second exploded as it hit the water alongside the bridge, stoving in hull plates, showering the machine gun crews with deadly shrapnel, and sweeping some of them into the sea with the cascade of seawater that followed. The third bomb hit just behind the aft funnel, and the fourth on the stern quarter.

As the B-25 climbed away, its single tail gun and the twin guns in its dorsal turret raked the hapless ship.

The third bomb may have hit torpedo tubes, as, after a delay of a few seconds, a devastating explosion blew the twin funnels overboard. The ship lost way as fire began to take hold. More explosions blew large pieces of metal high into the air, probably as depth charges at the stern exploded. Burning figures threw themselves into the sea.

The B-25 banked into a right-hand turn, and climbed to about 500 feet. Once on a reciprocal course it flew straight and level for a minute, then turned towards us again. This time it did not attack the dying ship in its low pass, a pass so low that we could see the silhouettes of its crew against the bright sky.

Mesmerised by the sight of waves now washing over the sinking stern of the destroyer, I whooped, 'Jack, we live to fight another day.' There was no answer. I looked around. Jack lay back, gasping for breath. He was deathly pale despite the tan. 'Jack, is it your heart?' I shouted. Jack was clutching at his chest, but when his hands dropped away, I could see blood. Lots of it. Momentarily stunned, it took me a few seconds to see the foot-long splinter from the transom that was sticking out of his chest.

'Pull it out, pull it out,' he implored. I did, fearing that I would cause a gush of blood. More bleeding followed for a few seconds, then stopped but for a trickle. The wound was shallow.

'You'll be okay Jack, don't worry, it'll take more than that to kill you,' I shouted, and laughed hysterically. He tried to grin also. It was more of a grimace, and he didn't attempt to rise from his prone position. 'Hang on, I'll get you comfortable. I used our kit bags to prop him up in the bow, and he patted me on the arm. I pulled off my singlet, tore it into strips, and used one of them to make a bandage across the wound. He closed his eyes and seemed to relax, but his pallid skin worried me.

I looked up when I heard a deep rumble and the hissing of steam. The destroyer was sinking, stern first. Oil was spreading, and men were tumbling off the sides, into the oil-covered sea.

Most were not wearing any safety gear. Then I was galvanized into action: several strong swimmers had seen our old boat as their only salvation, and were only yards away. I reached up and grabbed the flapping boom. We'd slowly swung into wind, so it took a few seconds to figure out which way to push the boom. The sail flopped about for a few more seconds, then filled with a welcome thud. I held on with all my might, and the boat suddenly accelerated. If I'd have lost my grip, the sail would have swung away and lost all its drawing power, so I hung on grimly, almost being pulled out of the boat. Hands reached out, but none were able to get a grip as we slid past, and in a couple of minutes we'd gone far enough to be clear of even the strongest swimmers.

We left the surviving Jap sailors to look after themselves. I felt no remorse, because I knew it was them or us. Within half an hour we could see nothing of the horror we'd left. The destroyer had gone to the bottom.

I was focused so much on re-rigging the boom with a makeshift mainsheet, watching Jack, and getting us away from our near miss, that I didn't notice that the behaviour of the boat was changing. It was slowing and wallowing. It then dawned on me that there was more bilge water than usual. From our launching, the boat had leaked enough to require a little baling every few hours, but this was something altogether worse. I guessed it had been only an hour since I'd last bailed, so this didn't look good. I'd left my RAAF-issued watch for Kala as a parting gift, so it was hard to be really certain. Now I monitored the level carefully.

By dark it was obvious that we did have a serious problem. Despite almost continuous bailing, the water level had risen enough to make it hard to keep Jack dry. I felt around under the water near the transom, and to my horror, found a steady stream entering where a plank on the starboard side joined the transom. Leaning over the stern, I ran my hand down the join. I found a deep furrow where a Japanese bullet had shattered a rotten plank. A few fibres of wood were all that stood between the boat floating or sinking rapidly. I felt around under the water to see if we could cover the hole in some way. I almost poked a new hole with my finger. Any attempt to jam something in the damaged area was only going to disturb the soft planks even more. The only option left to us was to bail even harder.

We had one old metal bucket. By this time Jack was in a parlous state, and it was all I could do to keep the water level from soaking him. I bailed all night, with brief rests when I just couldn't carry on any longer.

The wind dropped sometime during the night, and we drifted aimlessly. I could tell that we were slowly spinning because of the rotation of the stars. We bumped into something around midnight, at a guess. I was taking a brief rest, and I was jerked awake. I could see nothing, and only heard the occasional hiss of a wave running alongside, or the thud of one hitting the side or stern. I wondered if it was a shark that bumped us, or some other denizen of the black water.

I must have fallen asleep just before first light. I came awake still sitting with the bucket in my hands, but now the water level had reached the simple plank seats. Jack was lying half in water. I called his name, and he grunted and lifted his hand in tired acknowledgement. I resumed bailing, but made little headway. I despaired that we would sink within the next hour or two. I was scared. As a country boy I had swum in rivers, but I'd rarely seen the sea before joining the RAAF. The immensity of the ocean, the constant wave motion, and the thought of what creatures could be lurking somewhere beneath us was deeply frightening.

Jack motioned for me to come near. When I crawled forward, he spoke to me croakily. I could barely hear him.

'Ricky, I have to tell you something.'

'Can it wait Jack? If I stop bailing, we'll go under.'

'No, no, it can't wait. Rick, if we sink, I'll be done for in minutes. I've had it, Rick. I think I've had my days.' He grabbed my arm, but couldn't hold it for more than a few seconds.

'Nonsense Jack, I've had a rest, I'll start bailing again.'

'No Rick, I don't think you can keep that up much longer. But you're young and fit, you never know, you might survive long enough for some boat to come along, so I have to tell you something.' He grimaced with the effort of talking.

'Okay Jack, talk while I bail.'

'Alright. A couple of years ago,' he wheezed, 'for something to do, I went panning in the creek that feeds the inlet, about half way between my hut and the where this boat was stored. Rick, I found gold. Quite a lot of it. I spent all my spare time in that creek, working my way right up into the hills, and I found gold wherever there was still water. I found lots of fine grains of gold, and even a few nuggets as big as your thumb. Altogether, I reckon I have collected about 500 ounces, Rick.'

I tried to interrupt, but Jack waved me to silence. His shoulders heaved as he fought for breath.

'I reckon I know where the gold is coming from. The reef must be in the hills above my hut. I have started a tunnel. I haven't reached the lode yet, but I reckon it's there.'

'So why are you telling me, Jack?' I gasped between buckets of bilge water.

'Rick, if you make it, wait until the Japs leave, then go back to my sleeping hut and dig a hole in the middle of the floor. That's where the gold is.'

With that, Jack sank back against the hull, and closed his eyes. I thought about what he had just said as I bailed, then dismissed it. He was probably delusional in his sickness and pain. Why would he have stuck it out in New Ireland in a flimsy reed-lined hut, with the occasional company of a native girl, if he'd had a fortune in gold buried beneath his feet? Surely, he would have escaped when the Nips were advancing through New Ireland?

Whatever the truth, the prospect of a fortune in gold meant nothing to us now. I would have swapped any such fortune for any method of stopping that steady inflow.

I lost track of time, but it must have been at least an hour after Jack had last spoken, when the wind began gusting to 15 or even 20 knots. If we'd had a dry boat and a good sail, we'd be flying along. As it was, the boat was so heavy with bilge water, that it barely responded to the wind, other than wallowing in the steepening waves. Seawater constantly washed over the sides, which made my bailing even more of a losing battle. I could so easily have given up, but every time I glanced at the old man, I found the strength to empty a few more buckets over the side.

I thought I heard the drone of an aircraft. I was so close to exhaustion that I couldn't lift my head to locate it. My eyelashes were now so encrusted from salt spray that I couldn't see clearly anyway. I stopped bailing for a moment and listened carefully, but then the drone had gone. I thought I must have imagined it. Another bucket, then another, then I heard it again, and this time it was much louder. I dropped the bucket, splashed my face, opened my eyes and was startled to see the gunnels were now only inches above water. I was in such despair that I didn't care if the aircraft above was friend of foe. If we were machine-gunned by the Japs, at least we'd be out of this torment.

The drone continued. The aircraft above was circling, and getting lower. I strained to see, and at last caught a glimpse. It was a P-40 Kittyhawk, maybe RAAF, or could be RNZAF, I couldn't tell. It continued to fly in lazy circles. It couldn't help us, so I forced myself to ignore it and resumed bailing. What good was there in just circling above us, I thought?

Then another sound. Not the crackle of an inline V-12, but the rumble of big radial engines. I dropped the bucket again and stood up. The sway I caused allowed seawater to slop over the gunnel into the boat, but I steadied myself before causing the boat to slip under. Unbelievably, a big blue flying boat, a Catalina, or PBY as the Americans called them, was skimming the waves not five hundred yards away. Instantly I knew that the pilot was running a big risk, as the sea was far from smooth. One big wave and the crew of that aeroplane would be in the same boat as us, literally.

Feathers of spray were being flicked up by Catalina's deep V hull, and for long moments I thought that the pilot was going to abort. Then the intermittent spray slowly grew into a white wave as the big bird settled down into the sea, rapidly losing speed as it did.

The extended splash-down had taken the Catalina a mile past us. The pilot gunned one of the big Pratt & Whitney R-2800 radial engines mounted on the high wing, flattening the waves behind and turning the flying boat towards us. It looked like it would take too long, as the waves were now regularly slopping over our stern. It seemed to take forever, but we were still afloat when the Catalina came abeam of us, not fifty yards away, the pilot expertly turned into the now howling wind. I could see that it was a US Navy aircraft.

A crewman slid open the large Perspex blister on its rear fuselage, and two others pushed out a small inflatable dinghy. With a gas cartridge they quickly inflated it, and one of them jumped aboard and began paddling towards us. Our old boat chose that moment to stop fighting the inevitable. With hardly a sound, suddenly it just fell away beneath us, and I was treading water. I spun around to see only the top of Jack's head above the surface, surrounded by bits of rotten wood and an empty hessian sack. With a few strokes I caught him, and brought his head above the surface. Seconds later the inflatable reached the pair of us. It was tiny, barely big enough for three. Nothing was said, but the Yank seaman gripped Jack and tried to haul him aboard. He was such a dead weight that the seaman couldn't manage alone, but with me pushing, Jack's body tumbled into the dinghy. I tried to climb aboard, but my tired arms refused to hoist my own body out of the water.

Then I realised the Catalina was getting closer. We were being reeled in like a fish, with the seaman holding Jack tight, and me holding onto the rope handles around the dinghy.

CHAPTER 11

Homeward bound.

The Americans flew at 110 mph all the way to the Australian base at Milne Bay, which is on the very eastern end of the New Guinea mainland. That's about as fast as the PBY could go, as it had not been built for speed. The noise inside the flying boat was deafening, but the Americans knew what we needed without speaking; blankets, and as much hot coffee as we could drink. They bandaged Jack's chest, and gave him a shot of what I presume was morphine. I wouldn't have traded that ride for a seat in the most luxurious airliner in the world.

After mooring and shutting down, and while awaiting a tender to come from shore, the young American captain, who looked barely old enough to shave, explained that it had been a three services effort to save us.

'Our B-25 that sank the Jap destroyer was based in Moresby, but was patrolling for Jap ships seeking to supply any pockets of enemy troops remaining on the north coast. In the attack run, the captain realised that the crew of the enemy ship was preoccupied with shooting at something, and therefore hadn't seen his B-25 coming, until too late. The bomber crew was very grateful for the distraction, because, as you know, attacking destroyers is a risky business. They all wanted to say thanks to the couple of natives in the little sailboat. When they did the low pass, they could see that you weren't natives out on a fishing trip.

'Anyway, they alerted the RAAF base at Nadzab, which was the closest. They in turn contacted the New Zealand base on Green Island, and the Kiwis sent out a couple of P-40s. One of them located you this morning. We were at Milne Bay, and were called in to pick you up.'

✶✶✶

From the dock, Jack and I were carried by army ambulance along a muddy road straight to the series of large tents that constituted the army hospital. Jack had regained consciousness, but was clearly in a lot of trouble. He was whisked away, and I was assured that he'd receive the best of care. I was just buggered, still thirsty, and hungry, and the blisters on both hands were bleeding. After arranging telegrams to Dad and Lyn, I was allocated a bed. It had a soft mattress, (soft compared to a wooden slab), and crisp white sheets. I barely had the strength to climb into it. Moments later I succumbed to it all. I had the deepest sleep I'd had since leaving Molong.

Late in the afternoon they wheeled Jack into the ward. 'Come on Rick, you can't sleep all day, let's go and have a beer.' It took a moment to figure out where I was, and even longer to recognise Jack. I couldn't believe the transformation. He was clean shaven, his hair washed, cut, and combed. His skin colour had returned, and he carried a huge grin. I'd never actually seen his grin before, as his mouth had always been hidden behind the bushy mo. A minute later he was followed in by a doctor dressed in a white coat, who introduced himself, and gave us the drum.

'Rick, you need to rest for a couple of days. You're dehydrated, badly sunburnt, and no doubt exhausted. Otherwise, you are okay to return to your squadron when you are ready. Jack, you're a different matter altogether. We've got to watch that your chest wound doesn't get infected. You are obviously aware that your heart is weak, and the strain of the last few days hasn't helped it. You are also sunburnt and dehydrated. I'm giving you some pills to help you with your heart, but my advice is to return to Australia when you feel fit enough to travel. Go and see a cardiac specialist there, but I'm sure he'll tell you that your days of adventuring are over. Go and find a quiet retirement home. Meanwhile, you can have a beer, maybe two, but don't overdo it.'

✶✶✶

Jack and I spent the next three days lazing about the hospital, and each night one of the nurses smuggled us a bottle of beer to share. We talked and laughed a lot, but clearly Jack wasn't too fond of the idea of spending his waning years in some decrepit home where he'd only have old people to talk to.

'I've been my own boss for years, and busy all my life, Rick. No way am I going to sit around all day with nothing to do.'

As he said that, the perfect solution came to me.

'Jack, get onto a boat to Sydney. From there you can catch the train to Molong, and I'll arrange for my dad to pick you up. You can live on our farm for ever and a day. Dad would love the company, and when you're fit, you can pull your weight alright. There are plenty of jobs on the farm that you can do, jobs that aren't too physically demanding, and it will free up Dad's time.'

'You'd really let me come and live on your farm? Are you sure about this?'

'Sure I'm sure. I'll write to Dad tonight.'

The idea grew on Jack quickly. By the time I received orders to rejoin my Squadron, he was enthusiastic. I wrote to Dad explaining Jack's situation, and I wrote out in detail the directions for him to get to Molong. We parted company in high spirits, and with shouts of 'See you at the farm.'

***

It was now July 20th, 1945, and I learned that as the Japs had been forced to retreat northward, 101 Squadron had moved on from Noemfoor to Morotai, an island in the Dutch East Indies. I jumped aboard a C-47 transport that was taking medical supplies from Milne Bay to the 101 Squadron base. It was an uncomfortable flight on an unpadded jump seat on the freighter, but I'd become accustomed to discomfort ever since arriving in New Guinea. Upon arrival, I was told to report to the new Squadron Leader, John Rowe.

'Well young Richards, I've heard about you and your exploits. You're back from your holiday, I see.' He grinned and shook my hand. 'I've read your report. Jolly good show, I must say. We'll be glad to have you back. Just don't bugger up another P-40, eh. But before you do get back into the air, you'll have to have a medical.'

'But Sir, the doctor at Milne Bay said that all I'd needed was rest, and I've had that. He said I was ready to come back to the squadron.'

'Yes, I know that you've just been discharged from hospital and the doc said that you are okay. He's an army doctor. You know as well as I do that you'll have to see a RAAF doctor now. Just a formality of course.'

It wasn't just a formality. The RAAF doctor took one look at the scars on my head and frowned. I had little choice but to explain about the head injury and what Jack did to help me.

'Subdural haemorrhage, eh? A penetrating injury they call it, when you've had to have a craniotomy. Well, son, your Kittyhawk days are over. The only thing you'll be flying is a desk, if they can find you a job in admin. Too much risk of seizure. You say you haven't had a seizure since the crash, but you might have one, maybe tomorrow, maybe five years from now. Sorry, but I'm declaring you medically unfit. I'm going to recommend that you be returned to Australia and, if they can't make use of you on the ground, to be discharged from the RAAF.'

I argued, but it was of no use. As he ushered me out of the tent, he asked me what my profession had been before the war.

'A farmer, eh. Well, go back to being a farmer, Son. If you have a seizure driving a tractor, you won't have so far to fall.'

It was a crushing blow, but there was no appeal. My flying days were over. Now, all I wanted to do was get back to pick up Jack, then arrange for us both to get back to Australia. Before I left the RAAF doctor, he had some more advice.

'Your skull probably has some rough edges inside where it has been drilled. Those rough edges can cause the seizures I mentioned. Go easy, boy. Don't get into any fights. Don't bump your head into anything solid, for at least five years, maybe ten.'

✶

During the slow and uncomfortable ride to Morotai, I'd been excited at my imminent return to 101 Squadron, and to flying. That made the discomfort bearable. The same slow and uncomfortable ride back to Milne Bay was torturous. I was no longer a priority: I was more like useless baggage, and half a dozen times I was shunted off flights for more important cargo. Over two weeks had passed since I had left the hospital when I went to find Jack and give him my tale of woe. I found his bed empty. A nurse was passing and I asked where Jack had been moved to. 'Oh, sorry, the old gentlemen passed away a few hours ago. He was doing fine, and had a good sleep this afternoon, but when he got up, he said he felt a bit dizzy. He collapsed, and we couldn't revive him.'

✱✱✱

On August 7th we heard that an atomic bomb had been dropped on Hiroshima, and four days later another on Nagasaki. Three weeks later, the surrender of Japan was announced. It was a massive relief, as the predictions of losses on both sides for the invasion of Japan were horrific. As awful as it was for the civilians of Hiroshima and Nagasaki, there could be no doubt that the atomic bombs saved countless lives.

Now everybody wanted to quit the war and go home. There was no available transport for the deadweight I'd become. Each day there was the possibility of jumping aboard a RAAF or USAAF C-47, or even a USAAF B-24, but each day the chance evaporated. Having accepted that I was going home, now all I wanted was to get there. Much later I learned that some RAAF personnel in Timor waited almost a year for repatriation.

On my fourth day at Milne Bay a bag was dumped in my lap. 'Letters for you. Some have been held in Moresby since you went missing, others are recent. They'd been sent on to 101 Squadron at Morotai, but must have arrived at the same time you left. Finally, they've caught up with you.'

I eagerly sorted the letters by date stamp, and who they were from. The first pile was from Lyn, the second from Dad, and the third was from anyone else. I was thunderstruck when I realised that the first pile consisted of only four letters, whereas the second had more than double that number.

I read the first three of Lyn's letters quickly. They were similar, in that they related her day-to-day activities, and expressed her undying love. The third letter had been posted a day before my final mission. There was a big gap then to the last letter, dated just two days after our delivery by the Yank PBY to Milne Bay. It was fairly short.

My dear Ricky,

I am so, so happy that you have returned, so to speak, from the dead. Our prayers have been answered. Your father called me when he received his telegram, and he was so emotional that I could barely understand him. Mine arrived while he was on the line.

We've had only the sketchiest details of what you've been through this last six months, but I'm sure you must have been very brave.

You must understand how difficult it has been for me also. We fell in love, then so soon you were gone. I saw you only once in the year of your training, and then you were off to New Guinea. I worried every day, knowing that you were in danger on every mission. Then, of course, we got the awful telegram. "Missing believed killed in action," it said. Can you imagine how I felt in that moment?

Rick, I'll always love you, but I had to move on. I'm sorry. When there was no further information over so many months, I sought comfort from an old boyfriend. We have come to realise that we are meant for each other. We have become engaged, and will marry in three weeks.

I hope you and I can be friends. I am very fond of your father and would like to keep in contact.
Yours,

Lyn

I put down the letter, and sat stunned for minutes. It slowly dawned on me that I wasn't nearly as devastated as I should be. By the next day I was even able to laugh about the opportunities I'd missed whilst being true to Lyn.

Dad's letters from before my final mission were full of farm and district news, how proud he was of me, and how he longed for the day I would safely return. The last one was very long. It gave me local news, and finished with the message that he counted the days until I returned home. The middle of the letter went like this.

When I received the telegram that you were missing in action, I have to admit that my world crumbled for a time. If it wasn't for people like your Lyn, Mavis Doak, and the Hetheringtons, I might have given up altogether. Mavis made me pull out of the total despair I felt.

Over the last six months, I have come to rely heavily on Mavis. We have found great pleasure in each other's company, to the point that I no longer wish to be without a life partner. I have thus asked Mavis to marry me, and she has accepted.

With the miracle of your forthcoming return, we will put off setting a date, but I hope you will give me your blessing in this new partnership.

Which brings me to the second important item I must inform you of. Son, as you know this farm was my father's, and I have been so pleased all these years that you have taken up the same feeling for, and love for this land as I have had. As I get older, my greatest comfort is the knowledge that when I'm done, you will have it. My marriage will not change that. In my will, you are to inherit the farm and all its equipment, free and clear. Mavis is to have the right to live in the house on the farm free of rent until the day she chooses to leave, or dies. I have a life insurance policy that will keep her in comfort until that time.

Of course, as you also know, many good rural properties have to be sold or broken up to pay death duties. I want no such thing to befall you and this farm. Since you were a small boy, I have been putting aside some funds in term deposits to cover all taxes that apply when I inevitably do pass on to the next world. These funds have been invested through the local Commercial Bank, and now will cover the likely tax at the current farm value.

I'm telling you all this not because I expect to pass on any time soon, by the way!'

✳✳✳

Dad met me at the station. I think he'd been waiting a long time for the train to arrive. When I jumped down, RAAF duffle bag over my shoulder, Dad could barely speak. I think he was frightened he'd burst into tears. He'd kept news of my impending arrival to himself, but others were also there to welcome me home, including the owner of Molong's weekly newspaper. He asked for a story, but I simply said it was great to be home, and I'd talk to him later. A couple of my old friends were holding up a hastily-painted banner that said "Welcome home Pilot Officer Richards". I was embarrassed when they treated me like the returning hero, but I promised I'd see them in the pub in a few days.

On the way home, and once I was able to convince Dad that I was in good health, and none the worse for my experiences, he told me how shocked he was that Lyn hadn't waited for me.

'Every Sunday she came. For more than a year. She got on famously with Mavis, and I was looking at her as the daughter I never had. I really thought she'd be with you forever.'

'Dad, we were both too young. We both thought it was forever, but a lot has happened in the last three years. I know I've changed a lot, and I guess she has too. The surprising thing is, after I got over the shock of her last letter, I realised that it was almost a relief. You know, Lyn's a great girl, but I never felt any magic. Maybe I'm wanting too much,' I laughed.

Dad shook his head. 'I can only hope that you find the magic I did when I found your mother,' he said. He was also at great pains to explain his relationship with Mavis.

'Rick, I loved your mother with all my heart, and I've missed her every day for these eighteen years since she's been gone. At times it was hard, and I was often lonely, especially when you were young. I sometimes doubted I could carry on, but I had to, for you. When you left to join the RAAF, it left a giant hole in my life. It just happened that Mavis came into it at the right time. She'd brought up young Phil on her own, and I guess she felt the need for companionship at the same time I did. Of course, I'll never love her the same way I loved your mother, but we like each other very much, we get on fabulously, and I want to enjoy my remaining days with her in my life.'

As we entered the farm gate, I saw with a start that we had a new name. Dad had always resisted giving the farm a name, so it had been simply "the farm" for two generations. It now bore the name "Kittyhawk," proudly emblazoned on a panel wired to the open gate. Dad was a little embarrassed when I queried him. 'Seemed appropriate,' was all he'd say.

As we parked beside the house, the kelpies started barking. Friendly, high-pitched barks. They saw me as soon as I got out of the car, and the barking tempo increased. I had to walk over to their pen and give each dog a hug. Then the screen door swung open, and Mavis stood there, pulling off her apron, a smile from ear to ear. After hugs, she ushered me straight into the kitchen, warm from the baking she'd prepared for my arrival. For the next hour I was grilled about my time in New Guinea. Then it was my turn to hear the Molong district news.

There was some good news. Crops had been good, and the weather cooperative. There had been some births, and some marriages, some comings and goings. Unfortunately, there was bad news too. Several lads from the district had been killed while serving overseas. Many others were still away, but were hoping to return home soon. The news that floored me was about my best mate, Max Hetherington. He'd been severely wounded in battle on one of the islands, and was shortly to be shipped home. It was uncertain if he'd ever fully recover. Moreover, his father had lost his job as manager of the property next door, when the farm was sold by its absentee owner. He'd managed to find another position, just as a farm hand, near Dubbo, some distance to the west. Max's little sister was now at high school there.

The new owner was Reg Wilson, our town councillor, solicitor, and real estate agent. According to Dad, Max's father had been given a raw deal, being put off after two decades at the farm, with nothing more than a fortnight's notice.

Mavis's son Phil was helping Dad out on a casual basis, but Dad confided to me that the youngster, (he was eighteen going on nineteen), wasn't the best worker around.

'He's a bit lazy. He'd rather spend time with his mates than work on the farm. He sleeps over at various places, and only stays with his mother a couple of nights a week. I don't know why she puts up with it. The one thing in his favour is that he handles the dogs really well, and they respond to him. When he's here, he fusses about making sure they don't have any burs in their bedding, and their water is clean.'

I'd looked forward to climbing into my own bed on the farm

for so long, but after turning the light out I couldn't sleep for thinking about the last three years of my life. I'd become a fighter pilot, I'd fought the enemy, winning some battles, losing one. I'd made many friends, but lost too many of them. I'd been engaged to be married, and lost that too. I thought of Jack, and Kala, and how I'd left her with barely a goodbye, after all she'd done for me. I wondered if a life completely devoted to the farm would be satisfying enough for me now.

✳✳✳

Some friends did return home, including Max. There were too many who never would. Despite my fears, life returned to pre-war normality surprisingly quickly, and I was content. Many men were still overseas in military service, so there was a shortage of labour. Therefore I was in demand at our farm, and when I had time, helping other farmers. The shortage of men meant that I was also in demand by the local girls. That situation, sadly, would be the case for a long time.

One night I was to meet some friends at a pub in town. I walked in to find that I was the first to arrive. Instead, a group I'd have preferred to avoid turned as I entered.

'Well, if it isn't the conquering hero. Our very own flyboy,' William McLaren called out loudly.

'Hello William,' I replied, and turned to go out the way I'd come in.

'What, too good for us farm boys, are you MISTER Richards?'

William advanced on me, and I noticed that he was slightly unsteady on his feet. He'd obviously been in the pub for a while. Still, he was a good three inches taller than me, probably fifty pounds heavier, and was spoiling for a fight. I wasn't, and was also mindful of what the doc in Morotai had said about getting into a fight. His mates approached too, flexing their fists. The problem was that, short of turning tail and running, I was cornered.

Just then three older men stood up. Two I vaguely recognised as local farm hands, and one I don't think I'd ever seen before. They fronted William.

'Righto young McLaren,' one said, 'you've had your say, now go back to your good-for-nothing mates. Rick here is with us. Want to fight him? You've got to go through the three of us first.'

✳✳✳

In November 1945, Dad and Mavis were married. Dad's farmer friends used it as an excuse to have a big party, the first since December 1941 when the Japs started the Pacific war. The local hall was bedecked with flowers and banners, the tables laid with a collection of table cloths and plates of food, and a great time was had by all. The newlyweds took the train to Sydney, and spent a fortnight at Bondi. Swimming in the surf was a new experience for them both.

When Mavis moved in, so of course did young Phil. Our third bedroom became his. Apart from Herman and very occasional visitors, nobody had ever lived in that room, and so I had to do a hasty clean out of stuff that had been stored there. The type of stuff that had no use anymore, but appeared too good to be dumped.

Phil brought his record player and his big appetite with him. He also brought a reluctance to do any work, unless it involved handling the kelpies.

At first, I tried to treat him like a new little brother, but that didn't work. He rejected any attempt at closeness. Neither was he inclined to take any advice, let alone instructions from me. He'd disappear or reappear without warning, using his pushbike to get to the bus stop. He stayed away for more nights than he was at home. I said nothing, deciding that I'd leave Dad and Mavis to sort him out and lay some ground rules.

The wheat harvesting was done before Christmas 1945, and work on the farm slowed enough for us to take a breather. I had time to think, and I thought about resuming my university studies. I contacted the Engineering School, and the dean himself offered to help.

'We can get you started on year two, but you'll have to study after hours to recap your first year. You'll then have to sit for special exams.' It was a very good deal.

At the dean's suggestion, on the first day of term one in 1946, I presented myself to his office. 'Come with me,' he said, 'I'll introduce you to your classmates. He took me to the lecture theatre where the very first class of the year was about to start. He called the class's attention. 'It's good to see so many of you back for your second year. You all know each other by now, so I'll introduce you to Eric Richards. Eric had almost completed year one in 1943, but was called up to join the RAAF. He served with distinction in the Pacific, flying fighter planes, and is now ready to resume his studies with us. Please make him welcome.'

There was a smattering of applause. A few looked at me keenly, including a couple of girls in the front row, whilst others barely bothered to clap. I wondered if they came from families that hadn't been touched by the war. I smiled, and no doubt they thought I appreciated the welcome, but I'd just realised that for many young people, already the war was in the distant past, and although I was only about three years older than most of them, they probably looked on me as some sort of relic. It occurred to me that the next generation probably wouldn't even know that World War Two had happened, nor have any inkling of the enormous sacrifice made by so many to protect the free world they enjoyed.

I thanked the dean, and sat through most of the lecture, but

I quickly made up my mind. I'd seen and done too much to sit in lectures for the next couple of years in a dingy theatre. I slipped out just before the finish, and caught the next train home.

CHAPTER 12

A black day.

Time went swiftly by. Apart from a bit of tension whenever Phil was about, Dad and Mavis were obviously very happy together. She had never lived on a farm before, but readily took to looking after Dad, the house, and helping out with the dogs and sheep whenever an extra pair of hands were needed.

The only argument I ever heard was over Phil. Dad commented one day that Mavis shouldn't be so generous handing out cash to him. She shot back that she had the money from the rental of her cottage, it was hers, and she could do what she liked with it. I refrained from commenting, but I did frown when I saw Phil borrowing the farm ute to go into town. I insisted that it should not be away overnight, as I needed it on the farm, and Phil scowled at that.

With Dad and me both on the farm, we had time to relax now and then. I joined the Molong district cricket club, where I found a place as a fill-in bowler. My batting was only so-so, and I could rarely make more than a few runs, but I was a good stonewaller, and could hold up an end all day if needed. My specialty was spin bowling. Sometimes I took a hammering, but more often than not I'd manage a wicket or two, and if the pitch conditions suited me, I could be a match winner. My best effort was ten wickets in one match against an Orange eleven.

After each match the beers would flow, and although I sipped when others skulled, it was good to be part of a team again.

In April of 1946 I made a trip to Narromine to see the Hetheringtons. I was shocked to see Mr Hetherington reduced to a position not much better than a labourer. However, he gave no indication of being dissatisfied, and was still the big, affable, good-humoured friend he'd always been. Worse was to see what a Japanese bullet had done to Max. He'd been shot in the chest, had lost a lung, and would be physically compromised for the rest of his life. He was able to do some less taxing work around the farm his father lived and worked on. He also planned on doing a book keeping course, so he could earn extra money helping farmers in his new district with their paperwork.

His little sister had left in February to board at a college at Sydney University. She wanted to be a vet, and she'd managed to get the marks required to get into Vet school there. The Hetheringtons said she'd be sorry she missed me. They seemed content, but to me their family home wasn't the same noisy, happy place I had spent so much of my youth in. I guessed too much had happened in the last four years to expect that.

✳✳✳

As was the case on many a farm, neither Dad nor I took regular wages. The farm paydays came three times each year, after the sale of wheat, wool, and lambs, so the standard practice was that household expenses came out of one account, farm expenses another, and we took money for ourselves if and when each of the income streams came in. It meant that I had no regular savings, but I knew that my efforts would only improve the farm I would one day own.

Dad was clearly slowing down. He was beginning to tire quickly, and before long I was really doing most of the physical work on the farm. That was fine with me, I revelled in being busy.

1948 was a good year, and Dad said we had to spend some money or the tax man would have it. He bought himself a new cream Ford sedan, a V8. He handed me a wad of cash, most of which I put straight into the bank.

He was very pleased with the Ford. It was comfortable, could seat six, had a synchromesh gearbox, and hydraulic brakes on all four wheels. It also had a nice exhaust note, a low and throaty rumble. On my weekly night out, Dad let me use it. It was no P-40 Kittyhawk, but I sure felt good behind that shiny new steering wheel.

By 1951 little had changed. I had a good circle of friends, and had taken up playing a little tennis as well as cricket. No matter how hard I tried, I was pretty average at tennis, and although I was fairly ordinary to look at, there were quite a few attractive and sporting young ladies who were keen to help me improve my game. Although nothing lasting came of it, I was never short of a date when I wanted one.

It was somewhere in the middle of that year that I noticed that Dad was taking long tea breaks, and that he struggled to help me with heavier tasks. One day, I saw him clutch at his chest. After the terrible experience with old Jack, I was thoroughly alarmed. He asked me not to tell Mavis, but I refused. She immediately demanded he see the local GP, who then recommended him to a specialist in Sydney

He didn't want to go, but we insisted. It was lamb marking and tailing time, he said, so we reluctantly agreed to put off the appointment for a fortnight. The next day we penned the first lot of ewes and their lambs to begin the rather unpleasant job of marking and tailing.

The timber- railed yards were all part of the shearing shed and its set-up. Dad insisted on helping me all day on the first lot of lambs, and at three o'clock in the afternoon, we released them back into the paddock nearest the shearing shed. We'd run out of some house supplies, so I volunteered to drive the twenty minutes into Molong. I was away just over an hour all told. When I turned into the farm gate, I almost ran into Mavis, who was running, red faced and with skirt hitched up above her knees, to meet me.

It was obvious something drastic had happened. Immediately I thought of Dad, his heart, and the long day he'd just worked. I jammed my foot on the brake of Dad's Ford, and swung the door open as Mavis reached me. She could barely get the words out for gasping for breath

'Ricky, come quick. It's your father. He's been bitten by a snake. A big one. We've got to get him to hospital in Orange.'

Dad was lying in a recliner on the back veranda. His face was drawn, and he was holding his hand over the tourniquet that Mavis had applied. I half lifted, half dragged him to the Ford, and layed him across the spacious rear seat. Mavis sat beside me in front. Orange was half an hour away, even using the shortcuts I knew so well, so I put my foot as hard down as I dared.

Dad insisted he tell me what had happened, despite obviously being in pain, and becoming more and more breathless.

'Not long after you left, I was sweeping up in the shed when I heard a lamb bleating. The silly thing must have squeezed through the railing from one of the pens and somehow got under the shed floor. It was bleating its head off, and its mother was responding, pacing back and forth at the paddock gate. So, I climbed under the floor to grab it. Didn't see this snake coiled up there. Too dark. He got me good, right on the forearm.'

'Dad,' I said, exasperation probably evident in my voice, 'from the time I was a little kid you've warned me never to crawl under that floor. Snakes go in there after the mice.'

'Yeah, I know. But I couldn't leave that lamb there all night. It'd be dead by morning.'

'What sort of snake was it?'

'An eastern brown. A big bugger. And he got his fangs right in before I knew what was happening.'

Mavis cried in anguish, 'And you, you silly man, spent precious minutes catching the lamb before coming and telling me what happened. I tried to start the farm ute, but I have never driven it before, and I think I flooded it. I was still trying when I heard you, Rick, coming through the gate.'

In 1951, there was no antivenene for snake bite. The standard treatment was little more than to bleed the wound, and keep the patient still. Decades later, even after the advent of antivenene, people still died from the bites of our deadly snakes. I knew Dad was in trouble.

I was doing 90mph when I came to the last hill before reaching the city of Orange. As I topped the rise, a pale blue police car pulled out of the trees beside the road, and with siren wailing and blue beacon flashing, began chasing us. I figured that to enlist the copper's help made more sense than trying to outrun him, so I jammed on the brakes and screeched to a halt. I leapt out and ran to the police car, yelling through the open window to the burly sergeant behind the wheel.

'Snake bite. Brown snake. My Dad's in a bad way.'

'Follow me,' the copper yelled, and pulled out, wheels spinning in the loose gravel.

He was a good driver, and together, we made it at blistering speed through the city streets, other cars pulling over to allow us to speed by. The copper had also used his radio to alert the hospital. In record time Dad was stretchered in to the emergency operating theatre, and Mavis and I sat in the waiting room. We must have looked a pair. Mavis was wearing a house dress that was far from new, and I still had on trousers that were stained with lamb blood and a few spots of dung. We were both tired, thirsty, and hungry, but we sat together, silently for the most part, both lost in our thoughts.

Periodically a doctor would update us. The message they gave was that it wasn't looking good. The bite had been, as Dad had said, "a good one." The venom had gone deep into Dad's muscle. Dad's heart was already weak, and the last thing it needed was the blood-coagulating venom of an eastern brown.

It was after midnight that a doctor gently shook my shoulder. Despite our anxious state, both Mavis and I had fallen asleep in the hard wooden chairs, sitting upright, heads leaning against the brick wall.

'I'm terribly sorry. We did all we could. His heart just couldn't take it.'

Dad was just 61 years old.

∗∗∗

Dad's funeral was hard for Mavis and me. So many people came to the church, and to the cemetery, and most wanted to convey their condolences. Mavis had spent days baking and making sandwiches for the many who came for the wake, and had the house looking spotless. We both put on a brave front, but in reality, I think neither of us could wait for it to be over so that we could grieve alone.

The Hetheringtons came from Narromine. Mr Hetherington had his best suit on, its baggy trousers showing it dated from well before the war. He was in tears when he gripped my hand. Max looked thin, a shadow of his prewar fitness. Even his little sister came. Ellie was now eighteen, going on nineteen, tall and skinny, but healthy looking. She smiled shyly at me and I caught a glimpse of metal braces before she quickly ducked behind her father. I tried to engage her in conversation a couple of times, particularly wanting to tell her that the image of her and her galloping horse had helped sustain me through my years away, but her embarrassment was obvious. I was so grateful they'd come, and even more so because of the distance they'd travelled.

It was probably worse for Mavis than for me, because I had no choice but to resume the lamb marking and docking early the next day, which was a difficult job by oneself. Of course, Phil was nowhere to be seen until the job was over. Mavis had nothing to distract her from her loss.

***

The following twelve months went by very quickly. Mavis argued against employing any help, maintaining that between Phil and myself, we could handle all the work. At his mother's insistence, Phil did now spend more time at home, but in many ways, he was more a hindrance than a help. He would not do what I asked, nor would he do things the way I suggested. The only thing he was good at was rounding up sheep, because the kelpies responded well to him and they worked their little doggy butts off to please him.

CHAPTER 13

A change of direction.

I was cleaning up in the sheep yards one mid-winter afternoon, and my bare hands were aching with cold. I looked up to see Phil driving out in Dad's cream Ford V8. This was too much. I dropped the broom, and ran to head him off. He jerked the car to a stop and wound the window down.

'Yeah, what is it, Rick?' I bent down to the open window and put my hands on the door.

'What are you doing in my dad's car? It's only three o'clock and we've still got work to do.'

Phil sneered. 'It's about time that you stopped trying to order me around, Rick. From now on I'm the one who'll be doing the ordering, got it?'

I was speechless for a moment. I stood back, and said 'Get out of Dad's car, Phil,'

'Be fucked if I will. It's not your car anymore. It's mine. The whole farm's mine, or soon will be.'

With that he dropped the clutch and sped away, kicking

up dust and revving the engine hard in first and second gears. I stood flummoxed for a few seconds, then marched into the house, where Mavis was reading a magazine, feet up, and tea cup at hand. I plonked myself opposite, and willed myself to speak calmly. I told Mavis what had just happened. She listened without commenting. I continued.

'Mavis, I know you pay Phil a wage out of the farm account, which I guess is fair enough. I don't take a regular wage, because it's my farm. What isn't fair is that Phil isn't worth what he's being paid. He could be, but he won't work with or for me, and I end up doing his work as well as mine. The other thing is, I simply won't have him driving Dad's Ford. You should use it as much as you want, but not Phil. Not unless he starts pulling his weight.'

I waited. Mavis slowly put down her magazine. She was obviously thinking carefully on what she wanted to say before opening her mouth.

'Well, Rick, I guess that this conversation has been a year in coming. From what you have just said, I guess you haven't put two and two together, so I'll do it for you. Rick, you're a nice chap, and you work hard. You are welcome to stay here and we'll work out a regular salary. But the fact is that you don't own this farm. I do. Your father died without leaving a will. As his widow, I inherited everything, and that includes the Ford that I'm letting Phil use. As of now, Phil is the farm manager, he'll own it one day of course, and from now on you report to him.'

I was so totally gobsmacked that I sat back, and it took me a few moments to answer.

'That's ridiculous, Mavis. You know full well that Dad willed the farm to me, and gave you the right to live here as long as you want to.'

'If he intended that, he should have put it in a will.'

'I'm damned sure he did. He told me in a letter that he had.'

'Rick, if you don't accept the facts, you know what to do.'

'Mavis, you've lived here for six years. It's a year since Dad died. Do you mean to tell me that you'd kick me off my own farm, having worked here without a proper salary all that time? I haven't taken any money at all since Dad died. I don't believe you'd do that.'

Mavis also sat back. Her face looked different. She now looked hard, emotionless.

'Sorry Rick. I have to look after my own. Phil is my concern now. He needs a shove, and I guess now is the time to give it, whereas you are the type of man who'll make a go of it no matter what the odds. I think our time working together is over!'

***

So, at twenty seven years of age, I packed my clothes, a few precious photos, and my RAAF logbook into my old RAAF duffle bag, and drove out of the farm that had been my home for my entire life. I left the old ute at the main road, and hitched a ride into town. I took a room at the local hotel, and next morning was waiting at Reg Wilson's office before it opened at 9am. His secretary tried to fob me off by saying I had to make an appointment. I have never been the pushy type, but I quickly convinced her that I wasn't leaving until her boss showed up. He sauntered into the office an hour later. He gestured me to follow him into his room and closed the door. Before I had a chance to say a word, he said 'I believe you've had an altercation with Mavis Doak?'

'Mavis Richards, actually, since she married my dad. But you know that. You were a guest at their wedding.'

'Mavis rang me this morning and explained the situation. She's right, you know. Your father died intestate, and that means his widow automatically inherits. Mavis now owns the farm lock, stock, and barrel.'

I think my face must have gone white. I could only stammer 'And what about the funds on term deposit, the funds Dad saved over twenty years to pay death duties so that I could keep the farm?'

'Same thing. Mavis will use them for that very purpose.'

'Dad wrote to me while I was in New Guinea, saying specifically that he'd written a new will, and it had been lodged with your firm!'

'Your father made a couple of appointments with me to draft a will, but cancelled out at short notice both times. Must have been too busy dagging sheep or whatever to look after trivia like his will.'

I had never particularly liked old Wilson, because from my first memory of him he seemed a bit slick. I could never understand why Dad had ever even socialised with him. I was still unprepared for his attitude towards me, nor the demeaning look he gave me when he sneered. 'If a will exists, I suggest you go and find it. Otherwise, leave Mavis alone, and leave me alone. You'll be wasting your time hassling either of us. Now piss off out of my office.'

∗∗∗

Suddenly, to me Molong was longer the friendly town I thought I knew like the back of my hand. It was instantly an alien place, and I felt I had to get out immediately. I hitched a ride to Orange, and booked into the Telegraph Hotel. I made an appointment to see another solicitor. That afternoon I explained the situation to David Frew, (Attorney at Law). He shook his head, then began to speak.

'I've dealt with Reg Wilson. I have to admit that I have reason to avoid dealing with him if I can. But the fact is that without a will you have no case. It might be different if you were still a dependant of your father, but that's clearly not the case. After all, you were away from home for about three years while in the RAAF, and you are obviously fit, healthy, and quite capable of finding a job elsewhere. About the only option you have is to sue for the wages you weren't paid after you returned from the war. But I'm sure Mrs Doak, er, Richards, would dispute your rate of pay, the hours worked, the benefits of board and lodging, and the use of her vehicle, etcetera, to lessen the sum a court might grant you. Legal action is costly and slow, and quite frankly I suggest you just put it all down to experience.'

***

I'd suffered a few low points in my life, like having holes drilled in my head with a brace and bit in a dingy hut, the death of my dog Spinner, and of course Dad's death by snake bite. This felt almost as bad, because I'd been betrayed by a person I was close to and trusted implicitly. I felt powerless, and for the first time, totally alone.

That night I fronted the bar of the hotel and tried to drown my sorrows. It didn't work: it just gave me a bad headache in the morning. I paid for a second night, and spent most of the day sitting in the dark hotel room, with its yellowed wallpaper and creaking timber floor. On dusk I switched on its only light: a naked bulb hanging from the centre of the ceiling. Lying on the bed staring at the cracked plaster above me, I resolved that if I was ever to get my own back on Mavis and Wilson, I had to get back on my feet.

The first step was to get a job. I had a fair bit of cash in the bank, because the RAAF paid me for the whole time I'd been in New Ireland, and of course I'd had no chance to spend any of it there. On top of that, in lieu of salary, Dad had given me small annual cash bonuses, so I could afford to wait for the right opportunity to arise. As it turned out, I didn't have to wait long at all.

The newspaper advert was headed: "FARM MANAGER WANTED. A young and fit person is required to manage a sheep run near Tamworth. The successful applicant will be experienced in all matters concerning merino sheep. Call xxxxxxx"

I made the call using the hotel's pay phone. When I explained my situation, I was offered the job immediately. "Ten quid a week, free accommodation. Supply your own food." I accepted. Now I had to figure a way of getting to this farm.

Orange had several car dealers. One sold Holdens, Oldsmobiles, and Chevs, one sold Fords, and one sold British makes like Austin and Morris. Although I liked the look of the new Holden sedan, I wasn't too keen to blow such a large hole in my savings.

'Sixty horsepower, one hundred and thirty-two cubic inches, three forward gears, with synchro on second and top. The 48-215 can seat six, and the boot can carry two big suitcases. She'll get twenty-five miles per gallon cruising at forty miles per hour. These are selling like hot cakes, but we have just one ready for immediate delivery. Isn't this a great colour? It's called jade green.'

The salesman's pitch was tempting. I even agreed to a quick "run around the block." Compared to Dad's big Ford, now a few years old, it had a spartan interior, but it was light and nimble on the road. I stood looking at the shiny new car when a mechanic wheeled an old motorbike past, and propped it in the back corner of the lot. It had a sign on it: CHEAP.

'How much is cheap?' I asked the salesman. He laughed. 'Five quid and you can ride it away.'

I did, relieved that I now had transport, a job, and my kitty was largely intact.

The bike was an Indian. It had once been an expensive piece

of kit; good looking too. However, the previous owner had left it in a shed in 1940, gone to war, and had never returned. Chrome had pitted, and rust was replacing faded paint, The leather seat was as rough as crocodile skin, and the horsehair padding was escaping from a large crack in it. However, the single cylinder engine fired after only a few kicks, and the resultant cloud of smoke dissipated as the engine settled into a steady rumble.

I rode straight to the hotel, strapped on my duffle bag, and pointed the bike towards Tamworth. So began a love affair with the old Indian. It was to serve me well for a couple of years.

I'd never driven much further north than the central tablelands of New South Wales, so I enjoyed the road trip. I first rode south east to Bathurst, then turned north, reaching Mudgee on the first day, via backroads that were not in the best condition. I went through Dunedoo, Coolah, and Gunnedah on the second day, admiring lovely country for wheat, sheep, and cattle farming most of the way. On the morning of the third day, I calculated I had only sixty miles to go to reach Tamworth, where I'd find the new farm.

The closer I got to Tamworth, the more excited I got. The soil got darker and richer the further I rode. 'This farm must be a wonderful place,' I mused, 'four thousand acres of this land must be worth a fortune!'

My instructions were to go to Dalgetys stock and station agents, and I found them quickly enough. There I met Brett Thomas, the manager.

'Our client is the widow of one of Tamworth's leading businessmen. She has moved to Sydney. Her husband bought this land a few years ago, and put a manager on to look after it. The owner had every intention of developing it fully, but he contracted cancer, and died a few months ago. The manager proved to be unreliable, and we've sacked him. It is a big opportunity for you.'

Brett gave me the directions, suggested I stock up with some supplies, as he did not know what the manager had left, and shook my hand. 'See you in a few weeks,' he called as I rode off to find a general store.

✷✷✷

There isn't a lot of room on a motorbike, and my duffle bag filled most of what there was. However, I bought some of the basics, including a bag of potatoes, a loaf of bread, some flour, some sugar, a few fresh vegetables, a packet of salt, a bottle of fresh milk, a bag of tea, and a big jar of coffee, stuffed them into a hessian sack that I threw onto my back, holding it there with some twine, and took off, following the mud map I had been given.

It wasn't easy to find. The farm, a term that had been applied rather loosely, was much nearer Walcha than Tamworth, and down a road that wasn't much better than a track. I saw with dismay the change in the soils as I neared my destination, from the deep and rich red-brown loams around Tamworth, to thin silty grey clays, interspersed with outcrops of sandstone.

The farm gate was rusty, and the hinges gave only after a hefty shove. The driveway beyond was nothing more than wheel tracks through a belt of uncleared dry, grey and drab eucalyptus forest. Windfall showed that no vehicle had used it for some time.

There was no house. All that had been built was a concrete slab about thirty by thirty feet, with a low-pitched corrugated iron roof supported by steel poles. There were no outside walls, but in the centre was a walled off square, again in corrugated iron, that contained a kitchen. It had a door frame but no door, and a window frame without glass. Inside this kitchen was an old Coolgardie safe, a filthy black wood stove, and a pitted enamel sink. A leaking water tank stood just outside the roof, and a grey Ferguson TEA 20 tractor was parked on the slab and alongside the kitchen. It couldn't have been more than two or three years old, but it was caked in mud, one mudguard was slightly bent, and one of the pod-mounted headlights was hanging by its electrical wiring.

It appeared that someone had bedded down outside the northern side of the kitchen, as there was a heap of hessian bags there, and the remnants of a mosquito net hung from the exposed rafters. A rusty kerosene lamp hung nearby. A half-full one-gallon drum of kero sat on the bare floor. There was nothing else.

It was late afternoon, and I was tempted to ride away without looking back. The thought of the cold night ahead wasn't at all appealing, but neither was another hour's ride back to Tamworth in failing light and plummeting temperatures, not to mention dodging kangaroos that had squatter's rights to the road at sunset. I resolved to camp for the night and reassess in the morning. It didn't take long to gather some fallen timber from the tree belt, and stoke up the stove until it belted out some heat. I found some rusty cans from an old rubbish dump, and one served that night as my cooking pot. I boiled a potato and a carrot, spread them generously with butter and gave them a healthy sprinkling of salt. I was so famished I enjoyed every mouthful. Coffee with milk and sugar, as hot as I could drink it, rounded off my first meal at this so-called farm.

The darkness beyond my open-sided shelter was total, and the air frigid. The Walcha area is at a higher altitude than Tamworth, and I soon discovered that even the locals regarded it as a bloody cold place. It certainly was that night. I lay down, fully clothed, on the hessian bags, saving a couple to use as blankets. Within an hour the warmth generated by my meal had gone, and the cold penetrated from both sides, above, and below. I ached and shivered. I also cursed myself for even thinking of taking on the impossible job of making something of this rubbish land. I picked up the hessian bags and carried them into the kitchen, and lay down beside the still-warm cast iron stove. Around midnight I stoked it with more wood, and that made the night just bearable.

The following morning, I rode back to confront Brett Thomas. Probably sensing that I'd be back, he'd made himself scarce, and his secretary had no idea when he'd return. So, I dictated a letter for Mr Thomas. It said that I offered two options. The first was that I would leave a shopping list for food supplies, a camp bed, a mosquito net, some cooking utensils, some basic tools, and some building materials, to be delivered to the farm by nightfall. He was also to forward a letter with those supplies confirming the doubling of my salary to twenty pounds a week.

The second option was that I quit.

✶✶✶

The Dalgety truck, a shiny red International, did arrive just on dark. The driver, Alf, wheezed as he helped me unload. He had a bad head-cold.

'Mr Thomas sends his apologies. He couldn't arrange all the things on your list, but what's missing will be here within a couple of days. Oh, nearly forgot. He gave me this note.' The note simply confirmed that my starting salary was now twenty pounds per week.

After a quick cup of coffee, Alf climbed into the truck's cab, and started the engine. As he shoved the gear lever into first, he said 'Looks like you could use some company out here. My neighbour picked up a stray dog the other day. Nobody knows where he came from, but he needs a good home. I was going to keep him myself, but I think you need the company more than I do.'

'Not sure you could describe this place as a good home. What sort of dog is he, anyway?'

'Mostly kelpie by his looks. But it's anybody's guess what the rest is. He's probably about six or seven years old, and looks like he's had a rough time. Might make a good sheepdog, anyway.'

✳✳✳

Alf was back late the following day. He was a big guy, I guessed in his mid-forties, and he was very strong. He spent all day every day loading and unloading the truck at farms all over the district. His legs were like tree trunks, and his upper arm muscles stretched his shirt sleeves, but he opened the passenger door, reached in and picked up a kelpie with gentleness. Well, mostly kelpie, as Alf had claimed. The dog was anxious to run around and explore my domain, but kept well clear of me. After a few minutes he returned to Alf, whom he seemed to trust, but glanced at me nervously. I thought Alf was right, somebody had given this dog a tough life.

Alf held him while I slowly went to him. He cautiously sniffed at my boots then looked into my eyes, unsure of the reaction to expect. I offered the back of my hand, he sniffed it, then I patted him. 'Hey beautiful boy, what's your name?' I knelt down and gave him a hug. If there was a son of Spinner, he was it.

Working alone all day had never bothered me, but I have to admit that the bleak and lonely nights alone in the poorly-lit half-shelter did test my resolve. When the wind blew the freezing air through the kitchen, not even the warmth of the stove could mitigate the feeling of isolation. After Horrie, short for Horace, came to live with me, he was very jumpy for weeks, as if he expected a belting at any moment. The fear gradually left him, and he and I formed an easy companionship. His gentle and undemanding company lifted my spirits, and our rough digs became bearable.

I didn't have the training skills that Dad had, but Horrie already knew the basics of herding. Under my inexpert tutelage, he would never be a champion sheepdog, but after a few weeks, he was more than pulling his weight when I had sheep to move. At night he listened attentively to everything I said, and never argued.

✳✳✳

For twelve long months I toiled on the farm without a break. The first task had been to repair all the fences, and until that was complete, I couldn't prevent sheep escaping into next-door's paddocks, nor could I rotate grazing to rest paddocks. Fencing was easy enough on the few flat parts of the farm, but very hard work on the hilly and rocky sections. The second priority was to ensure that every paddock had reliable water, from either a bore, tank, or dam. The third priority was to fix the primitive stock races, holding pens, and shearing facilities.

The fourth priority was to improve the pasture. Like much of Australia, the soil was chronically deficient in phosphorous and nitrogen. Spreading superphosphate annually could ameliorate the former, but the only economical way of providing the latter was to introduce sub clover to the native grasses. Fortunately, Brett Thomas from Dalgetys had by now become an ally. He was obviously happy with progress, and after my first six months, backed my request for expenditure on two small second-hand implements: a fertilizer spreader, and a six-tyned scarifier. Either could be mounted behind the little grey tractor. He also supported my demand for a small truck. I received a second-hand dark-green Bedford, which, despite its previous hard life, proved to be a reliable work horse for lugging bags of seed and fertilizer, fencing tools etc. around the farm.

In my original demands, I'd included some building materials, and carpentry tools. After work hours, I built simple outside walls around part of the slab, and clad them in weatherboard, to make a living room for myself and Horrie. I scrounged an old window and a door from a house that was being renovated in Tamworth, and a couple of rolls of carpet. The completion of this room improved our comfort enormously. A proper table, some chairs, and a three-piece lounge, all discarded from the same renovation in town, made the room positively cheerful. Life was now much easier and more satisfying, but despite Horrie's best efforts, I did get very lonely.

I joined a cricket team in Tamworth. My indifferent batting and fielding skills meant that I didn't play every Sunday, but when the pitch was a bit sticky and a spin bowler was needed, I was the first person the captain would call. Now I had a few team mates, and a couple became lifelong friends.

***

My method of improving the stock capacity of the land was probably not the most effective way, but it was simple and cheap. I mixed sub clover seed with superphosphate, spread it using the Fergie tractor, then swapped implements to break up the crust on the soil and give the new seed a chance to establish itself.

That would work well for the one thousand acres that I could drive the Fergie over. I figured it would take about two years, with the time available, as I could only cover about ten acres on a good day.

Horrie was always with me. I made a small tray on the back of my Indian, and he would expertly balance on it regardless of the terrain. He much preferred the comfort of the green Bedford, with his front legs and most of his upper body precariously hanging outside the open window. When I drove the tractor back and forth in what Horrie must have considered mindless repetition, he'd pick a shady spot and keep watch from there.

Scarifying and spreading at barely above walking pace didn't take a lot of skill, nor attention. It gave me a lot of time to think about many things. I thought a great deal about Dad, and how much I missed him, and 'Kittyhawk', as I still called our farm. I missed my best mate Max, and the camaraderie with the Hetherington family. I thought too about Jack, and Kala, and my flying days, where I'd grown from a simple farm boy to become a RAAF fighter pilot. It didn't take long to decide that the little twenty horsepower Fergie tractor was doing a sterling job for me, but it was no substitute for my twelve hundred horsepower P-40!

I also laughed aloud when I thought again of the opportunities with the opposite sex that I'd passed up, in my loyalty to Lyn.

One day, as the Fergie purred along, I began to think of the problem of how I could spread superphosphate over the three thousand acres that were too rough and / or too steep to drive the Fergie. The proverbial light bulb flashed on in my brain. An aeroplane, of course! I'm a pilot, aren't I? Go and fit an aeroplane with a bin to carry superphosphate, with or without seed mixed in, and it won't matter how rough the country is! I resolved to investigate the possibilities as soon as I could get a break from the farm. On my next visit into town, I made some enquiries, and found that yes indeed, the use of aircraft for super spreading was already well established, and in fact was in great demand. I immediately pictured myself in a new career. There were just two big obstacles, the first being that I didn't have an aeroplane. The second was that I didn't have a civil licence to fly one. To sell my services, I would need a commercial pilot's licence.

Further discreet enquiries were not encouraging. My 'penetrating head wound' ruled me out from passing a pilot's medical. But, though the air force had all the details of my injury, the local doctors didn't. I found one who conducted civil aviation medicals, and presented myself for an examination. He poked and prodded, tested my eyesight, and took measurements of my height and weight. If he noticed the scars across my hairline and over both of my ears, he didn't mention them. When it came to my medical history, and the question that said something like "Have you been admitted to hospital for any illness or injury?" I could honestly say No. Nobody could describe that dark, thatched hut in the jungle as a hospital, and the army hospital in Milne Bay was just for recuperation.

With commercial class medical in hand, I sought out the local flying school at Tamworth. John McIvor ran a one-man operation, with a single Tiger Moth. John took one look at my RAAF logbook, and said 'Let's go. We'll see if you remember how to fly a Tiger Moth.'

I did. It looked even smaller and more primitive after my hours in the P-40. It took me a few minutes to reacquaint myself with the featherlight controls of the docile old biplane, and the slow speed at which it did everything. I could feel myself getting smoother, and after twenty minutes or so John shouted to me from the rear cockpit and through the gosport tube. I could barely hear him over the roar of engine and slipstream around the open cockpit. 'How about a few straight forward aeros?'

Aerobatics gave me no particular joy, but they are a great way of improving the precision of one's flying. I gave him the thumbs up, did a clearing turn, then rolled into a 90 knot dive. I pulled a neat loop, followed by a barrel roll, then a stall turn.

'Now shoot a couple of touch and goes!'

A good landing starts at the top of descent. I slowed the Tiger on downwind and proceeded with the pre-landing checklist every pilot knows by rote. Base turn, final turn, and keeping above 30 knots, I touched the wheels on the grass, applied power and pulled gently on the stick to climb for another circuit. I repeated the first touch-down, and on the third circuit brought the nose up and cut the power so that we touched wheels and tail skid simultaneously. I heard a brief clap from the rear seat.

After shutting down, John said, 'Tell you what. If we go through the full rigmarole, I can bleed you for months before signing you out. But instead, I've got a proposition. We'll start a civil logbook for you, putting some dates in, stating that you've passed your commercial licence after a hundred hours flying time. Then, you can work for me on weekends training some young hopefuls, until you really do have the hundred hours up. I'll even pay you two quid an hour while you're doing it!'

***

Every Sunday for the next eight months I instructed ab initio pilots for John. They were all locals, of both sexes, and of ages from sixteen to sixty. I soon realised that I really didn't have the patience to become a full-time instructor, but as it was for only one day per week, I successfully hid my true feelings.

The Tiger's Gypsy Major engine wasn't in its first flush of youth, and spat a fine mist of oil that would curl back into the rear cockpit, and so I took to wearing my RAAF coveralls, Word then quickly spread between the students that I was an ex RAAF fighter pilot who had seen real action, and in no time I had a fan club. It included several very attractive young ladies, and so for the time I worked for John, I did not lack for a social life.

Horrie enjoyed Sundays even more than I did. He quickly figured out the need to keep everyone well back when I was about to start up, and to keep them there until I'd shut down after return. As soon as the prop flicked to a stop, he'd shepherd the waiting student to the aeroplane. It was that kelpie herding instinct, I suppose.

Horrie didn't get paid for his diligent efforts, but was well rewarded by attention from these same young ladies. He had a particular affinity for the fresh-baked biscuits they brought.

∗∗∗

Now that I had my licence, I began looking for a suitable aeroplane of my own. By 1953, dedicated agricultural aircraft were being built in America, but they were way too expensive for us here in Australia. All local operators used converted Tiger Moths. To make a Tiger into a crop duster, the front seat was removed, and in its place a hopper was bolted in. A simple lever opened a gate under the fuselage. A bit more complicated were the sprayers, that had spray nozzles at intervals along a pipe attached to the lower wing. There was even a company at Bankstown Airport that would do the conversion.

It was this company that put me onto a Tiger Moth for sale. I had to travel to Bankstown to see it, which meant leaving Horrie for a few days. Alf offered to look after him. When I handed him over, Horrie gave me a reproachful look, but I knew Alf would keep him well. I heard later that Horrie loved travelling with Alf on his rounds. He hung out the window between every farm, and said hello to all the farm dogs at delivery stops. At night, Horrie slept in Alf's own bedroom.

The Tiger Moth was still in its RAAF training yellow, somewhat faded from spending the entire war training new pilots. The air force roundels had been crudely over-sprayed with new yellow paint, making shiny patches on the old matt finish. It had flown over four thousand hours, and was on its fourth engine. The good part was that in RAAF days it had been regularly serviced, and the current engine had only a few hours of use on it. A Sydney businessman had bought it from RAAF disposals, but quickly found that flying was harder than it looked. The asking price was six hundred pounds.

RAAF wages during the war were far from generous, but if you didn't spend much and you weren't into gambling, you could save a major part of it. I had five hundred pounds, and I offered that much for the aeroplane and a full tank of fuel. My offer was accepted.

I couldn't afford for the conversion to crop duster yet, so I flew the Tiger back to Tamworth and parked in John McIvor's hanger. When I picked up Horrie, he reacted like I'd been gone forever, and despite his exciting holiday with Alf, seemed pleased to be home.

CHAPTER 14

A very big weekend.

It was now early December of 1954, and I needed a break. I was just turning 30, I'd been at the Walcha farm for 3 years, and hadn't had a holiday. I decided on a road trip on the Indian: I would go and see Max Hetherington on the property that his father now managed, just west of the Harvey Ranges, nearer Narromine than Dubbo. Once again Horrie stayed with Jack, and I left assuring him I'd be back in five days. That allowed two days riding each way, and one with Max.

It was quite a hike, and by four pm on the second day I was tired, wind-blown, dusty, probably a bit smelly and in need of a shave. When I found the right driveway, I turned in, and rode the last half mile to a pleasant-looking farmhouse surrounded by green lawns and a few eucalypt shade trees. I pulled up and switched off the rumbling motor in the open area outside the low front gate, and I walked up the paved path towards the front door, which was open, but its screen door was closed. I was a couple of steps away when it swung open.

There before me was the most stunning woman I'd ever seen. Because I'd looked down at the step I was about to stand on, and she stood two steps above me, the first part of her I saw were her bare feet. Her toenails were painted red: I'd never seen anything like that before. Her tight- fitting slacks went all the way up to curvy hips. She wore a broad leather belt around her narrow waist, a cotton shirt, finely chequered in red, white and blue, curvy too in the right places. Her long and shapely neck was topped by a face that rendered me speechless. Her eyes were green, her nose smallish, her skin lightly tanned. The mass of hair, tumbling past her shoulders, was dark, and tinged with red.

I stepped back involuntarily. She smiled, a wide smile showing perfect teeth. 'Hello Ricky, welcome to Billabong Farm. It's so lovely to see you.'

I couldn't think of a thing to say. At least I had the presence of mind to close my open jaw.

She laughed. 'You don't recognise me, do you. I'm Ellie, Max's little sister.' Of course I recognised her, Max's annoying baby sister. The skinny girl I last saw at Dad's funeral. It took some seconds for me to process how she'd changed, but at last, I found my voice.

'Hello Ellie,' I said. It came out as a croak. I guess my throat was dry after riding for hours. 'You've grown.' I immediately winced inwardly. What a dumb thing to say to this goddess.

She laughed again, came down one step and leaned forward to take my hand. 'Come on in, Max's out the back. He can't wait to see you.'

Ellie led me down the hallway into the kitchen. It and the attached family room occupied most of the house's rear. They overlooked a healthy back lawn, with shady trees both sides. The Harvey Ranges were just visible in the distance. As we entered, Ellie said 'look who I found at the front door.' She still held my hand.

'RICK,' Max, his dad and his mum shouted all at once. They all rose to hug me. I was a bit embarrassed by the effusive welcome, and was relieved when Ellie took charge.

'Okay, let him take his jacket off. The poor man must be so tired and hungry after riding such a long way. Mum, you sit and I'll put the kettle on.'

During the next few hours, from afternoon to the roast dinner, I tried to ask the Hetheringtons about their life on this farm, and how they had settled into the district after so many years at Molong. I particularly wanted all the details on how Mr H had recently risen from farm hand to farm manager. They barely answered my questions because they wanted even the smallest detail of my experiences in New Guinea, and what had happened that Mavis Doak now owned 'our' farm. I was uncomfortable talking so much about myself, but had little choice. As one they laughed, cried, looked horrified, or pleased as my story unfolded.

One thing I did learn was that Mr H had done well. I already knew that he was a good farmer, as honest as the day was long, and deserving of his promotion to farm manager. At about 9 pm he announced that he had an early start the next day, and he and Mrs H departed for bed. Max looked tired, and soon he too retired. Ellie said, 'Come outside for a bit of fresh air. It's a beautiful night.'

We sat on the front veranda, and, with my tiredness suddenly gone, we talked until midnight. She told me of her life at university, how she had just found out that she'd passed her final year of vet science, and was now about to look for a job in the district. I could have sat there until morning, listening to her, but the one question I really wanted to know, I couldn't bear to ask. Did she have a boyfriend? Suddenly she patted me on the knee, stood up, and said, 'Okay flyboy, you need a bath. There's a towel on the bed in your room. Bathroom's down the hall. It's all yours. I'll see you in the morning.'

I went to sleep that night wondering what had struck me. Was I dreaming this whole thing? I hadn't felt this good since Dad had died. Somehow I knew that my outlook on life had just changed forever.

✶✶✶

I was awake at first light, and I could hear the muted clatter of activity in the kitchen. After dressing quickly, I walked into a scene of activity and the smell of frying eggs and bacon 'We thought you'd sleep in, after that long ride,' Mrs H said.

'I guess after being brought up on a farm, you always get up with the sun,' I replied.

'Come sit down,' Ellie said. She stood behind me as I sat, and put both hands on my shoulders.

'Mmm, you do smell a whole lot better than you did last night,' she said. We all laughed. 'I think even the horses might have taken exception.'

'Horses?' I queried.

'Yes, horses. The owner of the farm loves horses. We have six here, and he likes us riding them to keep them exercised for when he visits himself. This morning we'll do a tour of the farm, on horseback.'

Mrs H asked 'Do you still ride, Rick?'

'Mrs H, I last rode horses when we were kids. You might recall that Ellie did teach Max and me to ride, with limited success in my case. But I guess it's like riding a bike, or flying an aeroplane. You never forget how.'

Max needed assistance to mount his horse. Ellie fussed about him, making sure everything was just right for him. We then set off. First stop was at the large shearing shed. It had eight stands, which was far too many for a two-thousand acre farm. Max explained. 'Twenty years ago this farm was six thousand

168

acres. Death duties and an argument between inheriting sons caused it to be broken up. Fortunately, this block had the shearing shed and shearer's quarters. We'll show you both.'

Half the shearing shed had been converted to a single open space, and the slatted floor had been replaced with polished floorboards. 'Once a year the owner busses a lot of his friends here, and they'll have a big party,' Ellie explained. 'Wait until you see the shearers' quarters.'

Outside, the shearers' quarters looked like they'd been built rough, decades ago. Inside, all walls had been plaster-lined, painted white, and the floor polished. There were individual rooms for at least half a dozen couples.

The rest of the tour was interesting, because the owner could afford the latest in machinery. He had a new MF 65 tractor with three-point linkage, a disc plough, and a wonderful fertilizer / seeder combo. Mr H met us there and immediately asked my advice about a problem he had getting the discs to cut evenly. Although I hadn't used such a modern implement myself, logically working through the setting on the plough and the tractor's linkage soon had the problem solved.

We rode the boundary fence line, and headed back towards the homestead for a late lunch. We had about a quarter mile to go, and I noticed that this last paddock had been cropped the previous year, then had been returned to pasture. It still had a few patches of stubble, but was nice and smooth: an ideal landing ground. Ellie suddenly called, 'Last one home is a rotten egg.' It was a call we often made when we were kids. She had the head start, but Max reacted quickly. My horse responded before I did. We galloped home, Ellie just beating Max, and me a poor third.

We were all laughing when Ellie and I dismounted. As at every stop, Ellie was quickly at her brother's side, to help him.

✶✶✶

It was a cold meat salad for lunch, as much as I could eat. We sat talking for half an hour, then Mrs H asked Ellie if the three of us could drive into Narromine for some urgent supplies. At the last minute, Max begged off, saying he needed to rest. I scolded myself when I realised that I was secretly pleased. Ellie drove the farm's new FJ Holden ute into town, smoothly manipulating the clutch and column gearshift. When I commented, she laughed, and said, 'there's a lot about me you don't know, Ricky.'

We angle-parked in Narromine's wide main street, and I followed her into a big grocery store. There she was greeted by a middle-aged chap, short, a bit overweight, a fringe of grey hair around his bald pate.

'Hello Ellie, nice to see you. Hey Marge, come and see who's in the shop.'

Marge was about the same height, but a good few pounds heavier. Ellie gave them both a quick peck on the cheek, and introduced me.

'Rick's an old friend. He was in the air force, but he's now farming near Tamworth.'

After a further jolly exchange, we did the rounds of the shop, and we left with two heavy boxes of fruit, vegetables, and various cleaning products. I hate shopping for myself, and get it done without delay, but I found myself quite willing to accompany Ellie H no matter how long it took. We left the store, placed the boxes in the tray of the FJ, and were about to jump in when someone called.

'Hey, Ellie, hold on a minute.'

A tall fair-haired fellow, about two inches taller than me and a few pounds heavier, strode towards us. He was neatly dressed in jeans and T shirt, and his hair was freshly combed. He had a square jaw, high cheek bones, and a wide and friendly grin. Until he saw me. He then frowned.

'Ellie, when did you get back into town? We've missed you.'

'Hi Chris. Finished uni a couple of weeks ago. Home for a bit now. How have you been?

'Okay I guess. Busy. Why didn't you give me a call?'

Ellie didn't answer the question but swung around towards me. 'Chris, this is Rick. He's an old friend of ours from Molong days. He's…' Chris interrupted with 'Yeah G'day Rick. Listen Ellie, there's a party on next weekend at Mike Lowe's place. How about coming with me?'

'Call me.' Ellie replied as she swung her lithe body into the seat, and pulled the door closed. 'See you, Chris.'

We drove half way back to the farm in silence, during which I was feeling a damn fool for allowing myself to even dream that Ellie might not already have a social life that excluded an old neighbour from Molong. Suddenly she said 'That guy Chris. He's a bit of a jerk. Thinks he's God's gift to women. I won't be going to any party with him.'

My mood lifted instantly. I asked about her job prospects, and we talked happily about mundane things until reaching the homestead.

Everyone was tired that night, and we were all just about talked out. We went to bed early, after another big meal of shepherd's pie and green beans. As I lay in the H's spare bedroom, I realised that this had been one of the best days of my life. I also kept telling myself that Ellie was a wonderful girl, that she was popular because of her friendly personality, and she'd been very nice to me over a great weekend. But that's all it was ever going to be. Unfortunately.

✶✶✶

We were all up for the usual early breakfast, and Max had helped me tie my swag onto Horrie's tray on the Indian. That done, we walked back into the kitchen for fond farewells. I thanked

Max, Ellie, and the senior H's for having given such a wonderful weekend. They made me promise to come again soon.

Ellie said, 'I'll walk you to your bike.'

As I swung my leg over the saddle, she said 'Ricky, why don't you come here for Christmas? We'd all love to have you. Stay for New Year too.'

I hesitated because I didn't want to stretch the friendship with the H's. 'Actually Ell, I can't. There's a guy who has done me a lot of favours. He lives alone in Tamworth, and he's asked me to have Christmas lunch with him.' It was true, Alf had.

'Oh, well in that case, how about New Year's Eve? Mum and Dad are having a party. They have a few friends coming from Molong, and they'll all stay over in the shearer's quarters. Some local couples are invited too. I'll have a few of my friends here. I'd love you to meet them.'

'Okay, I'll try. I'll let you know if I can.'

I kicked the start lever and the Indian rumbled into life. Ellie took a step back, and hugged herself against the early morning chill.

I let the bike warm up for a minute, selected first gear, and with a wave let out the clutch. The engine stalled.

As I lifted my foot to kick the start lever again, Ellie ran forward the few steps.

'Ricky, wait,' she said, and put a hand on my arm. She drew in her breath and said, 'Did you know that I had a crush on you from the time I was about two years old?'

I leaned back on the bike, raised my eyebrows, and said, 'Really. When did that end?' Immediately I berated myself for saying such a stupid thing.

'Who said that it did?' she replied softly.

For the second time that weekend I was gobsmacked. After what seemed like an eternity, I said something else that immediately sounded stupid.

'Well then,' I replied, 'what are you going to do about it?'

She looked seriously into my eyes, and said 'No, the question is, what are YOU going to do about it?'

I know I can be a bit slow on the uptake at times, but this time I knew I had to grab this opportunity right there and then. She still had her hand on my arm. I grabbed her other arm, pulled her against me, and kissed her. I put my hand behind her head to stop her pulling away. I didn't need to. She responded, and she held me tight for a long moment.

Ellie suddenly jumped back, and called, 'Safe travels, fly-boy! Come back soon.'

I started the bike, and as I pulled away, I called: 'Wait for me Ell, I'll be back on New Year's eve.'

The old Indian fairly flew all the way back to Tamworth, and I think I hummed and sang to myself all the way.

CHAPTER 15

A tiger, a kelpie, and the shindig.

Whenever I had a few spare hours, I rode over to the Tamworth aerodrome and worked on the Tiger. I removed the cylinder head, decoked it, checked the bores, (they were good), and ground the valves. I sanded and revarnished the fixed-pitch wooden prop, and the interplane struts. I tidied up the cockpits with new leather coaming, and sprayed a new coat of the RAAF trainer-yellow paint over the entire machine. I'd have swapped it in a second for a P-40, but for a Tiger, it looked pretty good.

The last job was to make a harness for Horrie. I used some old leather straps that lay about in the hangar. I wanted him to be able to sit on the seat without being able to climb out, nor jump down to the floor where the rudder pedals were. It took me half a day to get it right, but I was satisfied with the result. Horrie could sit up and look out, or he could curl up on the seat, but he couldn't interfere with the controls. To top it off, I modified an old leather flying helmet to fit him. It shielded his ears from the engine noise, but allowed the tips of his ears to poke through.

A few days before Christmas, Alf dropped by. He had a message for me to call Ellie, during business hours, at a number I didn't recognise. That afternoon I rode into Tamworth and made the call. It wasn't a good line, but I heard clearly a male voice, answering 'Narromine Vet Clinic.' I asked for Ellie Hetherington, and after a moment was put through.

'Hi Ricky, thanks for calling back.' Her voice was like music, despite sounding like it was coming through a rusty pipe a mile long. 'Just wanted to make sure you're coming for New Year's Eve?'

'Ellie, do you have a new job?'

'Yes I do, but let me tell you all about it later. I can barely hear you. You are coming, aren't you?'

'Sure am. Wouldn't miss it for the world.'

'Great. Can you be here by lunch?'

'I'll aim at that, Ell. Just one thing. Can I bring a friend?'

There was a hesitation. 'Of course. We'll have room.' At that point, the line dropped out.

***

Christmas came with a rush, and as promised, Horrie and I spent the day at Alf's place. He invited another couple of friends for a barbeque and a few beers. Horrie cleaned up lots of scraps, and then we discovered that he had unusual taste buds for a dog. One of the friends had brought a dessert dish called lemon delicious. It was like a very soft cake with a lemon flavoured syrup all over it. Horrie was given one of the plates to lick, and to my amazement, the lemon flavour won him totally. He spent hours licking that plate, until not a molecule of flavour was left on it. He couldn't leave it alone. When tired from standing over it, he lay on his side, head in the bowl, still licking. Strange dog. I'd had more than my usual limit of two drinks, so we stayed that night.

Soon it was New Year's Eve. Horrie and I were at the Tamworth field before dawn, but first light had revealed thick low cloud. It began to rain shortly after I opened the hangar door. The forecast was that the rain would clear, but would be followed by strong winds from the west.

This Tiger had very basic instruments, not the full blind flying panel I'd have needed to fly through this murk. Open cockpits are also extremely uncomfortable in rain, and I wouldn't submit Horrie to that. Even when the rain stopped at ten a.m., and the clouds lifted, I wasn't too sure whether to go. The Tiger is such a slow machine, cruising at about sixty knots, that even a twenty knot headwind slows you by one third of your groundspeed. A twenty knot crosswind can push you off course very quickly too, so a tiger pilot on a cross country flight plots his position every ten miles if he doesn't want to risk getting lost.

We waited another hour, and the forecast 20-30 knot winds hadn't arrived. It was now or never. I strapped the harness on Horrie, to his bewilderment, then hoisted him into the front cockpit and buckled his harness to the seatbelts. (With the Tiger Moth, the pilot in command sits in the rear seat, the passenger or student in the front). I stuck some ear plugs I'd cut from foam rubber into his ears, and strapped his helmet on. He shook his head to dislodge them, but didn't succeed. I hand-swung the prop, because Tigers have no electrical systems for starting, or anything else for that matter. With the engine ticking over and my leather helmet buckled up, I climbed in.

Horrie took to flying quite calmly. While we were still low, he took great interest in seeing people, cars, and tractors from this new perspective, but once above 4000 feet he curled up on the seat and went to sleep. I levelled off at 4500 feet.

It took three hours to reach the Hetherington farm, so I was too late for lunch. What I didn't know was that there were about fifty guests who had made it on time. I decided to show off a bit, so I held my altitude until only a couple of miles out, pushed the nose down into a maximum speed dive, all of one hundred knots, and brought the throttle back to about 50% power. Sensing the change, Horrie came awake and sat up expectantly.

The people gathered on the back lawn didn't hear my approach above the babble of conversation. When we were about to go over the house, at about fifty feet, I rammed on full power and pulled into a steep climbing turn. Back at six hundred feet I surveyed the paddock behind the house, checked the wind direction from ripples on a farm dam, did the downwind checks, and descended on base and final turns, over the boundary fence, for a neat three-pointer landing. I taxied up to the back gate, swung the Tiger through ninety degrees, and switched off the magnetos.

Only then did I see fifty startled onlookers. Almost every person had mouths agape, but I didn't immediately see why. I didn't think aeroplanes were that unusual these days. Of course, anyone without any knowledge of aircraft would assume that the pilot sat in front, and the passenger behind, therefore it must have looked ridiculous to see the upright ears, long nose, and alert eyes of a black and tan kelpie apparently flying the aeroplane.

A gorgeous tall and lithe figure materialised out of the crowd. Ellie rushed to the side of the aeroplane as I climbed down from the cockpit. In front of everybody she hugged and kissed me. She said 'I've been worrying for hours that you weren't coming.'

'Sorry Ell. Held up by bad weather. But let me introduce you to my friend Horrie. He must be getting a bit anxious, as he's been in there for over three hours.'

I unstrapped Horrie and lifted him to the ground. He gave Ellie a quick lick, a thrashing of his tail, and then he sprinted for the nearest gate post. Ellie suddenly stepped back, looked momentarily cross, and dug me in the ribs.

'You rotter. You had me thinking you were going to bring a

girlfriend.' We both laughed. 'I think after that grand entrance, you had better meet some of the people.'

There were people of all ages. Many were Mr and Mrs H's age group, but there were quite a few in their early twenties to thirties. A couple had young kids, who drew back in fright at the sight of me in my old RAAF flying suit. Once over the initial shock, everyone was extremely friendly. That is, except for three guys in their early to mid-twenties. They hung back, and I soon realised that they saw me as a rival. I pretended not to notice, and was particularly friendly when shaking their hands. Ellie introduced me to several young ladies, who batted eyelids and twirled their hair around their fingers, but Ellie kept an arm around my waist while we chatted.

It wasn't long before people began to disperse to their accommodation in the shearing shed or shearers' quarters, with instructions that the big barbecue would start at eight o'clock. I had time to give Ellie her Christmas present: a khaki RAAF flying suit, second hand but well cleaned. I explained that the other half of her present was a ride in the Tiger, first thing in the morning.

Lights had been strung up, and a big fire pit set up in the middle of the lawn. The grilled meat was swiftly carried to the shearing shed, which now looked like a small ballroom. Music came from a record player, and by ten pm, people were dancing.

I'm afraid that I'd never had much opportunity to improve my dancing, but Ellie didn't seem to care. She also danced with others, and allowed me to shuffle around with some single girls, but quickly reclaimed me each time. I was so glad of that.

Twelve o'clock and the new year came with the usual excitement, but very soon people drifted off, leaving just a few of the younger set. The music was still playing softly, and Ellie and I found a dark corner. We were slowly moving to the music, arms entwined, kissing, and I think we were both heady with passion, when I felt the tap on my shoulder. It was Mr H.

'Okay you two. Break it up. It's just another day tomorrow and just another early start.' I was embarrassed, and began to apologise, but Ellie cut me short. She laughed. 'Don't worry Dad. I'll be a good girl. I'll put him to bed in a minute.'

She laughed again as she kissed me goodnight. I checked on Horrie, who was sound asleep on the back veranda, having been pampered by people all night. I quickly showered and jumped into bed wearing just shortie pyjamas and a singlet. I was about to turnout the light when there was a knock on the door. I called to come in, not knowing quite what to expect. It was Mr H.

'Rick, can I have a word?'

'Yeah, sure Mr H, come in.'

'Rick, I'm not sure how to say this, but here goes. Mrs H and I are very happy that you and Ellie seem to have gotten together. Your father was a gentleman, and you take after him. I just ask you to treat her properly. If you're not serious, please let her down gently. You probably didn't know that she adored you when she was a little girl, and she's held this image of you even when you were away for so long. Max read out all your letters to us, and she hung on every word. Now you come storming back, first the dashing figure on the motorbike, then the war hero in his fying chariot. You've reinforced every image she's held of you all these years…'

'Hardly a war hero…' I tried to interrupt.

'Yes you are, Rick m'boy. And Mrs H and I look at you as a second son. Have done for twenty years. We're proud of you. I just ask you not to treat Ellie lightly. She's a good girl, and I'd like you to treat her honourably. And I don't want to see her hurt.'

I promised Mr H I would do just that. I also knew that being honourable was going to be very hard, on my part at least.

***

Ellie and I had a plan. At first light we met in the kitchen, and again she stunned me. She'd taken the second-hand RAAF flying suit, and while I slept soundly, had trimmed it to fit her figure. And did it fit! No RAAF flying suit had ever looked so good. The trousers clung tightly to her long legs, and the upper part emphasised her small waist and ample bosom. I whistled, and she grinned and put a finger to my lips. We sneaked out to the Tiger. Only Horrie awoke, and he accompanied us to the aeroplane. I'd put enough motor fuel into the top tank the previous afternoon, so after telling Horrie that I'd be back soon, I buckled her in. When I checked the tightness of the shoulder straps, my hands could feel the firmness of her body. The thought struck me that I'd just made that promise to Mr.H. 'Keep your hands to yourself,' I said to myself.

The staccato crackle of the Gypsy Major settled into a purr, and we taxied for take-off.

'All okay?' I yelled above the engine, and Ellie waved from the front seat with thumbs up. We lifted off adjacent the buildings, no doubt waking most of the guests. I climbed to a safe 2000 feet, turned 180 degrees, nosed over into a 90 knot dive, then pulled a simple loop. Coming out of the loop I went immediately into a second, but this time, just after the top of the loop, rolled upright and dived again. As soon as we regained 90 knots, I pulled and rolled into a climbing barrel roll, followed by a wing over turn that brought us back over the landing strip, this time diving to about 100 feet. With plenty of speed in hand I put on full power, pulled into a climb, and executed a four-point slow roll. Throughout the routine, I could hear Ellie whooping, and when we did the last slow roll, she held her hands above her head. Nothing could frighten this girl!

Back at 500 feet, downwind checks complete, I did a neat turn onto base leg, then final. We touched down lightly, taxied straight for the back gate, and swung 90 degrees as I cut the engine. A few of the guests had returned to their homes after midnight, but that left a sizeable audience that had emerged from their beds and congregated on the lawn. They poured through the gate as I held Ellie's hand as she jumped down, still with my spare leather helmet and goggles on.

Horrie was the first to greet us, then came everyone else. Ellie nestled close, put her arms around me, and adopted a pose that a supermodel would have been proud of. There were ooh's and ah's, clicking of cameras, and much laughter. I heard someone comment that we made a lovely couple. I think my chest swelled with pride when I heard the word "couple."

After breakfast, a few more people left, leaving a core of men and women about Ellie'e age. They decided to have a game of cricket. There was a suitable hard patch of ground in front of the machinery sheds, and someone produced a couple of empty four-gallon drums to serve as wickets. Horrie had seen cricket matches before, but was always tied up on the sidelines. This time he was intent on joining in. He caught onto the idea immediately. With every ball struck, he was off like lightning, usually beating the fieldsman. If the ball was in the air, he rarely missed the catch. Then it must have occurred to him that if he stood in the middle of the pitch, he had double the chance of intercepting the ball, once when the bowler bowled, and if he missed that, when the batsman hit it.

This completely destroyed any semblance of a match, but nobody seemed to care. They laughed heartily, and at the conclusion, declared Horrie as the man of the match.

I stayed two more days, but duties back at Walcha forced my return. This time there was no hesitation, we clung to each other, and I promised to return as soon as I could. She waved, and called out, 'Come back soon, fly boy, I'll be waiting.'

CHAPTER 16

A new life.

By early 1955 I'd put enough money aside to have the agricultural conversion done on the Tiger Moth. In addition to the hopper replacing the front seat, brakes were installed on the mainwheels, and a tailwheel fitted in place of the fixed spring-steel tailskid. Having brakes made ground manoeuvring very much easier. I was then ready to go to work. With Brett Thomas's permission, I placed an advert for my services in Dalgetys' shop window. I intended to carry out any work I picked up on weekends.

Work came in immediately. In fact, within weeks I realised that I could make super spreading my full-time occupation. My weekends filled out, and it became difficult to find time to fly to the Hetherington farm. In late March I gave Brett three months' notice: I had to quit running the Walcha farm.

At the same time, I rang Ellie at the vet office, to tell her I could get a few days off at Easter. I'd fly the Tiger to the Narromine farm as usual. 'No,' she said, 'I want to see what you get up to in Walcha. I'm coming to you this time.'

'I'm hardly prepared for guests, Ell, and how will you get here?'

'I'll drive myself. I have a brand-new Holden. It was delivered last week, and I want to run it in.'

I'd made my living quarters a little more comfortable over the three years I'd been at Walcha, but they were still a bit rough. I had walled off the living room properly, installed a large window, and a pot-belly heater. Horrie and I slept in that room, him in a proper doggie bed, me in my swag on a camp stretcher. I had also constructed a bathroom on part of the slab, with a shower over a bath, and a basin with a mirror. A toilet was only a few steps away, separate from the slab.

Hastily I constructed a separate bedroom, just 10 feet by 12 feet, on the slab, and purchased a single bed with iron frame and comfortable mattress. I bought two new fancy sleeping bags, ones that could be zipped together, if the opportunity arose. I left my camp stretcher in the living room.

How I looked forward to that Easter! I really did count the hours. I worried about Ellie driving all that way alone, but I knew that the roads were improving all the time, and that she was a careful and confident driver. Horrie picked up on my excitement, and when Easter finally arrived, he was the first to hear the engine of the shiny sky-blue Holden sedan as it came up the driveway.

Ellie stepped out of the car looking like she'd driven ten miles, not hundreds. We hugged and kissed, and held hands as I led her to my home. Horrie gave her an enthusiastic welcome too. I was embarrassed as I opened the door, but she shut me up with a kiss. "I came to see you, not to judge your house."

We talked as the light faded. I told her I would show her the farm tomorrow, and we ate a simple meal of grilled steak and vegies. She suddenly looked around, and saw the single bed with its single sleeping bag in one room, and the camp cot and similar bag in the other. She looked at me coyly, with hands on hips. 'You haven't been too extravagant with the sleeping arrangements, Richards!'

I was at a loss for a few moments, then stammered, 'I didn't want to be too presumptuous, Ell. Anyway, I made a promise to you father…'

'Did you now.' She arched an eyebrow, then laughed. She came to me and put her arms around me, and said 'Well, Dad's not here right now, and I didn't drive all this way to sleep in a single bed, all by myself.'

The single bed proved quite wide enough, and two new sleeping bags zipped together worked out just fine.

***

Easter came and went far too quickly. For those few days my camp was a place of joy and laughter. It seemed lighter and brighter inside the drab four walls of my camp, and even the farm itself looked greener than its usual olive-green colour. I was the happiest man alive, until Ellie had to drive away. Horrie and I must have looked forlorn as we stood in the middle of the driveway long after the tail of her car had disappeared, and the dust had settled. After a time, I felt Horrie gently touch my hand with his wet nose. We looked at each other, and I said 'Okay Horrie, it's back to just you and me again,' and we simultaneously turned to plod back to the shack.

Then it was back to work. I had another ten weeks of running both the farm and my new weekend aerial business. Super spreading wasn't easy. Alf would deliver the bags of fertilizer to the landing site, and I'd have to hoist the hundred-weight bags from the pile, across to the Tiger, climb a small step ladder, and empty each bag into the hopper. I'd repeat this three times per load. This load usually covered just three acres. So, typically, I'd be flying for minutes, shutting down, loading the fertilizer, swinging the prop, and taking off again several times an hour. At the end of the day, my back would be killing me, and I'd be windblown and exhausted. It wasn't an efficient way of doing things, but I did make money. Quite a lot of it.

Dalgetys found a new manager for the farm, and he seemed a capable sort of chap. We worked together until my notice was up, then I became a full-time pilot. On my last day I was given a bonus cheque, as both Dalgetys and the absentee owner were more than happy with the improvements I'd made to the farm.

Horrie and I moved in with Alf, so my dog spent working hours riding with him on deliveries. This suited him fine. He got to see all the farm dogs for miles around, and when I got home at night, he'd tell me all about it with licks, wriggles and the occasional yelp.

I knew I couldn't keep up the demand for my services while working as a one-man band, so I bought a little grey MF TEA 20 tractor, nearly new, that had a hydraulic set-up for a grader blade. I had the blade removed, and replaced with a hopper on an extended boom. It carried three bags of fertilizer. That meant the hopper could be filled at ground level, which was much easier than balancing on a small ladder with a hundredweight of super on your back.

I bought a five year-old red International truck, and put an advert in Dalgetys' window for a loader driver. Alf saw it, snatched the hand-written note off the wall, and said 'I'm taking the job.' Alf was burly and strong, but even he had trouble keeping up with me. While I was in the air, Alf would heave three heavy bags into the tractor's hopper. As soon as I taxied to a stop, he'd carefully manoeuvre the tractor to place its hopper directly above the one in the Tiger. In seconds the three hundredweight load would be transferred, and the instant Alf backed away I'd be off again. By the time he'd loaded another three bags, I'd have taken off, spread the load, and returned for another. I would now keep the engine running, so Alf had to be very careful not to strike the prop with the hopper. Being Alf, he always was.

I then hired a young guy from a local farm. He was fit, strong, and used to heaving heavy bags. Between him and Alf, they could load super faster than I could spread it. We made a jovial and efficient team

Horrie was there all the time of course. But I noticed that he was sleeping under the truck during much of the day. With a shock, I realised that he would now be about age ten, and was getting on in years.

Three months after starting Tiger Aerial Agricultural Services, TAAS for short, I went to the Commercial Bank of Australia, and showed the manager my figures. I owned the Tiger, the tractor, and the truck, so he had no hesitation in giving me a small overdraft. With it, I bought a second Tiger and hired another pilot. He too was ex RAAF, but had joined too late to see action during the war. He was pleased to find a job that put him back into the air, even if it was in a lowly Tiger Moth. Rex Langford was to stay with me for many years, and he never let me down.

July and August are cold in Walcha, and business slowed enough to allow us to catch up on maintenance. I also realised that there was no future in working fourteen hours a day, from sunup until late in the evening doing bookwork or answering calls from farmers who worked equally long days. I decided to buy three more Tigers, hire three more pilots, more loaders, and to hire both a manager and an engineer. Tigers were easy to come by and fairly cheap, and there were plenty of ex RAAF pilots and engineers around too. I also figured I knew a guy who'd make an ideal manager.

Colin Rodgers was in his early twenties, had been born and raised on a farm in the district, and had spent the previous three years at Sydney University, studying law. He'd washed out, admitting to everyone that he'd spent too much time partying instead of studying, and really wasn't cut out to be a lawyer anyway. He was a keen sportsman, playing in the same district cricket team I did, and a local football team too. He was a regular at the golf course, and at the golf club bar. He knew all the farmers for miles around, and they liked him.

Col proved to be as good as I'd hoped he would be. He quickly took over all ordering of fuel and other supplies, kept the accounts accurate, neat, and tidy, chased overdue debts, and he brought in new work by the loads. My new engineer, Johnny Land, took over all maintenance and repairs, and Alf was handed another truck, a brand new International, a new MF tractor, both red, and two extra loading hands. Apart from doing some flying myself, I only had to schedule the aircraft and pilots.

I rented a nice house in Tamworth, and prepared to move in. The day before I packed my belongings at Alf's place, I woke early to find Horrie still and cold. He'd died in his sleep. Alf was heartbroken, as was I. A few months later I bought a kelpie pup. 'Here Alf,' I said. 'This one's all yours.'

✳✳✳

Ellie came to see the new house, proclaimed it a vast improvement on my old digs, and went shopping for a double bed. The night it was delivered, she looked at me with a serious frown, but, as usual, mirth in her eyes, and asked 'Okay Richards, when are you going to make an honest woman of me?' Nothing could have made me happier to answer that question. I just wished Dad had been alive to see me now. We were married in October 1956. I was 31 years old, and Ellie had just turned 24. TAAS was busy, but I was confident the crew could handle the work for a few weeks without me. The wedding was held at the Hetherington farm, and Max was my best man. Alf came, as did most of my TAAS crew. Mrs H was clearly thrilled, and Mr H seemed very happy too. At the reception, he called me aside, put his arm around my shoulders, raised an eyebrow, and asked 'did you keep your promise to me?'

I hesitated too long, and he laughed. 'If you don't know already, you'll soon find out that our Ellie is a very determined girl. When she left to spend Easter with you, we had a fair idea what she had in mind. When she came home glowing, we had no doubt.'

'Sorry Mr H, I tried. I'm afraid I'm only human.' He squeezed my arm and said 'about time you called me Peter, isn't it?

✳✳✳

We spent our first night in Dubbo, and afterwards we took off in Ellie's car to spend a week driving to Shute Harbour in the Whitsundays. We were able to hire a thirty-foot sloop for five days, and while I knew nothing of sailing, I soon applied my knowledge of aerodynamics to the sails, and we had no trouble making way.

The weather was perfect, with just cumulus clouds and light breezes. Ellie wore cotton tops and shorts, and when we swam, she wore a white bikini. Years later, as I write this, the picture of her standing at the bow, in that bikini, is still fresh in my mind.

The bond between Ellie and me was now so strong that I couldn't imagine life without her. I was truly content, and now only occasionally had momentary anger and dismay when I thought about the loss of Kittyhawk farm four years earlier.

In February 1958 we bought a small farm outside Tamworth. Just two hundred and fifty acres, but mostly good level land with rich, brown soil. It had a healthy pasture, but few trees. There was just enough length along one side to have an airstrip. One corner had a creek running through it, but the creek dried up each summer to little more than a trickle. We built a low dam wall, just high enough to keep a large pool of permanent water, and fenced off about a hundred acres around it. We planted lots of native trees and shrubs inside that fence, and in an amazingly short time, nature began to reclaim the land.

Within five years there were quite tall gums and enough understory to attract native birds. A few grey kangaroos found it too, and adopted it as home. The highlight came one late afternoon when one of the staff saw first the bubbles, then the ripples, and finally the head of a platypus. This haven was my equivalent to the bushland strip Dad had kept back on the Molong farm.

The remaining paddocks kept Ellie's small string of horses very well fed.

We commissioned a local builder to build our new house, with large windows looking across lawns to the bush haven, as we now called it. A large hangar, with office attached was built alongside our small airstrip. We moved TAAS operations to the new property. Ellie found a job with a vet clinic in town, but had to give up full time work just six months later.

In October of that year, the first of our two sons was born. Young Max was a handful from day one, having boundless energy and curiosity. I bought Ellie a new FC Holden to celebrate, and I took over her old car. Two years later our second son was born. Peter was just like his brother. When he turned one year old, Ellie began working at the vet clinic one day each week, just to keep her mind active, as she put it.

With the business running strongly and smoothly, we were able to take holidays. We spent time on the Hetherington farm, and I hired a four-seat Piper Cherokee to fly Ellie and the two boys to places all over eastern Australia. Life was very, very good.

1961 was a particularly good one for our business and we

needed some tax deductions, so in March of 1962 I bought a new company car, which I immediately handed to Ellie. It was a stylish Chrysler Valiant R-series sedan, in leaf green, with push-button automatic transmission. She loved that car so much it was years before she'd part with it. I took over the FC Holden.

In 1963 Ellie brought home a puppy. It had been left at the clinic by someone who suddenly decided they didn't want a pet after all. It was a beautiful female Dalmation. She had a white face, the big black eyes of a seal, and large black spots over her white coat. She adored the kids, and they her. Chloe grew into a smart, energetic but gentle girl, very much part of the whole family. I would grin when seeing Max jnr, Peter, and Chloe, tail swinging, heading off into the bush paddock for another adventure. It reminded me so much of my early days with Max and Spinner. Ellie complained that Chloe dropped her hair all over the house, but wouldn't dream of banishing her to the outside. Chloe was one of us.

1966 brought several changes. The Tigers had served us well, but they had limited capacity and were getting old. Maintenance was getting more expensive as they wore out, and parts were becoming hard to find. They didn't have a very good safety record in the industry, though TAAS had been accident free, so far at least. The Civil Aviation Authority, CASA, was making moves that would ultimately ban the use of Tigers. It was time to look for something new.

Alternatives came that very year. The Cessna 180, Piper Pawnee, Fletcher, and Callair, all built in America, were quickly being adopted. The new Cessna 230HP C188 Agwagon appealed to me. It was purpose-built for aerial agriculture. It had a load capacity far superior to the Tiger, with 1800 pound weight versus 330, and it flew at twice the speed. Its fuselage was much stronger than the old Tiger's, and thus the pilot had more chance of surviving any accident. We ordered three, all red, for delivery in 1967. Meanwhile, the Commonwealth Aircraft Corporation had built the CAC 25 Ceres, largely from Wirraway components. It used the venerable 600 HP P & W 1340 geared radial engine that I was so familiar with from RAAF training days. We could have a Ceres immediately, so we took it. It was silver, but we did paint the engine cowling red.

Despite its poorly laid-out cockpit, straight from the Wirraway, I liked the Ceres. It was big and bluff, (it weighed more than two tonnes empty), and it felt like the aircraft I'd flown during the war. When the C188s did arrive, we found that their modern horizontally opposed six-cylinder engines were much more reliable and fuel efficient than the aging 1340, so we ordered a fourth C188, and after 1968, the Ceres was kept in reserve.

The final purchase in 1966 was a Cessna C337A Skymaster. This was an extravagance, because it was to be our personal tourer. The 337 is an unusual machine, having a Continental IO-320 engine of 210 HP driving a variable pitch prop at each end of the fuselage. Twin tail booms supported the tailplane. We fitted VH-WWC with a full IFR panel and twin radios. The rear-retracting undercarriage looked complicated, but the salesman assured me it was of a sound design. This one had been ordered by a businessman who then couldn't come up with the funds to pay for it. I grabbed the opportunity, because this aircraft had six seats, the safety of two engines, and the ability to get off the ground with a relatively short take off run. Our field was only seven hundred yards long. VH-WWC was overall white, with midline blue and grey stripes.

Ellie, the boys, and I used the aircraft as personal transport for many years, including for three trips to PNG and one to New Zealand. It was a costly machine to maintain, as Cessna parts were outrageously expensive, but it did everything we asked of it. I always had my concerns about the complex retract system, but it never gave us trouble. Some six decades later, in another pilot's

hands, the undercarriage did fail to lock properly, and poor old
Whiskey Whiskey Charlie ended its days at Bathurst airport.

In 1967 I parked the green Valiant in the shed, and bought
Ellie a new Jaguar Mark 2 sedan, white with red upholstery. It
was a 3.8 litre version, with manual gearbox and overdrive. It
was a seriously nice car to drive, and with 215 HP, it was quick.
In fact, it was the fastest 4-door car in production anywhere in
the world at the time. Ellie thanked me, but said it was far too
pretentious, and asked me to return the Valiant to our garage.
So, I kept the Jag for myself.

***

The TAAS crew was a happy one, and by the time I turned forty-
six in October 1970, I'd been able to reduce my workload to what
most people consider normal hours, and just five days a week.
The boys were happy at school, Ellie liked pottering in her big
garden, tending and riding her horses, and working as a vet just
one day per week. The bond between Ellie and me only grew
stronger over the years, if that were possible, and every day when
I looked at her, I'd tell myself that I was the luckiest man alive. If
life had continued like that forever, I would have been as happy
as any man can be. Unfortunately, trouble can find you no matter
how much you'd like to avoid it.

Every Friday night, the TAAS staff got together for a debrief.
I would lay on plenty of beer and wine, and Ellie would organize
a BBQ or pizza. On one such night, a few of the guys were sitting
around, sleepily sipping their beers, and Col Rodgers asked
me if it was true that I'd been shot down during the war. I'd
rarely spoken to anyone outside the family about my wartime
experiences, but that night it all seemed so long ago, and I began
to reminisce. Maybe the wine had loosened my tongue, but
almost against my will I began to relate my story

'No, Col,' I said. 'I was NOT shot down. I shot up a Jap Betty bomber that was taxiing for take-off. It must have been loaded with bombs, because the damned thing blew up with bits and pieces of it going in all directions, including directly in front of my P-40. I must have copped a couple of big pieces of debris in both the oil and coolant radiators, because the engine seized very quickly, and I was suddenly a four-ton glider.'

'Geez, Rick, did this happen in New Guinea?'

'New Ireland actually, a big island to the north of mainland PNG.'

The whole crew came wide awake with this, and questions came thick and fast. In the end, I told them pretty much all of it, including being rescued unconscious by natives, about Kala nursing me to health, how I tried to steal a Jap fighter, but ultimately had escaped with Jack in his rotten old wooden boat. I finished with details of how we were saved by the B-25 attack on the Jap destroyer, and were then picked up by the US Navy Catalina. The guys listened intently. The only sounds I heard were the periodic gasps of horror.

I finished the story, lay back in the easy chair and took another sip of the crisp chardonnay. A thought crossed my mind, for the first time since 1945. Why I said aloud what had long been dormant, I can't explain. 'You know, poor old Jack was semi delirious after the Japs had shot-up the boat, and he'd been wounded by this enormous splinter. He came out with this fanciful tale of having panned a lot of gold from the creek that ran past his camp, and that he'd buried a bag full of it in his hut. He said that he'd figured out where the reef was, and he was only weeks away from finding his Eldorado at the mine he was digging. When he was in the hospital at Milne Bay, he was still going on about it. I think he'd convinced himself it was all true.'

Col had hung on every word of the story, but he was wide-eyed when I got to the part about Jack's gold. He stammered 'You mean that bag of gold could still be there? Nobody has gone in to finish digging the mine?'

'Col, it was all in his imagination. He said nothing about it the whole time I lived in the hut. It was only when he thought he was dying that it came out.'

'But he told you then only because he knew he'd never live long enough to go back.'

'Possibly. Far more likely, it's never existed. Do you think he'd be living in semi squalor, with a native girl his occasional and only company, if he had a bag of gold under his bed?'

'Maybe. Maybe he wanted to prove that the motherlode existed before telling anyone?'

'Could be, but I'd think Kala would have known. I'm sure she would have, and this was twenty-six years ago. Kala might have found the bag of gold since, if it existed, or maybe someone else has. There might even be a proper commercial mine there now for all I know!'

✷✷✷

Weeks went by, and not a word about my tale was spoken, so it receded to the back of my mind. One afternoon I had just returned to the office from a spreading job when Col asked if he could talk to me in private. We went into his office and shut the door. He looked serious. I thought that either we had a major problem, or he was about to resign his job. He began.

'Rick, remember we were talking about your mate Jack's gold?'

'Oh, right. The mythical Eldorado.'

'Yeah. Look, my brother is a geologist. He's working in Western Australia, and I told him your story. He's never been to New Guinea, but he knows geologists who have. They reckon that gold has been found in the Tabar Islands, which is just off the coast of New Ireland…'

'Yes I know Col, I did some flying in the area, as you might recall.'

'Well, the point is, Tabar Island isn't that far from this place Borpop, so if gold exists in one part of the area, it might exist elsewhere.

'Yep, true,' I replied.

'I was able to have some checking done in Port Moresby. There is no mining lease anywhere near Borpop, so it's wide open to be exploited. I reckon we should form a company, find some investors to buy shares, take out a lease, and go there.'

I sat back and laughed. 'Col, you make it sound so easy. I know nothing about mining of any sort, and neither do you. All you are going on is my story, and for all you know, I could have made it all up.'

'Rick, I might be your employee, but we've also been mates for quite a while. I know you aren't the type to make up a bullshit story.'

'Well, what I told you is how it all happened, but if I thought there was a fortune in gold back there, I would have been motivated to find it years ago. Anyway, even if you do believe that Jack was dinky di, how are you going to get to Borpop? It's one of the most isolated places in the world.'

Col grinned. 'You're asking me? Have you forgotten that you own an aeroplane?'

The discussion went on for a time, with Col insisting that we, that is he, his geologist brother, and I, should go there, find the hut, the bag of gold, and the mine, if they existed. If they didn't, all we'd have lost was some travelling expenses.

CHAPTER 17

Memories rekindled.

Faded wartime memories began to resurface as Col kept up a campaign to convince me to go back to New Ireland. Although I had no illusions about becoming rich from Jack's gold, one recovered memory persisted. More than that, it threatened to become an obsession. Kala.

Kala had risked her life for Jack and me. After several years of dedicated service to Jack, and then the intense few months of helping to save my life, she'd been hastily left with nothing more than a hug and my RAAF-issued watch. What had become of her? Had she escaped retribution by the Japs? Had she married? Had she had children? Was she even still alive? The life span of natives in New Guinea was nothing like ours. I had to find out.

Of course, I had told Ellie the full story about Kala before we were married. Although she'd then ribbed me about my 'dark skinned angel' and what we may or may not have gotten up to, she quickly understood my growing unease about how Kala had been left.

'So, it's been twenty-six years. Better late than never,' she said. 'You're a pilot. We own an aeroplane. Let's fly to New Ireland and see if we can do anything for Kala. Let's take Col, and he can cure his gold fever, one way or another. He spends half his time thinking about it now. He'll be useless if we can't prove to him that it was all in Jack's imagination. Anyway, I feel the need for an adventure, so I'm coming too!'

'Oh really.' I cocked an eyebrow. 'And who'll look after the kids while we're away?'

'Mum will. She'd love to come and stay for two or three weeks. Dad will probably come too.'

With both Col AND Ellie hassling me about flying to New Ireland, I had no chance of convincing them that it was a bad idea. We laughingly agreed we'd split any gold we found three ways, after I'd deducted my expenses. That was easy to agree to, because I never expected to find any. The date was set for August 1971, and I began to plan how best to get there.

In 1944 it had been easy. My P-40 had speed, and I had the support of that wonderful flying club called the RAAF. The C337's economical cruise speed was a comparatively slow 155 knots, whilst burning about 90 litres per hour. With full main and auxiliary tanks, it was good for an endurance of four hours, with a forty-five minute reserve. That meant our longest leg had to be no more than six hundred nautical miles. Four hours is long enough to be cooped up in the cockpit of a 337, anyway.

We removed the rearmost pair of seats to make a decent luggage space, and hired an emergency raft in case of a ditching. We bought two lightweight tents, and some lightweight cooking gear designed for hikers. Emergency food and water, a few tools, a selection of clothes for every sort of weather, and we were good to go. Max and Peter were initially horrified that we'd leave them, but the excitement of having Nana and Grandpa to stay overcame that.

Ellie sat in the right-hand seat, and Col had the two seats immediately behind to himself. With full load, I needed all 420 HP to get off our fairly short strip. Once airborne, with wheels and flaps up, I throttled back to 25 inches of manifold pressure and 2500 RPM. At top of climb I selected 22 inches and 2300 RPM, synchronised the props, leaned the mixtures, intercepted the planned outbound track, and switched on the autopilot. I would repeat this procedure on every leg of the trip.

We overnighted at Bundaberg, Townsville, and Horn Island, just off the northern tip of our contintent. It was then a short hop overwater to Dumpu, on the south coast of Papua New Guinea, where we went through customs. Another fairly short flight took us to Port Moresby, where we took a taxi into town and stayed at the Hotel Papua.

Neither Col nor Ellie had been overseas before, and they were in turn amused and horrified with what they saw. Hordes of happy kids playing in the streets and waving as we went past delighted them, but the ramshackle houses and filth in the streets horrified them. They were both surprised how dry and dusty Port Moresby was.

The leg over the mountains was best tackled early in the morning, because by midday the peaks are often covered with cloud. The 337 was slow to reach sufficient height with our load, but we managed to cross the snow-capped spine of the mainland at a safe height. The northern side of the PNG mainland is of course much wetter, and the jungle dense and lush. This was the PNG my passengers had expected.

We refueled at Lae, then set course across the Solomon Sea. About half way to Rabaul, when we had nothing on the horizon but brilliant blue water. I pointed to the east, and said to Ellie and Col, 'it's probably only thirty or forty miles out there to the spot where the Jap destroyer almost got Jack and me. That ship and the poor bloody crew are down there somewhere, hundreds of them, including the bastards that were going to machine-gun us.'

Ellie looked ashen. 'Oh my God,' she said, 'when you described that time in the little boat, I visualised you crossing a big bay, not this wide ocean. I can't imagine how helpless you must have felt when they began shooting at you.'

I nodded, and replied 'not half as bloody helpless as when the boat was sinking under us a few hours later.' The sea, so unfriendly in 1945, now looked benign.

We crossed the coast of New Britain at Gasmata, once an important satellite field to Rabaul. From early 1942 and for two years this Japanese airfield had taken a pounding from RAAF Hudsons, Beauforts, A-20s and P-40s, plus USAAF B-17s, B-24s, B-25s, and B-26s. It looked so peaceful from 7,000 feet now, that it was hard to imagine the hardship and destruction the site had seen just over thirty years earlier. We tracked up the mountainous and volcanic centre of the island before approaching Rabaul.

Coming into land at this old Japanese stronghold took us over a bay of sparkling blue water, iridescent green fringing reefs, and white sandy beaches. The two-story Rabaul Hotel was a comfortable stopover for the night. It was my first visit too. If I'd landed there in 1944 or 45, I would have had a very hot reception.

That night we sat at an outside table, with candles and a mosquito coil burning, and gin and tonics at hand. We absorbed the heavy tropical atmosphere as we watched the sun set. Neither Ellie nor Col had ever experienced the calm, balmy, and humid evening, redolent with the aroma of tropical flowers, that is so typical of islands in the Pacific. They revelled in it. For me, it wiped years away, and memories of my six months in New Guinea flooded back, almost overwhelming me. Ellie noticed how quiet I suddenly became, and quietly took my hand.

In the morning, we stocked up on fuel, food, and water for

the final leg to Borpop Harbour, just 60 miles due east, across the channel between New Britain and New Ireland, then across the mountain spine of New Ireland itself to its east coast. Nobody had been able to update us on the condition of the old Japanese airstrip. All they could say was that the road that ran along that coast, built back in the 1920s by hand labour, was rough, often slippery, and frequently cut in numerous places by the creeks and rivers that flowed down from the mountainous backbone.

Ellie and Col got more and more excited as we flew towards our destination. I was apprehensive. Firstly, I had to make a judgement on whether the airstrip was safe for us to land. Secondly, once we landed, I had to face the villagers of Huris, some of whom might recognise me as the one who had risked their safety by hiding out amongst them. Thirdly, I had to justify this venture by finding Jack's old camp, and maybe even his almost certainly mythical mine. There are times a pilot wishes he was on the ground looking up into the air, instead of vice versa. This was one of those times. I feared that when we reached Borpop, the strip would be covered with regrowth, making it impossible to land. How foolish would this adventure look then?

The Borpop harbour was impossible to miss, because of the high northern headland, and the naturally treeless inland plain behind it. We began our descent from four thousand feet, just as I had in 1945. I levelled off at 500 feet as we crossed the site of the old airfield, and turned for a right-hand circuit. As we passed over the headland, I could see the Japanese guns still mounted there. Last time I saw them they were spitting death at me; but now were silently pointing to the sky in their rusty immobility.

I turned onto final for the old runway in a descending turn, and with flaps down one third, reduced speed to 80 knots. We flew over the grass-covered strip at 20 feet or so, looking for hidden obstacles. Amazingly, the only encroachment by trees or bushes was along the inland boundary. Whilst the grass was a bit too long for my liking, it was dry and thin. We saw a few cattle, so obviously they'd been keeping the growth down. I made the decision that it was safe to land. We made another circuit, this time with gear down and full flaps on final. The ground run was a bit rough, but nothing the C337 couldn't handle. We taxied back to the southern end of the strip and shut down the engines near the village of Huris, and quite near where the Japanese maintenance tents had been in 1944 and 45.

There was silence for a few minutes, that is apart from the ticking of cooling metal. We climbed out, and the heat hit us like a blast from a furnace. Then we heard the shouting. About twenty or thirty native men, mostly dressed only in shorts, and followed by an equal number of women in sarongs, burst over the natural embankment that separates Huris from the airstrip. Neither Ellie nor Col had ever experienced anything like this, and they shrank from the excited mob that quickly encircled us. I can't say I blame them, because to the uninitiated, the islanders did look fierce. Most had mouths and teeth stained red from chewing betel nut, and they carried machetes as you or I would carry a briefcase or handbag. As they probably had not seen a white man in years, and certainly no aircraft had used the strip for much longer than that, our arrival was a big event.

It has always been a mystery to me where they learned it, but a few of the young men spoke very basic English. It took a few minutes to get across that I had come to thank some of the village people for helping me during the war against the Japanese. Were there any people who remember that time, I asked? I tried to be tactful, bearing in mind that the average life span here was probably twenty or more years shorter than our own. The answer was yes, but we had to walk to the village to meet them.

We followed in single file through tall spear grass towards the village that was situated half way between the airstrip and the waters of the bay. On the way, we met about a dozen kids, ranging from about four to fourteen years of age. Half of them were totally naked. The older ones were all grins and curiosity. The younger ones were terrified, and fled at high speed back to the safety of the village, howling as they went. This sent the adults into paroxysms of laughter. One skinny teenager climbed a coconut palm in the village as easily as if it was a ladder, and knocked down three coconuts. With three deft blows with a machete, we each had a drink of fresh coconut juice. Having had little else to drink during my time with Jack, I didn't need reminding that I wasn't partial to the taste, but I was polite and thanked them. Ellie and Col seemed to actually enjoy the novel experience.

As it turned out, I could recognise none of the young guys who had helped me in 1945. Six there claimed to remember me, but they were old men now. I couldn't establish whether the others had moved elsewhere, or had passed away. These six old men would have helped in shielding me from the Japanese. They greeted me warmly, shaking hands and grinning, and I thanked them most sincerely.

Then I asked about Kala. There were puzzled looks before someone remembered. Long, long ago she had married a boy from Warangansau, a village to the south, and had moved there from Huris.

'Could one of the younger men find my crashed aeroplane,' I asked, 'and Jack's old hut?' This caused some discussion, but eventually we had two volunteers. It was agreed that we'd walk there the following morning.

✳✳✳

Soon enough, the novelty of our appearance wore off, and the villagers allowed us to return to the 337 and set up camp. That left the afternoon to explore the bay, something I could never do in

1945. We walked past the village, and stumbled upon the decaying remains of a Ki-61 fighter. From the bent prop it looked like it hadn't quite made it to the strip, and had burned out after skidding to a stop. Just beyond, on a bare patch of rock, we found ten-foot-deep holes filled with the clearest fresh water I'd ever seen, that was constantly bubbling up from underground springs.

Amid a thicket of trees just above the beach was the twisted remains of a G4M bomber. Not much of it was left, so I think it had hit pretty hard, again not quite making the field.

On one side of the bay, just inland from a row of coconut palms that grew parallel to the beach, and below the headland, was a group of thatched huts. We walked to it, and were greeted by several women. It was hard to understand what we were being told, as none spoke English, but I gathered that this was still part of Huris village. We sat in the shade with them for a time, but then decided to have a swim. Out in the bay were two little fuzzy-haired kids, sitting in a small dugout canoe, fishing with hand lines. The bay's water was milky, and so warm it was more like a bath. We swam out to the kids, but they were so terrified of us their eyes were like saucers, and they froze, so we beat a quick retreat. Some women at the village saw all this, and were bent double with mirth.

Back above the main village, we walked along what was the Jap strip. There were remains of about twenty aircraft, most so badly damaged I couldn't identify their types. Some had burned, others were just smashed beyond recognition. Several wrecks had been bulldozed off the edge of the strip into the jungle on the western edge of the plain, no doubt by the Japanese themselves. I tried to figure out which of these wrecks were associated with the attack I was part of, but I couldn't be sure. Everything looked different from the ground than it had from the air some twenty-seven years previously. Where the Ki-61 fighter and the sentry had burned, there was nothing but dry grass.

A small mob of cattle watched us sleepily from the edge of the strip. I silently thanked them for keeping the grass low, otherwise we'd never have been able to land.

***

Our next task was to find Jack's hut and my old P-40. As the crow flies, it wasn't that very far from the airstrip. Back in 1945, we couldn't use the coastal road for fear of running into enemy patrols, and via the circuitous jungle paths it took most of a day to get there. We no longer had that problem, but it was still a hike of a few miles along the road south, then along jungle paths that struck inland. Fortunately, we were offered an alternative. Lying near the beach was the wreck of an ancient wooden dinghy that had been left there by a visiting yacht some decades before. Bolted onto its decaying transom was an equally ancient British Seagull outboard motor. The village elders managed to convey the offer that if we could fix it, they'd provide us with a suitable dugout canoe.

This outboard had been sitting there for more than 40 years. It was already old when I'd crash landed nearby, and the only part of it not covered with rust was the brass fuel tank. But a quick examination showed how simple the design was, primitive in fact, so I had a fair chance of getting it running with the basic tools I had with me.

Working on a rough wooden bench only partially shaded by coconut palms, I stripped the motor, cleaned out congealed oil, and brushed off as much of the corrosion as I could. I sent Col off to drain some Avgas from the 337, and because the Seagull is a 2-stroke engine, when he returned, I added some of the spare oil we carried to the petrol. It then took a number of pulls with a starter cord, but ran it did. Not smoothly, nor efficiently, but I doubt any Seagull was smooth or efficient even when brand new.

The dugout we were provided with had the typical rounded ends, and so we had to attach the outboard to a plank nailed and bound to the gunnels, and projecting out the right-hand side. With full throttle and producing maybe four horsepower, the motor propelled us along at a jogging pace, which is much better than we would have achieved walking along the coastal track. With two guides and the three of us aboard, we ventured forth at daybreak on our third day at Borpop.

The sea was a little choppy after we'd left the protection of the harbour, but the breeze wasn't too strong and we made good time. By 9am we were nosing into the inlet where Jack had kept his ill-fated whaler. Nobody had been there in years, and the footpath that led from there to Jack's hut had long since been overgrown by shrubs, vines, and in some places, speargrass. It took our guides another two hours of slashing with machetes to reach a clearing I could recognise. It was one that the villagers used every few years to grow bananas. From there, even I could find the location of Jack's hut.

That doesn't mean it was easy. The old path had disappeared, and we bush-bashed further inland. The heat and humidity were intense, and the jungle so still it seemed airless. Our guides laughed when we had to beg for frequent stops for sips of water. We struggled to breathe, our legs stung from grass seeds, thorns, and scratches from broken twigs. We slipped and tripped over hidden moss-covered tree roots, and the myriad insects never let up on us. Sand flies, mosquitoes, midges and ants attacked in waves. I had known what to expect, and didn't fret about dripping with perspiration, itching from bites, and being clammy and sticky. Ellie and Col didn't know what hit them, but they were stoic, and never complained. I think it was intense interest in my past that drove Ellie on, while for Col it was expectation. For me it was curiosity: I wanted to see how memories compared with reality.

We came across Jack's camp suddenly, but it was no longer a bare-earth clearing with several huts, and a fire pit. The jungle was well along with the process of reclaiming its own. Now the old camp was recognisable only because there was an area of about a quarter of an acre of the jungle that had no large trees, but only saplings to about twenty feet high, and a thick understory of tall grass and tangled scrub. The huts themselves had gone, their frames most likely eaten by termites, and their thatch rooves had rotted away completely.

The two guides wanted to hunt for a cuscus for their night's meal. They left the three of us sitting on scattered logs, Ellie and I together, Col near us, trying to recover some energy after the hike. Col looked dejected. I think he expected that everything would be just as Jack and I had left it all those years ago, and that he'd just walk in and dig up the gold from Jack's hut. Now, I think he was prepared to go home right away. Ellie put an arm around my shoulders, looked quizzically at me, raised one eyebrow, and said 'so this is where you spent your time with the exotic Kala. Not exactly the tropical paradise I'd imagined.'

I shook my head and replied, 'It was no paradise Ell, believe me. Not even then, but it did look a lot better in 1945.'

We sat for minutes, each of us lost in our own thoughts. Then I heaved myself upright, and began hacking at the growth in what had been the clearing, being wary of the snakes that I knew were common. I soon found remnants of an old pathway that had been delineated by small stones. It took me a while, but I figured out where Jack's hut had been. 'Okay Col, you've been dreaming of this moment for nearly a year, and you've carried that shovel all the way here. That's where the hut was. Jack said he'd buried the bag in the middle of the floor, now go for it.'

Col's fair complexion really didn't equip him for this climate, and his face was soon the colour of beetroot, but with his bare arms and torso glistening with sweat, he toiled manfully. After half an hour he'd excavated a wide hole in the middle of the site I had indicated. He dropped the shovel, sat back on his fallen log, and put his head in his hands, defeated. The three of us sat in silence for ten minutes.

I looked up when I heard the slow wingbeats of a Kokomo: two of them in fact, and they landed in one of the tall trees that surrounded what was left of Jack's camp. They were so like the pair that hung around this camp back in 1945. Maybe it was the same pair? The male bird let forth a typical call that sounded like a course and drawn-out human laugh. 'Haa, haa, haa.'

'Laugh at us, will you, you buggers,' I called back, then I picked up the shovel and prodded at the hole. A picture of the interior of Jack's hut began to crystallise in my mind. It dawned on me that he couldn't have buried anything in the middle of the hut, because the frame of his bed extended from the back wall to the centre. If he had buried anything, it would more likely be at the foot of the bed, just off centre of the floorspace. I picked away at that edge of the hole. Almost immediately I felt something pliable, but resistant to the shovel. 'Just a tree root,' I wondered? I dug a small trench around the obstacle, then pushed the shovel beneath it and levered it out of its resting place. Moist soil fell away to reveal a rubberized canvas bag, the top tied with a frayed cord. I lifted the bag out of the hole: it was heavy, really heavy. I put it on the ground and called 'Hey Ell, I wonder what this might be.'

I waited till she'd tiredly forced herself upright, and pushed through the grass and scrub to me. Then as she watched I tugged at the rotting cord, and it fell away. I carefully pulled at one corner of the bag's top, and exposed the contents. Gold. Gleaming, fine gold particles, some bigger nuggets, some as big as a pea, spilled out through the open top. Ellie gasped, and looked at me open-mouthed. A slow smile spread across her sweat-streaked but still gorgeous face.

Col appeared to have fallen asleep. He had his head in his hands, and was breathing heavily. I carefully lay the old canvas bag in his lap, open to reveal its contents. Col awoke with a start. His florid face went white, and his eyes bulged. He tentatively put his hand into the bag and let the gold dust run through his fingers, as if he expected it to be a mirage that would disappear before his very eyes. We were all silent for what seemed like minutes, then Col stood and began dancing around the open bag. He gripped Ellie's hand and mine, and the three of us danced around it together. Well, Ellie and Col did, I sort of stumbled around. Jack's gold was real after all.

✳✳✳

When the guides returned, one carrying a dead cuscus over his shoulder, we acted as if we'd already had a good look around, and there was nothing left to see. Well, there wasn't. We asked the guides if they knew of a big hole in the ground nearby. They consulted each other, and then indicated that we should proceed further up the creek that was a few hundred yards away. It trickled down from the hills ahead.

Progress was again slow, because any path that led uphill from Jack's camp had long ago been obliterated by the jungle. However, to our surprise we did find an opening in the side of the hill after less than half an hour. It was clearly man-made, but the spoil that spewed from its entrance had long ago solidified, and then had been colonized by ants and spiny bushes. The dark entrance to the tunnel was criss-crossed with spider webs. We quickly agreed that nothing could be gained by trying to enter. We had no torches, and there was every chance the tunnel might now be the home of snakes, scorpions, and bats. Anyway, Jack never claimed to have found gold there, but only that he was close to a vein of it.

So, we retreated along the new path we'd created, back to the old clearing. 'Now,' I said to the guides, 'can you find my crashed aeroplane?'

From Jack's camp we angled back towards Borpop, and away from the creek that led to the estuary. The jungle thinned out as we progressed, until we were walking through tall speargrass and scattered trees. It was another trial by sun and airless humidity, made a bit harder as Col and I shared the carrying of the backpack that contained the gold. I was third in line, after the guide who carried the dead cuscus, hanging from his belt. Its still bright and bulbous black eyes seemed to stare at me as we walked. Thankfully it was only an hour before the lead guide gave a shout. They'd found my Kittyhawk.

I'd expected to experience some emotion if we found it. Instead, I saw that its decay was well advanced.

It had been a magnificent living, breathing and deadly flying machine. Now it was a silent hulk, of little more relevance than a discarded drink can. I saw that the lower prop blade was bent backwards, and the spinner was badly dented. The engine cowling fasteners had rusted through so that the cowlings had fallen off, revealing the rusty V-12 Alison. The electrical cables that hadn't burnt were covered with corrosion fizz, and rubber hoses were faded and cracked. The inch-thick laminated windscreen had discoloured, and the Perspex canopy had gone brown, had cracked, then fallen in. The burned frame and skin of the fuselage had collapsed. The fabric on the vertical rudder had torn away, revealing its internal aluminium ribs. Bakelite fittings in the cockpit had gone altogether, either burnt or decayed. The parachute seat pack was missing. I guessed that for years the local women had had a source of fine silk for making clothing. The only unburnt panels were on the wingtips and tail fin, and there the paint had worn and oxidised, leaving powdery remnants of dull yellow-green primer. No roundels or squadron codes had survived.

I walked away without a backward glance. This remnant of history was a part of my life that was long past, and I'd had enough of revisiting it.

✶✶✶

That night we lit a fire on the beach near our canoe, and the two native boys singed their cuscus and ate the almost-raw meat with gusto. We offered to share our hikers' rations, but they were not impressed and stuck to their fresh fare. We all stretched out on the sand. The boys slept soundly, their heads resting on their hands. We three had inflatable pillows, but we itched, tossed and turned all night. It actually got cold enough in the early hours for us to use our sleeping bags. We were relieved when first light came, and happier still when the sun came over the horizon. The temperature was perfect for an hour or two, then sweltering by mid morning.

Our third and final task for this expedition was to find Kala. We launched the dugout, cranked the sputtering Seagull outboard, and headed south. Five hours later the boys pointed to a small inlet, and we motored into a tiny bay. Immediately we were greeted by villagers, and taken the few yards inland to their huts. Again, the local children either fled in fright or surrounded us, staring and laughing.

Nobody spoke English here, but our guides immediately conveyed our query: was Kala here? Indeed yes, but no. She and her husband lived in that hut over there, but they had just yesterday left to walk to Sum Sum, another village even further along the coast, to attend a wedding ceremony. They would be back in a few days. We had insufficient fuel with us to go further, so trying to reach that village was out of the question.

I left in Kala's hut a parcel I'd prepared a week earlier. It had black and white photos of Jack and myself in hospital in Milne Bay, one of his grave, and a colour photo of Ellie, me, and the boys. I included a copy of a report I'd made on my time in New Ireland and escape from there. Kala might find someone to read it to her. The last item included was a role of Australian banknotes, totalling two thousand dollars. I knew Aussie money was very acceptable in New Guinea, whether it be the old pounds or the new dollars, and that amount was equivalent to decades of earnings for a native labourer on a plantation, if such jobs existed here. Kala would be a wealthy woman in her village. It would probably enable her to build a good house and have her grandchildren educated at the capital, Namatanai.

✶✶✶

It was almost dark when we beached the dugout in Borpop's harbour. It was another 20-minute walk to where the 337 was parked. We were bone tired, hungry, dirty, itchy and sore, but we solved one of those problems by jumping into a bubbling freshwater pool along the way. We then used our hikers' cooking equipment to heat some cans of beef stew and vegies. By the time we crawled into our tents under the wings of the 337, exhaustion overcame all else, and we slept till sunrise.

After a slow start the following morning, we handed the guides fifty dollars each, a princely sum to them. We handed to the village elders another one hundred dollars, the repaired Seagull, a few gallons of our precious avgas mixed with oil, our tents and all the other camping gear we'd brought with us. The 337 fired up immediately, as if it were anxious to get back into the air and out of the stifling heat. I taxied to the southern end of the old runway, and fed in full power. Just 30 minutes later we landed in Rabaul to refuel.

Before we reached Port Moresby, we had to have a discussion on what to do with one rather large bag of gold. Who did it really belong to? Was it finders-keepers? None of us had a clue about New Guinea law, but we did know that corruption was rife, and if we let anyone know about the gold, there would be a queue of officials ready to relieve us of it. At the very least, we'd lose half in taxation.

So, we simply hid the gold in empty oil bottles. It filled all twelve bottles we'd taken. It meant dumping the unused oil, but a few dollars' worth of Shell 100 oil was worthwhile sacrifice. The same logic applied when we landed at Horn Island. The customs official gave us a cursory check, then we were on our way south again. We landed back on our own strip with Jack's gold intact.

When we weighed the gold, we found that we had almost exactly 18 kilograms. That converted to 634 ounces, which was worth close to $30,000 dollars, or $10,000 each. (We were now dealing with the Australian dollar, not the pound). That might not sound much today, but back in 1971 you could buy a nice house in a good suburb in Sydney for around $25,000. To Ellie, the trip had been an adventure, and she came home with the equivalent of more than two year's income working as a vet. To me, it had more than covered expenses, I'd met some self-imposed obligations, and had slayed some dragons. To Col, it was the beginning of the rest of his life. He was bubbling with excitement over the opportunities he saw ahead.

CHAPTER 18

Borpop Gold

Two weeks later, Col came to me with a proposition. He had it all planned out, or thought he did. Rather than having other employees overhearing his plan, I invited Col into our family room, where he and I sat opposite each other across a small table, and where we could look past our lush lawn and garden beds to the bush haven beyond. Ellie busied herself at the kitchen bench, where she was close enough to be part of the conversation. Col sat forward, oozing confidence.

'What we do, Rick, is we form a private company, and create, say one hundred thousand shares at a dollar each. You, Ellie, and I put in our $10,000 each, so between us we own thirty percent of the company. We appoint ourselves as the three directors, and then we find some investors for the other seventy thousand shares. That gives us $100,000 to fly back to Borpop, taking my brother. He can do an assessment, and when his report is favourable, we can barge a small drilling rig from either Rabaul or the PNG north coast up to the inlet. Once cores are analysed, we can start taking directors' fees. When we ultimately float the company. our one-dollar shares will skyrocket, and we'll be millionaires!'

I laughed. 'Col, I think you've simplified things a bit. There is whole range of obstacles between now and us becoming millionaires. The first thing, and the most obvious one of all, is that we found a bag of gold. It didn't come from a mine, it came from panning the creek. It's a small creek, and Jack may have taken all the alluvial gold it held. We have no idea if he was right in assuming he'd located its original source. You could spend a million dollars sending a team of experts up there, and still not find the vein that Jack dreamed of.'

Col's face fell. He had probably thought we'd share his enthusiasm immediately. 'Yeah, but my brother is a geologist, and he's working for a gold mining company now. For expenses, plus an option on some shares, he'll fly up there with us. If anyone can find the gold reef, he will.'

'Col, I know nothing about gold mining, but I think that finding this motherlode is a bit more complicated than having one geo wandering around with a pick in his hand. Besides, you can't just lob into Borpop and start digging. I'm sure that you would have to go to the PNG government and apply for a mining lease. That's bound to cost some money. Then, when the villagers get wind of what you are planning, they'll have their hands out too.' Col tried to interrupt, but I continued.

'Flying your brother up there won't be free. I've absorbed all the fuel and overhead expenses for the 337 last time, but I won't do it again. I'd need reimbursement. Then you would need to hire a rig and a barge, and the labour to run both. Can you see that your $100,000 will be dwindling fast?'

Col nodded, and took a swig of his beer. 'Okay, so we'll need more than $100,000. When we float, we'll have millions to invest. But in the interim, would you agree to taking my brother Geoff up there in the 337?'

I looked at Ellie, and she shrugged. 'Ellie,' I said, 'Do you want to put any of your $10,000 into this venture of Col's?'

'Frankly no.' She came and sat beside me, leaned forward and looked earnestly at our guest. 'Sorry to disappoint you Col, but there is too much of a leap from finding a bag of gold, to becoming mining entrepreneurs. But, if Rick wants to fly up there again, that's okay with me. I won't come. We had a great adventure, but I've had enough of PNG heat, humidity, mosquitoes and sand flies to last me awhile.'

Col slowly nodded. He could see his dreams of riches falling apart before the first step. I took pity on him.

'Col, I'll do this for you. You can have time off work on full pay. I'll fly you and your brother up to Borpop, and I'll stay with you for three days. If you want to stay longer, you'll have to find your own way home. I'll charge the 337 out at $2000 for the trip, but I'll take payment in shares. I'll buy another 3000 shares at $1 each. That's it. Neither Ellie nor I will be directors of the company. It's all yours.'

✳✳✳

As I'd mentioned, Col was a popular guy around town. He was well respected, and he'd used those assets to help build our business. Now he used them to spruik his gold exploration business. He called it Borpop Gold Exploration Co, and appointed himself and his brother as directors. As it was a private company, he did not have to have an official prospectus, and although I never heard his spiel personally, I heard later that he made some pretty extravagant claims as to the potential of 'his' mine, and alluded to have already extracted "substantial quantities" of gold. His story soon became the buzz of the town. He must have intimated that Ellie and I were shareholders, because several people asked us about 'our mine'. I suppose the fact that we helped him supported that idea, but we did explain the facts to anyone who asked.

The result of Col's efforts was that, to my amazement, he quickly secured dozens of investors, all prominent and respectable people in town, and each willing to put up amounts from $5000 to $30000. He knocked back a heap of offers to buy small parcels of shares. It seems that nobody wanted to miss out on the this New Guinea gold bonanza.

Col and Geoff began to push me hard to set a date for our return to Borpop. I really didn't want to go, as TAAS kept me busy enough, and I liked spending my leisure time with Ellie and the boys. But, a promise is a promise, and we lifted off our airstrip on June 1st, 1972. This time we had a heap of mining hand tools, and just enough supplies to keep us at the mine site for three days.

The trip across was much the same as the one before, and I enjoyed doing some long distance flying instead of the quick hops that crop dusting involves. But it wasn't the same without Ellie beside me. We'd fallen in love quickly and easily enough, but the bond had only grown from there, and I didn't feel comfortable leaving her behind. I don't know whether that was the main cause of my unease, or whether it was Col and Geoff's constant chatter about the new venture, but by the time we reached Rabaul, I found myself wishing I hadn't been so rash in offering help.

As it often does in PNG, the weather quickly deteriorated as we neared Rabaul, and I had to make an instrument approach through thick cloud and lashing rain. We broke through the overcast at six hundred feet, and I was grateful for the long, sealed runway as we rolled and pitched in the wind gusts that hit us just before touching down. The one good thing was that my two passengers shut up during the descent, and were quite white-faced by the time I parked and shut down the engines.

The forecast was similar for the following afternoon, so we left early in order to beat a front coming from the east. We didn't succeed. It hit Borpop just as we began our descent, and of course there were no navigational aids, no long, sealed strip, and no runway lighting. I fought a twenty-knot crosswind on final, and because of rain over several days, mud flew from our tyres when we touched down on the slippery grass. We were all glad to peg the 337 down on the side of the strip.

Despite the wind and rain, our welcome from the villagers was enthusiastic, no doubt helped by the donations I'd left last time. It was dark before we extricated ourselves from the village and once again pitched our small tents under the wings of the aeroplane.

***

The chief was more than happy to lend us the dugout and Seagull motor. I'd brought four jerrycans of fuel and oil mix from Rabaul, a new spark plug, and a spare propellor. The chief appointed two fit young guys to act as boatmen and porters. It seemed a fair trade. So, the trip to the inlet was in relative ease, but as usual, the hike to the mine was a different matter. In the stormy conditions, the humidity was even more stifling, and there were moments I thought my two companions would refuse to go on.

We did make it, and we gratefully dumped our camping gear, three days supplies of food and water, plus a bag full of mining implements. I set about putting up the tents, making a fire, and cooking us a meal. Col and Geoff scoffed down some rice and beans, and were miraculously revitalised. They left me to clean up as they set off for the mine.

I left them to work in the creek and the mine largely by themselves. I acted as a cook and carrier when needed, but made no attempt to get involved in the mine itself. That seemed to suit them also. Over the three days, they collected numerous bags of crushed rock, so many in fact that I had to call a limit.

'Look guys, it's a Cessna 337, not a DC-3. We've got a payload of 400 Kg, and that includes the three of us. If we dump all the camping and mining gear here, we can lift about 150Kg of your samples. That's it. No more.' They were a bit disgruntled, but Col should have known better. After all, he'd worked for our aviation company for years, and logistics was a major part of his job.

The villagers were happy with the excess gear, plus a wad of notes that Col gave them. I waved them fond farewell, thinking that I wouldn't ever be coming back to Borpop, beautiful as it may be. There was just one more item on my list before setting course for Rabaul: after take-off I levelled at five hundred feet and followed the coast south for eight minutes. Kala's village lay before us, and I circled several times at about three hundred feet. Adults and children waved, but of course we couldn't recognise faces at that altitude. What I did see was a new house being built on one side of the village. Building materials, a cement mixer, and sheets of roofing lay alongside the partially constructed walls. It was going to be much bigger than the other houses in the village. If it was Kala's new house, which I'm sure it was, it looked like my money was being well spent.

For the first time since leaving Kala all those years ago, I felt no guilt. I'd filled my obligations, and the New Ireland chapter was closed. Well, not quite. Col and his bloody goldmine were to haunt us yet.

✳✳✳

Normal living resumed for all of three weeks, then Col called a meeting of existing and potential new shareholders in the Borpop Gold Exploration Company. He'd asked if he could hold it at our TAAS office, but I declined, saying that I did not want to lead others to believe that I was any more than a minor shareholder. Instead, Col hired a room at the golf club for a couple of hours one Monday evening.

I arrived a little before the appointed time. I quickly found the meeting room. It was bare but for several rows of chairs, a lectern, and a few golf-related photos on the walls. Col and his brother were waiting expectantly. We chatted for 10 minutes before anyone else showed up, and I was beginning to think the venture had already sunk from disinterest before it even got underway. A few locals drifted in, and then it became a flood. I recognised all but two of the faces: some I knew quite well, as they were clients of TAAS. I noticed that many attendees had beers in their hands, and were treating the meeting like a social occasion. I nodded hellos, and I chose a chair in the back row.

Col and Geoff disappeared for a couple of minutes, but reappeared bringing more beers on two trays, which they offered around, the result being that a couple of guys had a beer in each hand. I declined, not only because I rarely drink beer, but I wanted a very clear head. I couldn't help wondering if free-flowing alcohol was just one of Col's promotional tools.

He began in his usual personable style, and quickly engendered an atmosphere of bonhomie. I had to admire his technique. He described the initial trip with me, pointing me out as 'Rick, our local war hero pilot that you all know.' That irritated me, but I tried to listen with an open mind.

'Gentlemen, on our second trip, again courtesy of Rick's aeroplane, we were able to enter the mine, and dig for samples. Because of the limitations on the equipment we could take in the small aircraft, we could not take deep cores, but, Gentlemen, we have had analyses done on a hundred small samples we took in the relatively shallow mine, and the result is an astounding gold assay of an ounce per ton. For those of you who are not mining experts, I'll let my brother Geoff, a qualified and experienced geologist, explain the significance of that figure. Over to you, Geoff.'

'Thanks Col. Gentlemen, it is rare to find gold at such shallow levels. The mines that I have worked in have seams at depths of hundreds of feet, even over a thousand feet. Of course, the deeper the seam, the longer it takes to reach it, and more expensive it is to mine it. Heavier equipment is needed, and tailings become more of an issue. This mine has economic gold virtually at surface level. Of course, when we can barge in heavier drilling equipment, we can ascertain just how deep and how extensive the seam is, so we can't get too carried away just yet. But, please note that an ounce per ton is an exceptional grade. Most mines around the world make good money with grades around under one third of an ounce. To summarise, the grade and shallow depth of gold in this mine make it a strong prospect that should be investigated immediately.'

Col stood up, beamed at his audience, and I knew he had them by their throats, or more importantly, their wallets. These were mostly simple country folk, and he was making an investment in Borpop Gold sound like an exotic adventure, and a sure thing. His story was threaded with verbal images of Jack the hermit, the brave RAAF pilot fleeing from a vicious enemy, hot and humid jungle on a remote and exotic island, and a tale of gold that turned out to be true. Many of his audience had never travelled further than Sydney, and they lapped up the word picture he presented. Then he moved in for the kill.

'Okay folks, you've heard our story, and you know that we are not pulling your legs. You know me, you know Rick and Ellie, so you know it's kosher. We're now offering you, our friends in Tamworth, the opportunity to partake in this adventure. Col paused, to allow this vision of riches sink in. He looked into the eyes of everyone in his spellbound audience. Then he continued.

'But of course, we can't make a fortune from gold mining

with little more than a bucket and spade. Geoff has drawn a comprehensive plan on how we should go about expanding the mine. We have a copy for each of you, but to summarise, to get to stage two, we'll need to barge in from Lae to Borpop several pieces of machinery. We need a small dozer to cut a track from the harbour all the way to the mine. It will then drag a mobile drilling rig to the site. We'll need at least half a dozen holes dug to get any idea of the extent of the reef. Then we'll know what sort of equipment we'll need to get to the gold itself. That will bring us to stage three. Could be we only need a good excavator before we can start mining properly. We'll need trucks to move the ore, a processing plant, and maybe even dredging equipment to open up the inlet for the barge.'

Again, Col paused for effect. Several listeners leaned forward in anticipation. He lowered his voice, making it sound like his pitch was just for this exclusive audience.

'What I am suggesting is that, to kick off stage two, we issue another 900,000 shares in Borpop Mining at $1 each. Fifty cents payable up front, and another fifty cents when we confirm that we've found the reef of gold. You good people have first refusal. Any shares not taken up will be offered to new investors. Then, when we have all the results from the drilling program, and we know the extent of the reef, AND have begun to produce our first commercial gold, we'll float the company on the Australian stock exchange. That, Gentlemen, is when you'll see the share value SKYROCKET!'

He paused once again, so I grabbed the opportunity.

'Col, aren't you making a big assumption? In fact, two rather big assumptions. Firstly, you're asking for a million dollars to send in drilling equipment based solely on samples taken at surface level. Then you are forecasting a huge jump in the share price because of assay results you assume will confirm what you hope it will...' Col interrupted me.

'Rick, you've been there. You have seen the gold that came out of the creek that flows directly through the site of our claim, and alongside the existing mine. You've actually put your hands in kilos of gold dust, and let it run through your fingers…' A murmur went around the room as Col conjured up that mental picture.

It was my turn to interrupt. I didn't bother to correct his statement that it was my fingers in the bag of gold.

'Okay Col, I'm not disputing that you and I found a bag of gold that an old prospector panned out of the creek, and I'm not trying to pour cold water on your ideas. I'd just like to point out to everyone here that this is a highly speculative venture, and that nothing has so far been proved…'

'Not nothing,' interjected Geoff. 'We have the assay results from the cores that you helped bring back from Borpop.'

Col jumped in. 'Yes, we all know it is a speculative venture, and since when did you multiply your money five, ten, maybe a hundred times by investing in something safe, like the local bank!'

Someone interjected, 'Yeah, I get about 5% on my money in the bank. Fat lot of good it is when the rate of inflation is probably 10%!'

There was a murmur of agreement, and just about everyone turned to look at me during this exchange. There were some obvious frowns, but I think that the sentiment was that I was being unnecessarily negative. In the rising babble of voices, I didn't hear anyone supporting my concerns. I decided to shut up. I figured that they all knew the risks, and some people like to gamble. I didn't. In the end, Col and Geoff triumphed. Their 900,000 shares were actually oversubscribed, and they raised a staggering $1.3 million dollars, half payable now. That's amazing considering that the average wage at the time was well under $4,000 a year. I left the meeting without putting my hand in my pocket. I had just 5,000 shares, and I was happy to let the others reap the rewards if and when the mine turned into a bonanza.

A few days after the meeting, Col handed in his notice.

'Sorry Rick, but I'm going to devote myself full time to the mine. I'll be heading up to Port Moresby soon to work out the mining lease, then I'll go on to Lae to organise the barging of mining equipment across to Borpop. You know that we could use you and your aeroplane up there, full time?'

'Thanks Col, but I'll pass on that. I've got plenty to keep me occupied here. And besides, as lovely as Borpop harbour is, I really have had enough of New Ireland heat, humidity, and bugs. I'll leave it to you young guys!'

'Alright Rick, I understand. I've enjoyed my job, and I'll miss it. You've been a great boss. But this is my chance to make it big, and I have to grasp it while I can.'

'Okay Col. We've enjoyed having you here, and we'll miss you too. You've done a great job for us. Just do me a favour, please. However it turns out with the mine, look after the Huris villagers, will you? I'd hate to see them badly done by.'

***

Six months went by with just a couple of letters to shareholders. According to them, a mining lease had been granted, and mining equipment, tents, camping gear, a small dozer, a small drill rig, and other bits and pieces were being readied for transport to Borpop Harbour. Another circular 3 months later indicated that the gear had actually arrived.

I promoted an ageing Alf to manage the office, as I figured that he was overdue for a break in the loading work, and found a new young chap to take over the loading crew. Then Christmas was upon us, and the result was that I forgot all about Borpop and the mining venture. It was early in the new year of 1973 when a formal letter arrived, telling all shareholders in Borpop Gold that a meeting of shareholders was to be held on February 1st.

It was with some ambivalence that I walked into that same meeting room at the golf club on the appointed night. I genuinely liked and respected Col, and I looked forward to seeing him again. I also hoped that his venture would be successful for him and his investors. On the other hand, I had a gut feeling that the whole thing had gone way too far, that Col was out of his depth, and quite a few people were in danger of losing their money. I tried to be invisible, sitting in the back row.

The beer flowed as before, and when Col and Geoff made their appearances, it was obvious they were there to spread good news. They pranced onto the stage like rock stars!

'Ladies and Gentlemen,' Col began, 'It is with the greatest pleasure that I can provide you with this update. As you know, with the funds previously raised, we have purchased a substantial amount of equipment, and have had it shipped to Borpop Harbour in New Ireland. Included in this equipment was a Caterpillar D4 dozer, and we have used it to cut a road from the unnamed inlet nearest the mine to the mine itself. We've also dredged part of the inlet to allow the barge to enter, so that in future we don't have to unload at Borpop and then move gear by the old road.'

This statement didn't gel with me, because I knew that the offshore coral reef would almost certainly prevent anything bigger than a small boat from approaching the inlet, but I let it pass for the moment. Col continued.

'The D4 was then used to drag the drill rig to the mine site, which allowed us to dig more than a dozen holes to a depth of two hundred feet. Analysis of these cores, copies of which we'll hand out later, have confirmed that the gold reef starts just beyond the end of the existing tunnel. It has assayed extremely well, just as previous test samples had promised. It is also shallow, as we previously indicated, so that mining will be cheap compared to most mines in PNG, where the gold can be over a thousand feet deep. All that we need to do now is, with further test drilling, confirm just HOW extensive the reef is. Then, Ladies and Gentlemen, we will have the processing plant we've ordered shipped over, and we can start producing GOLD.'

As Col continued with more details on what was happening right now, and what was going to happen over the next few months, I watched as his audience just sucked it all up. I was tempted to interrupt a couple of times when extravagant predictions were made, but I knew that there was little point. When the request came for all option holders to pay up the balance of the 50 cents per share outstanding, nobody raised an eyebrow. I quietly exited, thinking that maybe I'd missed an opportunity to make a lot of money, and how disappointed Jack would be if others got rich from his find and I didn't. Somehow, though, I still felt that two and two weren't making four, and I feared that there might be tears before Christmas of that year.

CHAPTER 19

Bad vibes.

Borpop Gold was a long way from the forefront of my mind for most of 1973. The boys were thirteen and fifteen, growing like weeds, doing well at school, and playing sport on weekends. They were old enough to benefit from and enjoy overseas travel, and so we took them to the USA and spent six weeks touring the American West. Magic! What a marvellous time we had! We hired a motorhome, and did a 7,000 mile loop from Oregon to Idaho, Wyoming, Montana, South Dakota, Colorado, New Mexico, Arizona, Utah, Nevada, and California, They begged for more, so we then flew to the Solomon Islands and spent two weeks on a boat, scuba diving and exploring. They saw at first hand relics of the Pacific War, and for the first time got some appreciation of what the previous generation had done to defeat the tyrannical Axis powers.

It was early December when another communication came from Borpop Gold. Addressed to all shareholders, it told of progress to date. It said that the exploration program was complete, that small-scale mining was underway, that the larger equipment required for full-scale mining had been ordered, and that it would be ready to ship to Borpop within weeks. It forecast economic production by March, and the first dividend by May 1974.

I have to admit that the rosy picture momentarily made me again feel that maybe I was missing out, and that others would get rich on "my" gold, while I sat on the sidelines. However, my niggling doubts persisted.

The last paragraph in the letter was in bold type. "All outstanding payments to convert partially-paid options to fully paid shares are overdue. Any shares not fully subscribed by January first will be offered to new investors." With some unease, I ignored the letter. My miserly 5,000 shares were fully paid up from day one anyway, and once again I put the venture to a far corner of my mind. It was June of 1974 before I was reminded of it.

***

Walking down the main street of Tamworth with Ellie one Saturday morning, I was buttonholed by one of Col's investors. John Lamming was a big, fair-haired man and a large landholder, owning several thousand acres west of the city. He was a member of the city council, and a regular at the golf club. He planted himself in front of me on the footpath, so that we nearly bumped heads. He was wearing his usual sharply pressed blue jeans, fancy belt and buckle, crisp collared light blue shirt, and tan Akubra hat.

'Eric Richards, can I have a word with you?' The three of us stopping in the middle of the busy footbath caused a minor jam, so I indicated we should step over to the curb. I assumed he wanted to get some crop dusting or spraying done.

'Sure John, what can I do for you?'

'You can tell me what's going on in New Guinea for a start.' His tone was belligerent.

'What do you mean, John?'

'Borpop Gold is what I mean. I want to know what exactly is going on.'

A little baffled, I replied, 'You've received Col's newsletters, haven't you? I'm just a minor shareholder, so I don't have any information other than that.'

'Haven't heard a thing for months. We should be mining now, and our first dividend was due more than a month ago. I've put up a hundred grand, you know, and I want results.' As John spoke, his fair skin became more and more florid.

'John,' I replied calmly, 'I repeat, I'm a very minor shareholder, and I have had nothing to do with running the mining company other than initially taking Col up to Borpop, and then later taking his brother also. I only know what I receive in the mail.'

John prodded me in the chest, and I took a step back in surprise. Ellie did too.

'That's not the way I see it. I believe that you sold Col on the idea of mining up there, and you've been up there twice, bringing back samples. I reckon you are in cahoots with Col, and I'm beginning to smell a rat.'

'John, that's not the case. If you ask me, the whole venture has been fraught with peril from day one, and I said as much at that first meeting at the golf club. If you've gone in over your head, it's your doing, not mine. I put $5000 into the company just because Col was a good mate and a good employee and I wanted to help him. So don't come running to me if there's a problem.'

I took Ellie's hand, and pushed past Lamming. He grunted, and stared daggers as we walked away. My long-repressed feeling of unease suddenly came rushing to the fore. Instead of going home, Ellie and I deviated from the main street into the side street where Borpop Gold had its small office. It was upstairs, above a shop that sold bicycles, and alongside the equally-small office of a local accountant. As I expected, both were closed on this Saturday morning, but what gave us a bad feeling was the pile of unopened letters partially shoved under Borpop Gold's door. It looked like that door hadn't been opened for some days, at the very least. I tried Col's old home number, but it rang out. There was nothing more I could do until Monday.

At 9am that day I climbed those stairs again. There was no change to the letters under Col's door. However, the accountant opposite was in. I vaguely knew him.

'Hi Bruce, just wondering if you've seen Col lately? It looks like he hasn't been into his office for a while.'

'Oh, hi, Rick. No, I haven't seen Col for many months. Somebody must come in and collect the mail periodically, but they must be doing it after hours. We do hear their phone ringing sometimes, but nobody ever answers it. Also, between you and me, I think our landlord is getting anxious. I think his rent is long overdue.'

The picture that was emerging wasn't good. I drove straight home and searched to find my file on the mining company. I remembered that at the last presentation, we were given a handout that included copies of invoices for the new equipment that was meant to be in place early in the year. After rummaging through a pile of folders in the corner of my office, I found it. There were several invoices, totalling hundreds of thousands of dollars, and they were from PNG Engineering Support Services, of Lae. I rang their number, and after going through a couple of sleepy clerks, got hold of the local manager. Harry Crossan introduced himself, and I explained that I was a minor shareholder in Borpop Gold, and that I had flown the directors of the company to the mine site a couple of times.

'Mr Crossan, I'm trying to contact Col Rodgers, or anyone else from the company. Can you tell me if you are in contact with anyone up there?'

'Hmm. It's Harry, by the way. Look Rick, I can't divulge details of our customers and what they buy from us. But, I'll tell you this. Borpop Gold Mining asked us to invoice them for a large amount of equipment, and they paid a very small deposit. That was the last we've heard of them. Apart from some really crappy old gear we sent up over a year ago, that's all they bought from us.'

'Harry, did that old stuff include a D4 and a portable drill rig?'

'Yeah, it did. The D4 was just about stuffed. We told them it wasn't worth shipping, but they said it only needed to last long enough to cut one road.'

My next call was to the National Analytical Service, also at Lae. Nobody in authority could speak to me, but I was promised a call-back. It came an hour later.

'My name is Fred Collins, I'm the manager of the local branch of National Analytical. I understand that you are enquiring about Borpop Gold.'

'Yes, Fred. I am a very minor shareholder in the company, but through a friendship with one of the directors, Col Rodgers, I did some flying in PNG for the initial exploration up there. I'm now trying to contact someone, anyone, from the company.'

'Well Rick, good luck with that. We've had no contact with them for a considerable time. If you do get in contact with Mr Rodgers, please remind him that we've never been paid for the second lot of assays that we did for him.'

'Oh. I'm sorry to hear that. Just as an aside, was there anything unusual about the samples that you assayed?'

There was silence on the line for a time. I was about to hang up, thinking that the line had dropped out, when Harry spoke again.

'I shouldn't really divulge this, but if you agree to giving me a contact number for Col if and when you find him, I'll tell you one thing.'

'Yes, I'll do that,' I replied.

'The samples, both the initial and second batch, a hundred samples in each, were unusual. Exactly half assayed zero gold or anything else of value. The other half assayed a very high gold content. Exceptionally high. That's all I can say.'

It was becoming painfully obvious where this was heading. Even then I'd have been prepared to bet that half were real cores, and the second half had been doctored, probably with Col's share of Jack's gold.

***

A week later I received in the mail a letter addressed to all shareholders in Borpop Gold. This time it was from John Lamming, the shareholder who had put in 'a hundred grand.' It proposed an informal meeting at the usual venue, to be held in ten days.

This was another meeting I was not looking forward to. I would have been absolutely dreading it had I known the direction it was to take. I guess that I should have seen it coming, as the shareholders were sensing doom, and were looking for someone to pin blame on. Lamming provided a target: me.

'Rick Richards was the initial promotor of this gold mine,' he boomed, 'and he convinced his then employee, Col Rodgers, to take up the running. You know the rest. Now it looks like everyone but Rick has done a runner. Why is that, I wonder? Is it because Rick has little interest in it now, just 5,000 shares I'm told. Is it because he's already had his payout, from all the money you lot, and I, have put in?'

A voice called, 'He should be arrested.' I couldn't see who it was, but everyone then turned and looked at Steve Drummond, the Tamworth police chief, and another Borpop Gold investor. He hesitated, looked a bit uncomfortable, then said, 'Rick, perhaps you and I had better have a talk. Nine a.m. tomorrow, at the station.'

I hadn't expected this. I stood, somewhat shakily, and replied to the room. 'I'll be at the police station tomorrow at 9am. But, for the record, everyone here heard me warn that this venture was extremely risky. You all heard me question Col and Geoff over the developmental path they were taking. You are also aware that I have only ever taken up 5,000 shares, and that's because I have always had strong reservations about the whole thing. I have NOT taken any money from the company. I was NOT reimbursed for the substantial costs of the first trip to New Ireland, and for the second I took shares in lieu of payment. Anyone who spreads any false stories about my involvement will regret it. Thank you.' I turned and left.

The next morning, I sat before Steve Drummond in a police interview room. I told him everything. He hunched over the table between us and took laborious notes, and finally sat back and looked at me.

'Rick, the small amount of evidence I have supports what you say. I'll take no further action at this stage.' It was hardly a ringing endorsement, but it was better than nothing.

Rumours spread quickly in country towns. I noticed a couple of times that people I knew looked at me quizzically, as if seeing me properly for the first time. I was beginning to learn that mud sticks, no matter how inaccurately thrown. I had to do something. One night I made a decision.

'Ellie, Max, Peter, we are going on an adventure. We are going to New Ireland, in the 337. We leave next Saturday.'

The boys had never found aeroplanes particularly interesting, because they'd grown up with them. That didn't mean they didn't enjoy going somewhere new by aeroplane, and this trip gave them that in spades. We took our time heading north, stopping over on the Gold Coast, where Surfers Paradise was still lovely before being grossly over-developed. Ellie and the boys swam at the beach, and bought tickets on an amusement ride that scared the dickens out of me. In the Whitsundays, we hired a yacht for a few days and taught the boys how to sail. From Cairns we took a ride on the Kuranda railway, and hiked through a rainforest looking at iridescent blue Ulysses butterflies and exotic flowers. At Cooktown we visited the site of Captain Cook's beaching of the Endeavour, and from Horn Island we took a boat and 4WD ride to the tip of the Australian mainland.

Port Moresby's heat, poverty and decay were an education for the boys, and the crossing of the snow-capped Owen Stanley ranges an incredible sight for them. We crossed a ridge line not far from the 13,250 foot peak, that towered more than one thousand feet above us.

We stayed at Rabaul for a few days, where we walked through the tunnels the Japanese had dug to shelter from Allied bombing during the war, swam over pristine coral reefs that teemed with fish of every size and colour, and the boys went fishing with a local guide. As Ellie and I sipped gin and tonics and watched the sunset, she asked if I was disappointed that neither Max or Peter had any interest in taking up flying.

'Hardly,' I replied, 'there are much safer ways of making a living!'

'But wouldn't you like them to at least have some interest in planes?'

'It's entirely up to them. They'll find their own interests.

Look at this new fascination with fishing. To me, fishing is on a par with watching flies crawl up a wall, and if you have the misfortune to actually catch one, you've got to gut and clean it. But they love it.'

Ellie laughed, we clinked glasses, and she said, 'You're right. All we can do is expose them to as many things as we can, and they'll decide for themselves on the path they want to follow.'

***

Ellie and I dragged Max and Peter away from Rabaul, only by promising them something even more exciting. I then hoped I could meet their expectations. I'd never talked to the boys much about my wartime experiences. They knew that I'd been a fighter pilot, and had been brought down in the islands somewhere to the north, but not much else. So, as we began our descent into Borpop, I followed the same approach path as I had on that fateful morning thirty-one years earlier, describing what it was like all the way in. Seeing the grass strip and the rusty Japanese AA guns still pointing skywards, my story suddenly came alive to them. To my surprise, when we landed, they wanted to see it all.

Firstly, we had to go through the usual welcome from the Huris villagers. This time, the local youngsters were far more forthright, and soon our two were off on an adventure with a dozen black kids, who were particularly fascinated by young Max's near-blond hair. They all wanted to touch it to confirm it was real hair. That left Ellie and me to set up camp under the 337's wing.

In the morning, we wandered around the harbour, looking at the two wrecks close by, the bubbling springs, and the guns on the northern headland. In the afternoon we looked at the remaining wrecks on the edge of the airstrip, both boys wanting every detail of the bombing and strafing we'd done, and which wrecks I'd contributed to. They were only mildly disappointed when I explained that Jap bulldozers must have cleared up after our raid, as I couldn't claim responsibility with any certainty for any that were still lying there.

They were visibly excited when we set off early on the second day, as this was to be the more important part of our visit, and not even the blazing sun could dampen their enthusiasm. Once again, we were able to borrow the dugout and outboard, and we used it to find the road that Col and Geoff had cut with the D4. This meant that instead of a couple of hours on an overgrown jungle path, we had easy walking all the way from there to the mine site. It was a shock to see what was there, even though it was not an unexpected one.

The old and rusty D4 was silent now. It appeared that it had broken down while pushing some dirt, and had been abandoned where it stopped. Not even a tarpaulin covered the engine or the open cab. Not far away was the portable drill rig, similarly unprotected from the elements. It looked like it was half way through drilling a test hole, except for the spider webs all over it. Near the mine entry, piles of spoil had been dumped, but weeds were already reclaiming the mounds.

I broke the silence. 'Well, so much for a million dollars' worth of machinery, and dividends before June.'

We found what had been Jack's clearing easily enough, and even my forlorn P-40. The boys were strangely quiet when I told them I remembered nothing between sliding through the kunai grass and waking up in Jack's hut many hours later. They were astonished that we'd had to hide from the Japanese for months. I skipped the part about Jack's surgery on my head. I thought I'd leave it for another day to tell them about the escape by small boat, and the terrifying encounter with the enemy destroyer. I think they had a new appreciation for their father as we hiked and boated back to the 337.

The village elders were once again happy to relieve us of the new camping gear we'd brought, some cash, and a drum of outboard motor fuel for the old Seagull outboard. They waved happily as we departed Borpop for the last time.

★★★

We'd been at Borpop for 60 hours, during which we'd had no VHF radio coverage. In addition, as is quite common, our long-range HF radio was picking up too much static to be useful, and thus we'd had no weather reports since departing Rabaul. Weather reporting in 1975 was nothing like it is today, where satellites and computers allow amazingly accurate forecasts a week or more ahead. Back then it wasn't much better than guessing from what you could see out the window. As soon as we'd climbed a few hundred feet I noticed a band of low cloud on the horizon east of us, and some mare's tails high above. They are the harbinger of bad weather. I knew we had to get the latest forecast as soon as we landed in Rabaul.

We cruised at 500 feet up the coast, circled Kala's village, noted the fine new house in its centre, then set course for New Britain's capital. After landing and organising refueling, I walked over to the briefing office. I woke up the met officer who was deep in slumber, his head resting on the latest weather charts. Somewhat startled, he proceeded to give me news I didn't want to hear. A cyclone, most likely a very severe one, was at this moment somewhere north of Green Island, and heading north-west. It was expected to hit Rabaul at around about five p.m. that evening. It would likely be accompanied by torrential rain, flooding was expected, and could ground all aerial activity for several days. The met officer recommended that if we departed immediately, we'd be ahead of the storm. We put in a plan to fly direct to Lae, leaving as soon as the refueler finished.

It was only ten am, but the sky was already darkening as we rotated, and the higher we climbed the taller the grey mass ahead appeared to be. By the time we reached our cruising altitude of 9000 feet, the anvil top had overtaken us. I'd flown through plenty of bad weather before, and had no qualms, but I knew my passengers were in for a very unpleasant ride.

Our initial track took us down the spine of New Britain, and as the wind strengthened, so did the turbulence caused by the strong wind bouncing off the mountains below us. It got so bad I couldn't hold my hand steady enough to change radio frequencies, and the autopilot couldn't keep the aeroplane on an even keel. We'd hit a pocket that would drop us 500 feet, only to hit another that would hurl us 500 feet above our chosen altitude. It felt like our stomachs were being left behind in the rollercoaster ride. One of the boys shakily queried whether the wings ever came off Cessna 337s? I assured him that ours wouldn't, but I climbed another 2000 feet, where the air was a little less rough. That meant plunging into the amorphous grey mass of storm cloud. We were then flying on instruments, which meant that I scanned the basic instruments of artificial horizon, directional gyro, rate of climb indicator, turn and bank indicator, airspeed indicator, and altimeter in rotation every few seconds. A pilot not trained for instrument flight who is foolish enough to enter cloud usually loses control within a minute, not knowing up from down. Loss of control in these circumstances almost invariably has fatal consequences. I ignored what my senses were telling me, and concentrated on the instruments. All normal for me, but scary for my three passengers.

I'd just about convinced them that, while not exactly sailing smoothly, we were going well, and within an hour or so would begin our descent into Lae, when we had another problem. What I didn't know was that the cyclone was travelling much faster than had been forecast, and the eye of it was much further south than had been predicted. At that moment, we were getting closer to the eye, not fleeing from it.

I was startled when ice began to form around the edges of the windshield. I couldn't see the leading edges of the wings, but pulling my eyes away from the instrument scan for a few seconds, I could see ice forming around the wing struts too.

Ice has killed many airmen. It can build up very quickly, deforming the profile of the flying surfaces, thus destroying lift, and it can add so much weight that the aircraft can no longer carry it. Big aeroplanes almost always have the luxury of anti-icing systems, with heated panels or deicing fluid sprays on wing leading edges, air intakes, and even on propellors. Small aeroplanes rarely do. We had one way of getting rid of ice: we had to descend to warmer air, and fast.

Of course, descending meant re-entering the more turbulent air, but a few extra bumps was a price we were glad to pay. Then the hail began. We were lashed with it, sounding like we were in a noisy drum being pelted by a million rocks. Sadly, I knew to expect some chips in the paint on my lovely aeroplane's wings.

To find Lae's airfield, I made an approach using their radio beacon. We finally broke through cloud at about 500', with Lae's glistening-wet but long runway directly in front of us. I think Ellie and the boys now had a new appreciation for the skills needed to fly an aeroplane in all weathers.

The rain pelted down for 48 hours, so we stayed in a hotel in Lae. It was another time that it was better to be looking up from the ground than looking down from the air.

***

I circulated a letter to all the shareholders that I had information on Borpop Gold, and requested they attend an informal meeting the following Tuesday, usual time, usual place. Again, Ellie and

I arrived early, but unlike at the official meetings, there was no free beer this time. Once all shareholders were seated, I began without preamble. I explained that I'd done some research, found that there were inconsistencies with what we'd been told by the chairman, and thus had decided to make a third visit to Borpop, at my own expense. I described what I'd found.

'So, in summary, ladies and gentlemen, I think Col and Geoff had every expectation of success with this venture, but I also think they had a back-up plan in case expectations weren't met by reality. I think that the assays they showed us all were of samples that had been salted with gold from Col's share of the original find in the hut. The real samples showed not a trace of gold. Old Jack had probably exhausted the alluvial gold in the creek, and if a reef in the mountain upstream exists, it is certainly beyond any digging done by Jack, and any exploratory drilling by Col and Geoff. Personally, from what I have learned about gold mining over the last year or so, I think it extremely unlikely an economic vein exists. I'm quite sure you've lost all your money. I've lost mine too'

There were long faces around the room. All were quiet, with one exception: John Lamming looked angry.

'Now,' I continued, 'a footnote to this unfortunate story. I am very disappointed in you all. I have served my country as a pilot during the war, and I've served this district as an ag pilot since, yet you all were just too ready to believe that I was partly responsible for this failed venture. I think you are now aware that I have made nothing from my input, and in fact took shares in lieu of repayment for my expenses. If, in future, I hear a single word from any of you linking me with the failure of Borpop Gold, I'll be down your throats with every legal avenue available. I'll now say goodnight.'

With that, Ellie and I walked out. As we passed through the door, I did hear one person clapping, so at least one of the shareholders appreciated my efforts. Nothing was said between Ellie and me until I started the car. Then she burst out laughing. 'Well, THAT'S telling them, Richards,' she said.

240

CHAPTER 20

Tragedy strikes again.

Outwardly, life in Tamworth settled back to normal, and we heard no more of Borpop Gold, nor of Col and Geoff Rodgers. I often wondered how the brothers managed to disappear so successfully, but I resigned myself to never knowing. Though Col had left me with a mess, I couldn't bring myself to feel any antipathy towards him. What continued to bother me was that so many people had been prepared to think the worst of me, that I could be party to diddling them with a gold scam. To them, I was guilty until I proved myself innocent. Later, quite a few people made overtures to resuming our previous friendships, but I found myself unable to reciprocate. After Borpop Gold, I could never feel quite the same about living in the district.

Despite my personal feelings, our aerial business was booming. At Wee Waa, about 200 km to the north west, cotton growing had expanded since the early 60's to being the major cash crop of the district. Every acre of it needed to be sprayed multiple times to prevent insect damage, and then again at defoliation prior to harvest. Oil seed crops also flourished. We could have doubled our fleet of aircraft and pilots, and we'd still have been busy. I put on more staff, and we all worked hard through the summers.

Demand in winter eased up, and I trusted our staff to manage the business when I was away. So, Ellie and I took the opportunity to take the boys travelling again. During 1975 and 1976 we flew all over Australia in the 337, once to New Zealand in it, and had an incredible two-month safari covering nine countries in Africa.

Also in 1977, Alf retired. He'd been crucial to the efficient running of our business from the very early days, so on his last day with us, I handed him a cash bonus so big that he was momentarily speechless.

'Alf, I hear that you're heading off on that lap around Australia that you've been talking about for years?'

'Yeah, Rick. I haven't been outside this state in decades, so I'm looking forward to a road trip. You know Betty from the RSL café? I was telling her about it, and she said she'd like to come with me.' He was a bit bashful letting me in on this, and kept looking at his feet.

'You sly old dog!' I exclaimed joyfully. 'Good for you! I also heard that you've been eyeing off a new Toyota Landcruiser Troop Carrier at the local dealership?'

Alf chuckled, and nodded. 'I was. It would be the ideal vehicle for a year's tripping around the country, but it was wishful thinking. Even with your generosity, Rick, I can't justify spending that sort of money. My old Holden ute will be okay.'

'No, bugger that, Alf. Do it in style. I heard that you were looking at that Toyota, so I got the sales manager to trick it up with upmarket tyres, a bull bar, air-con and a radio. It's registered in your name, so go and pick it up.'

Alf remained a close friend until he died fifteen years later. Betty stayed with him during that time.

∗∗∗

Two years after my final trip to Borpop, I received a letter, postmarked PNG. I unfolded a typed letter, out of which fell a bank cheque for $20,000. Somewhat startled, I began to read.

Dear Rick,

By now you will have figured out the facts about the Borpop mine. Of course you were right, the whole thing was a disaster. I was foolish for not having taken your advice. It wasn't meant to be that way. Geoff and I really did think it would be a success, and we had no intention of ripping off the good folk of Tamworth. After Borpop, Geoff and I changed our names and used the remaining funds to open up a mine in the Bulolo Valley, south of Lae. It was immediately successful, and we've just sold the mining rights to a large company. We'll now leave PNG before the past debts catch up with us. South America looks promising. As a token of our continued goodwill towards you and Ellie, we enclose this bank cheque. It might compensate you for all your efforts on our behalf. Use it as you will.

Goodbye old friend,
Col.

I sat for minutes before tearing up the letter. I then addressed an envelope to Borpop Gold's receiver, put in the cheque and a note explaining that the funds had come to me from PNG unsolicited. As a minor shareholder, much later I did receive a few dollars when the $20,000 was dispersed to shareholders, but I never received any acknowledgement by the receiver or the other recipients.

✳✳✳

It was with mixed feelings in early 1977 that we prepared ourselves for Max's departure for university in Sydney. Of course, we were excited to see him move onto the next stage of his life, but we knew we'd miss being involved with his day-to-day life, and those of his teenage friends. With that move only weeks away, we received terrible news. I came in from work at about 6.30 one evening, to find Ellie preparing dinner. Both boys were already at the table, so I poured myself a glass of white wine, and sat beside them. The phone in the kitchen rang, and Ellie answered with one hand, while stirring a pot with the other. I took no notice until she dropped the phone. Her hands flew to her ashen face. 'It's Dad. He's had a heart attack. He's been rushed to Dubbo Hospital.'

Less than an hour later, the four of us piled aboard the 337, There was just enough light for me to take off legally from our unlit paddock strip. We'd land at Dubbo Aerodrome, where the runways had good lighting, and Mrs H would arrange someone to pick us up. Ellie filled me in on the way, with as much as she knew.

'Poor Dad. Only sixty-seven years old, and about to retire. My poor Mum. This just isn't fair…'

Ellie knew few details, other than Mr H had not come in for dinner at the expected time that evening, so Mrs H had gone looking for him. She found him lying beside a tractor, barely breathing. She'd had to manhandle him into their car herself, and drive him to Dubbo's big hospital.

We got to the hospital, and found Mrs H surrounded by anxious friends. There were tears when she and Ellie embraced.

Only minutes later a doctor called to us with the news we dreaded. Mr H was dead.

⁎⁎⁎

During the next few days, we learned that Ellie's parents had decided to retire from the farm he managed within the next few months. They planned to return to their favourite area, around Molong, where they wanted to buy a house, preferably with an acre or two of land. Max, that is Ellie's brother Max, still struggled with his health and found that running his farm accountancy business was now too demanding. Therefore, he'd decided to go with them. A move by Mrs H and Max was now going to be necessary quite soon.

Ellie and I agreed that the two of them should come and live with us, at least temporarily.

'Plenty of room,' she insisted. 'In fact, our house will otherwise be very quiet, with Max (Jnr) going off to uni next month.' It made sense to me. Mrs H was easy going, and I looked forward to spending time with my best mate Max.

Before anything else was contemplated, we had the funeral to endure. I'd been to too many funerals while serving in the RAAF, after accidents during training and action in New Guinea. I remembered what an impact Dad's funeral had had on me all those years ago, and I dreaded this one now. The only mitigating factor was that Mrs H wanted Ellie's dad to be buried at Molong, his favourite place on earth, and where he'd be among old friends. I anticipated catching up with people I hadn't seen in years. Twenty two years in fact. It suddenly dawned on me that I hadn't been back there since 1955.

We all have our limited time on Earth and life goes on when we leave it. That doesn't lessen the immense hole left by the death of someone close. We would never see Mr H again. That fact was hard to come to terms with. It was a big hole for me, a chasm for Mrs H, Max, Ellie, and the boys. We stayed at the Narromine farm all week, helping Max and Mrs H with packing and tidying up loose ends, then drove to a motel in Molong for the funeral.

By 10am it was already hot, and most people had the sense to dress suitably for the funeral at Molong's Church of England church. I had one light grey suit I kept for official occasions, and it was of such fine wool it wasn't too uncomfortable in the heat. A few of Mr H's older friends wore heavy woollen suits, probably their only formal wear, and they wilted in the sun as we waited to enter the church. Even in the simple black dress she wore, Ellie looked amazing. The boys surprised me with their hair being neatly combed, (for once), and their clothing conservative, instead of their favoured semi-wild look. I was proud of my family, as I knew Mr. H had been. We greeted people as they arrived, and it staggered me that so many had come. I was surprised to find that I recognised quite a few of them. The church was over-flowing.

Mr H had not been a church goer, but he was a believer. The minister had known him well, and therefore was able to give a personal view of his life. It was a brief but moving service.

Ellie had organised with a local caterer to provide refreshments at the hall alongside the church. I'd been out of the lives of Molong people so long that I'd been worried that it was going to be difficult making small talk. In fact, it was uplifting, as they treated the Hetheringtons and myself as if we had never left. Stories were swapped, local news brought up to date, and old friendships rekindled. I guess that is one of the benefits in growing up in a small community.

As people began to drift off after more than an hour, one lady approached me tentatively. I couldn't place her initially.

'Ricky,' she said, 'You probably don't remember me. I'm Mandy Simms.'

I didn't recognize her face at all, and it took me a few seconds for the name to jog my memory. 'Of course, Mandy. High school. It's been a long time,' I said lamely.

'It has, and I know we've all changed. Look, I hope you don't mind me asking you a personal question, but I often wondered why you just disappeared from us all, back in 1955?'

'Yes, twenty-two years ago, Mandy, but I'm surprised you recall the year?'

'When you fell out with Lyn, I thought you'd be quite a nice catch. I batted my eyelids at you a couple of times, but you didn't even notice. Then you left town without a word to any of us. Why? You left your beautiful farm to Mavis Doak!'

'It's a long story, Mandy, but in a nutshell, Dad never left a will. Mavis got the lot, and I only discovered that after working on the farm for over a year after Dad died. When I did find out, I was so shattered that I just couldn't stick around.'

Mandy looked stunned for a second, and then leaned in close to me. Cautiously she said 'but that can't be right, Rick. Your dad left everything to you, with provisions for you to look after Mavis!'

I shook my head. I was wondering how this person could possibly know anything about my dad's will. Then I said 'I know that was his intention, Mandy, and he told me he'd written it in a will, but it turned out he never got around to putting it on paper. But why…'

Mandy glanced around, then satisfied no one was too close, again leaned towards me and said 'Rick, your father DID leave a will…'

'Sorry Mandy, but how would you know…?

'I typed it up, that's how I know. I worked for a while for Mr Wilson, the old skinflint. I was his secretary for about two years, and I can tell you that you were left the farm AND enough cash to pay death duties, and then some. Mavis was to have the use of the house plus keep for as long as she wanted, but everything else was yours. I remember it well. I thought it made you quite a catch for a girl like me.'

I don't know how long I stood there without speaking. My brain was working overtime though. Eventually I stammered 'Mandy, it's probably of no use now, but would you be prepared to go to a solicitor and write out a declaration to that effect?'

'Of course I would. But why wouldn't it be of any use?'

'Well… this is all a bit of a shock, Mandy, so maybe I'm not thinking too clearly… but I'd imagine that without proof, without WRITTEN proof, I doubt that what you say now proves anything.'

'If it helps, Rick, I can even tell you who witnessed your father's signature. Remember that Wilson's office was above a pair of shops? One was his own real estate office, and the other was Robert McDonald's pharmacy. It was Rob himself who came upstairs and witnessed your father signing his will. He did that regularly for documents requiring a witness.'

I rocked back on my heels. I began to think that maybe this wasn't some memory trick that had fermented in Mandy's mind over twenty-two years. The enormity of the betrayal by Mavis struck me, as did the consequences if I could find proof of Mandy's claim. I stammered 'Ttthanks a million, Mandy, I'll call on him tomorrow.'

'Oh Rick, by the way, I guess that you know that Wilson married your ex-step mother, AND he bought the farm next door that the Hetherington's used to manage. He bought it for himself, through his own agency, and the rumour is that he paid about half the going price for that type of land. The widow of the owner just accepted his valuation. She didn't know any better.'

***

We had planned to return to the Narromine farm early the following morning, but I asked Ellie and Mrs H if we could delay the journey for a couple of hours. I was waiting on the doorstep of McDonald's Pharmacy when it opened at 9am.

'No, sorry, Rob retired just a few weeks ago. I'm the new pharmacist. Joan is my name. Can I help?'

'Not really, Joan, but thanks. Can you give me Rob's home number, or give me his address?'

'Well, I can, but Rob and his wife have just left on a six-month round-the-world cruise. They've gone to Sydney. I think their ship leaves tomorrow.'

Hastily I wrote down all of the details of Rob McDonald's trip that Joan could give me. I then raced back to the motel, gathered up Ellie, Mrs H, and the boys, and headed off to Narromine. It was 86 miles, and we made it in just under an hour and a half. Thirty minutes later I was unlocking the 337's door at Narromine airport. At one pm I touched down on Runway 29 at Bankstown Airport, and by 1.15pm a taxi that Ellie had organised picked me up from the flight planning office in Airport Avenue. Thirty minutes later I was at the reception desk at the Hilton Hotel, in Sydney's Pitt Street.

The receptionist wasn't very helpful. All she could do was ring Mr and Mrs McDonald's room and leave a message. I waited in the lobby all afternoon. At 8pm I felt a touch on my shoulder. I must have fallen asleep in the big leather chair. An elderly gent, white haired, about six foot two but of slender build and slightly stooped, was standing beside me.

'Mr Richards is it? You wanted to see me, urgently I'm told. I'm Rob McDonald.'

Rob showed me into the room he and his wife shared. Under the circumstances, they were very gracious, as they were repacking suitcases in preparation to boarding a cruise ship the next morning.

'Yes, I often witnessed signatures for Mr Wilson's clients. I knew your father. I knew him for many years. I do remember signing his will. I have no idea what the provisions of the will were, but I most definitely remember witnessing his signature on it.'

'Rob, would you be prepared to sign a declaration to that effect?'

'Of course I will. I'll write it up tonight, and I'll find a JP to witness it first thing in the morning. I can post or fax it to wherever you want.'

At 10pm a taxi dropped me back at the airport, and at midnight I touched down at Narromine in the 337. Ellie picked me up herself. It had been a long and emotion-charged day, I was dog-tired, but still found it hard to sleep.

***

Ellie and I stayed at the farm for a few more days while we finished packing up the Hetherington's furniture and other belongings. Ellie, Max snr and Mrs H set off in the Hetherington's private car, while I flew home with the boys. Ahead was another period of upheaval, as Max Jnr finalised his preparation to go to Sydney, and Max snr and Mrs H settled in. We had a big house, and though all four bedrooms were full, (the boys temporarily sharing), we were comfortable.

It was two weeks later that Max Jnr left, driving off in his own car. Meanwhile, I had received the statutory declaration from Rob McDonald. I made copies of it and the one from Mandy, and flew in the 337 to Orange airport. I had a hire car waiting there, a brand-new Ford Fairmont sedan. I was on the road by 11am.

It was only a thirty-minute drive from Orange airport to Kittyhawk, Dad's old farm. I hadn't been there for over twenty years, and I expected changes. What I saw staggered me. The sign at the gate had faded and cracked, so much so that the name 'Kittyhawk' was barely readable. The two hundred metre driveway to the homestead, once fenced neatly on both sides, carefully mown, and with rows of healthy shade trees, was unrecognisable. Now, fences were broken, the grass long and dry, and the few surviving shade trees drooped in the heat. It was suitable preparation to seeing the house. The once regularly painted weatherboard was faded, and bare in patches. The corrugated iron roof had rusty streaks, and the guttering had rusted through altogether. One window was broken. The lawn, once lush, had ceased to exist, as had all but a remnant of the garden.

I pulled up at the back gate, which was hanging off its bottom hinge. As I walked towards the back door of the house, the screen door swung open with a bang. A scraggly looking women stood there. She was middle aged, had a thin face, her hair was unkempt, and she wore a stained floral dress. 'Yeah, waddya want?'

I stopped and stared for a moment. I couldn't believe the degradation of the house, nor its occupant. 'I'd like to speak to Mavis or Phil, please.'

She turned and yelled back into the house. 'Phil. Get out here. Some bloke in a fancy car wants ta speak to ya.'

She disappeared back into the house, allowing the screen door to swing shut with a bang. I heard low voices, then a minute later Phil appeared. He hadn't aged well in the intervening years. His dirty singlet barely covered his beer gut, which also strained his equally dirty pyjama pants. He hadn't shaved for a few days. His hair was tousled, and the way he rubbed his eyes led me to believe he'd been asleep. He woke up quickly enough though, when he recognised me. He sneered. 'What the fuck are you doing here?'

I'd intended to be polite and calm. The combination of shock at seeing the state of the place and its occupants was too much. 'I've come to kick you out, Phil. I want you out by the end of the month.'

Phil laughed. 'In ya dreams, ya wanker!'

'I can prove the farm was left to me, Phil. I'm taking it back. Go and pack your bags.'

Phil's sneer changed to a scowl. 'You're trespassing. Get off the property before I throw ya off!' With that, he reached behind and picked up a baseball bat that had been leaning against the inside wall. I was prepared to fight him if necessary, but not at an unfair disadvantage. So, I retreated. As I did, I noticed the sheds and stockyards were neat and tidy. I drove along part of our old boundary, and I could see a healthy wheat crop growing in one paddock, the filling seed heads waving as one in the slight breeze. In another, plump sheep were grazing on green pasture. The difference between the house and driveway and the rest of the farm was stark.

Next stop was Hetherington's farm. I now expected to find both Reg Wilson and Mavis there, but another surprise was in store. The old house had always been beautifully kept by the Hetheringtons, but it had been renovated and extended since I last saw it, and looked magnificent. The lawns and gardens around it were also extensive and manicured. Beyond the house area, a long and high colorbond shed housed what looked like a brand new green and yellow John Deere tractor, and matching auto header. Expensive equipment.

I caught Wilson as he was leaving the back door. He wore charcoal pin-striped trousers, white shirt and blue tie. A matching jacket was over one arm, and he held a briefcase with the other. He stopped mid stride.

'Well, young Richards,' he boomed. 'What the hell are you doing here?'

'Hello to you too, Mr Wilson. Actually, I have something to say to both you and Mavis. Is she at home?'

'Mavis doesn't live here anymore. What could you possibly have to say to either of us? I'm in a hurry, so I'll ask you to leave.'

I can't remember having been asked to leave anywhere before, but twice in a morning was certainly a record.

I responded, 'I'd hoped to be a bit more civilised about this, Mr Wilson, but I'll get to the point of my visit. I have proof that my father did leave a will, one that you prepared and that was signed by Dad in front of witnesses. I believe that you and Mavis conspired to destroy that will, and to steal Dad's property from me.'

Wilson paled visibly, and took a step back. In seconds he regained his bluster.

'Proof? There is no proof. This is bullshit!'

'No, it's not. I have a declaration from the person who typed the will, and one from the person who witnessed Dad's signature. I also have Dad's original letter saying that he'd signed a will, prepared by you, that gave the farm to me.'

'Hearsay. Just hearsay. Twenty-four years ago, your father was going to come in and prepare his will. Never happened. Now get out of my way.'

As I reluctantly turned to walk back to the hire car, I noticed the curtains twitch. A woman's face appeared momentarily, a face I didn't recognise. I surmised that perhaps Wilson had already traded Mavis for a younger model. That gave me an idea.

Wilson had called my bluff, and I was now by no means certain that I had enough on Wilson to bring him down. But perhaps I had a third shot. What had happened to Mavis, and where was she now? I had to take a punt. I drove straight to Wilson's real estate agency in town. A friendly young lady asked if she could be of assistance.

'Oh yes,' I replied. 'I've just been visiting Reg out at the farm, and as I was coming into town, he asked me to drop something off to Mavis, but I've mislaid the address he gave me.'

'No problem. I'll write it down for you.'

The address led me to a small but pleasant house two streets back. It had a picket fence, and gate to match. A brick-paved path led across a neat lawn to a portico, where the front door had glass panels set in a stained-wood frame. I knocked, and immediately heard footsteps. Mavis opened the door, and froze. She wore a simple but elegant dress, and her hair was neatly done, just as it always was. She'd obviously aged in the twenty-odd years, but hadn't put on much weight, and still looked good for a woman in her 70's. Her hand flew to her mouth, and it took a few seconds for her to recover.

'Rick, oh my goodness.' She hesitated, then said 'You'd better come in.'

We sat in her immaculate kitchen, around a small table that had just two chairs. Windows opened to a tiny back garden, which consisted of a square of perfect lawn, bordered by colourful flower beds.

She didn't ask why I was there. Somehow, I think she already knew. So, I said very little, sensing that Mavis wanted to open up to me. But first we had to go through the ritual boiling of the kettle. The tension rose as fast as the kettle's head of steam. Then she began, without any prompting by me.

'Ricky, I've been a fool. A silly old fool. Look what it has got me. I'm here alone in this little house, Reg has the farm with his new fancy lady, and Phil is a drug addled no hoper with an equally drug addled girlfriend. I did the wrong thing by you, and I'm so, so sorry.'

She sniffed, and buried her nose in her handkerchief. I waited, then I just said 'Mavis, I know about the will.' Mavis didn't look up, but her shoulders slumped, and she nodded. After a minute, she composed herself and looked into my eyes.

'Ricky, I know that there's no excuse for what we did, but I always knew you'd do well, no matter what the obstacles. I also knew that Phil was not cut from the same cloth. He needed help and guidance. When your father died, I hoped that you and Phil could work together and make a good living for us all, but Phil's laziness and obstinacy put paid to that. Then Reg Wilson started hanging around. I should have realised that the land was the attraction, not me, but I was lonely. He proposed not only marriage, but also a scheme to take the farm away from you. He said Phil would be appointed manager, and would ultimately own it. I know it was wrong, but I went along with it.'

'So, you knowingly went along with hiding the existence of the real will?' Mavis nodded, her eyes downcast.

'So, where does Hetherington's farm come into it?'

'Well, as you know, the owner died, and his widow trusted Reg to sell it, and he did. He sold it to himself at less than half its real worth. The widow lived in Sydney, and didn't know any better. Reg and I moved into the house there, and I supervised the renovation. Then I found out that all those late nights at the office were actually with his new girlfriend. Twenty years younger, and a real gold digger. We agreed to split. I got this house, and an agreement that Phil could live in your old house forever. Now he has that, he's forgotten about me. I haven't seen my own son in months. Meanwhile, Reg has done very well by combining your farm with Hetherington's, with the economy of scale, and he has a very good manager. Brian Stubbs is his name.'

I sat and pondered. I really didn't know what to say. There was silence between us as Mavis got up and put the kettle on the stove for a second cup. Then she said 'you know, that time with your father and yourself, and before Phil got into real mischief, was the happiest time of my life. I really was heartbroken when your dad died.'

I believed her. I sighed and said 'Well, these revelations are interesting Mavis, but the evidence that I have about Dad's will is unlikely to be of any real value, so I guess the crook wins.'

'Would it help if I write a declaration, confirming everything I've just told you?'

'It might. I'd be grateful if you'd do that, but nothing short of the original will…'

Mavis interrupted, 'Oh, I think Reg destroyed that, but I did keep a certified copy. Reg told me to burn it, but I never did. Wait a moment, I'll go and get it for you.'

***

Armed with Mavis's declaration to add to those I already had, plus of course an actual certified copy of Dad's will, I couldn't wait to confront Wilson again. As I drove out of town and towards the two farms, I saw him passing in the opposite direction. He was driving a white Mercedes Benz 220 sedan, a type of car you didn't often see in the bush, otherwise I probably wouldn't have taken any notice. I pulled over to do a U-turn, but had to wait for half a dozen cars to trundle past. By the time I got going again, the white Merc had disappeared. I drove through the main street, and cruised around the parallel streets both east and west of it. There was no sign of the car, or of Wilson. I went back to his real estate shop, poked my head in the door, and spoke to the same friendly young lady.

'Thanks for the address. I saw Mrs Wilson, and delivered the package. I just need a quick word with Reg. Has he come in from the farm yet?'

'No, not yet. I think he had an appointment in Orange. I doubt that he will be back until late this afternoon. He might even go straight home from there.'

It was 2pm. A few doors down was a café, so I ordered a toasted ham and cheese sandwich and a flat white coffee. As good as I'm sure they were, I barely tasted either. I couldn't wait to confront Wilson again, and I was getting nervy. At 2.30pm I decided to drive to the farm and wait. It was a long two hours parked just up the road from the gate, but right on 5pm I saw the Merc approaching. Wilson didn't even glance in my direction. As soon as he drove through the farm gate, I started the Ford and followed him into the neatly paved driveway. I stopped beside his car, just as he was getting out.

'You again. Didn't I tell you to fuck off my property?'

'Not yours much longer, MISTER Wilson. Perhaps you should take a look at this.' I handed him a stapled bundle of documents. On top, was a copy of Dad's will. Wilson blanched, and sank back against his car.

'Fraud, Wilson. A clear case of fraud. You have two choices. The first is to try to bluff it out. I think I have enough evidence to recover what's mine, put you in jail, and destroy your reputation around here forever. I'll also sue you for every dollar you've made off Dad's farm in the last twenty-two years. The other choice is to hand it over to me, as it should have been in 1955. Not only that, I know that you cheated the original owner of what used to be Hetherington's. Half the going rate, I'm told. You took advantage of a trusting old lady. So, you'll sell it to me for $1, as a going concern. That means all the equipment on the farm stays. I want all the paperwork completed within a week. Here's my card.' I threw it at his feet. Wilson attempted to straighten up, but almost fell when he tried. The back door of the house opened, and the woman I had seen earlier, a pretty middle-aged blond, called out.

'Reg, are you alright?'

He turned and snarled 'Go inside, you stupid bitch.'

She did. Hurriedly.

'Nice,' I said. 'By the way, when you do the transfer of

ownership for the Hetherington farm, make it out to Max Hetherington and Ellie Richards, not me.'

I turned to go, and realized that another man was approaching from the farm sheds. He was middle-aged, with close-cropped dark hair, and neatly dressed in khaki work clothes. He looked quizzically at Wilson and me. I stuck out my hand, he hesitated, but then took it. I said 'I'm Eric Richards. I guess you're Brian Stubbs, the manager here?' He nodded.

'I'm your new boss, Brian. Mr Wilson has just sold me this farm, with all stock and machinery, and is also vacating my farm next door. I like the way you run the two places, so I'd like you to stay. My first instruction is for you to supervise Mr Wilson's departure. Make sure he doesn't take anything that doesn't belong to him.'

I turned and got back into my car. As I drove away, neither had moved: Stubbs was staring open mouthed at me, and Wilson was slumped, head down, against the front wheel of his Mercedes. My next stop was Dad's farm. Well, now MY farm. I heard yelling as I got out of the rental car. The argument inside stopped when I banged my fist on the back door. A few seconds later Phil kicked it open. Unsurprisingly, he had the same filthy singlet and pyjama pants on, and still hadn't shaved.

I stepped back, and said 'Go and see Wilson. He'll tell you to clear out. Don't take anything but your personal belongings. If you are still here at the end of the month, I'll have you evicted.' For once Phil was lost for words.

Before heading home, I called in to see Mandy Simms and her husband. They were both delighted that Mandy had played a crucial part in Reg Wilson's downfall. As I left them, I noticed an ageing but well-kept Ford Falcon wagon in their carport. I called at Molong Ford and arranged delivery of a brand-new, top of the line Falcon wagon, registered to Mandy Simms. At the local travel agency, I arranged a two-week all-expense paid trip to Singapore and Malaysia for a family of two adults and three teenagers.

An hour later I was advancing the C337's throttles on Runway 11 Orange airport, to fly home. I couldn't wait to tell Ellie the news.

∗∗∗

Ten days later I received a bulky envelope in the mail. Included in it were a contract for sale of the Hetherington farm, made out to Max and Ellie, and the title deeds for Dad's farm. There was no note. I had Ellie sign the contract, I added a cheque for one dollar, and sent it to Wilson by return. On the first of the month, Ellie, Max Snr, Mrs H and I boarded the 337. Of course, Ellie now knew all the details, and we'd told Max and Mrs H about my farm's recovery. We hadn't said a word about the property they'd lived on for twenty years.

Ellie couldn't help herself. She told them 'Ricky has found a place for you at Molong. I think you'll like it. It's just like your old farm, only better. If you like it, you can move in anytime.' They were excited, and pressed for details. I fobbed them off. Ellie had a twinkle in her eye when she added, 'I know the owners really well, and they'll give you guaranteed tenancy for life. If you're happy with it, it will be your home forever.' Max looked puzzled, but said nothing.

They were even more intrigued as each turn of the road brought us closer to our valley. They were curious when we passed Kittyhawk Farm, and speechless when we pulled up outside the now fully renovated homestead at their old farm. When Ellie handed a copy of the title deeds to Max, he couldn't speak, and had tears in his eyes. The only sadness came when Mrs H said how much Mr. H would have loved to have come back to his favourite place on Earth.

We stayed a couple of hours. Max and I met with Brian Stubbs, who was a bit reserved initially, but warmed to us when I explained how I saw things being run.

'The two properties have different ownership, but I'm sure Max will agree that they be run as one. We'll have a management committee of three, that's the three of us. Max can't do much heavy physical work, but he's a whizz at keeping up with latest trends, and at keeping the books. I enjoy a bit of physical work when it's needed, and I'm good with machinery. I'll make sure all the equipment is maintained properly, and repaired quickly when necessary. I have other interests that will keep me occupied for at least half my time. Otherwise, you run the combined farm as you see fit. You've done a great job for Wilson, and I have no doubt you'll do the same for Max and me.'

Ellie and her mother were happily planning new furniture, curtains, and carpets, but I dragged them away. It was time to go to Kittyhawk. I feared that the takeover there might not be so simple. As we entered the driveway, we saw a ute and trailer parked at the back door, both loaded with suitcases, household goods, and furniture. Leaving the others in the car, I walked up the litter-strewn path towards the back door, but it flew open, and Phil's partner came down the step, clutching a handful of clothes. As she passed me, she gave me a verbal spray that would have made a sailor blush. I said nothing. She climbed into the mud and dust-streaked ute, and then yelled 'He'll be out in a minute.'

I waited. I could hear movement in the house. Finally, Phil emerged, wearing what looked like the same singlet, and some equally dirty track pants. He didn't look me in the eye, but said, 'it's all yours, now, you bastard!' He smiled when he got into the ute. He started it, stalled as he let out the clutch with a jerk, restarted, then took off down the drive at twice the sensible speed. As he and his partner shot past our car, I saw Phil grinning at Ellie. His girlfriend looked far from happy.

I turned to enter the house, but Ellie ran to me and grabbed my arm. 'Wait Ricky, I don't like this. Something's wrong. He's made it too easy.' She had fear in her voice.

'Come on Ell, he's just left. What can he do now?' I turned again to enter, when she cried 'No, WAIT Ricky...'

'Okay Ell, come back to the car, we'll talk about this.'

The car took most of the blast. Thankfully, nobody had opened windows on the left side of the car, which was sprayed by broken glass and pieces of wood. A sheet of tin lazily spiralled down and landed on the bonnet, cracking the windscreen. The blast hit me in the face, but nothing solid did. Ellie had just sat down and closed the passenger door, and I'd gone around to the driver's side. My only injury was singed eyebrows, but Dad's house ceased to exist in an instant.

When the dust settled, Ellie was sobbing in my arms. 'Don't worry Ell, we'll build a new house. A fresh start. It will be the best house in the district, I promise.'

We had no choice but to call in police, who in turn called in forensic experts from the fire brigade. They found evidence of explosives. It wasn't easy to fill in the accident report to Avis Hire Cars. Phil was arrested a few days later, and his girlfriend immediately spilled the beans, claiming that Phil set the explosive timer, wanting to destroy the house as we arrived. She added that she didn't think he planned to kill anyone.

Maybe that wasn't in his original plan, but killing me, and possibly Ellie, would have been a bonus to him. He would have succeeded, if Ellie hadn't had the premonition. Because there was no evidence that Phil had planned to kill anyone, he was not charged with attempted murder. The raft of charges he was convicted of included malicious damage and illegal use of explosives. He was given five years in gaol, but absconded from bail, and the last we heard was that he was still on the run.

CHAPTER 21

Back to Molong.

The new house was built just a few hundred metres away from the site of the old one. It was on a slight rise, so its panoramic windows took in the sweep of the paddocks, and the hills behind. Cathedral ceilings made the new house spacious and airy. Our Tamworth property and TAAS were sold at substantial profits, and we moved back to Molong in December 1977. Peter (Jnr) had finished high school in Tamworth, and was enrolled at Sydney University, to begin in March of the following year.

The local vet practice was delighted to offer Ellie a part time job. She spent the rest of her time making a beautiful, warm, and comfortable home of our stylish new house. The boys were established on their career paths, Max Snr and Mrs H were very happy in their old house just up the road, and the combined farms were soon running like clockwork.

I spent half my week with Max and Brian on the farm. Suddenly, I had everything I could have wished for. I was fifty four years old, and for the first time in my adult life I had not a care in the world, I had time to relax. That was wonderful, for about a fortnight. Then I decided that I needed a project.

✳✳✳

The Cessna 337 lived in a hangar at Orange airport, for which I paid rent. We now had 4,000 acres of land, and enough of it was suitably flat to make an airfield. A few fibreglass boundary markers and a windsock created it, and periodic heavy grazing kept the grass suitably low. I commissioned an Orange-based building company to erect a hangar big enough for two aircraft the size of the 337, though at the time I wasn't sure why.

Now I had the 337 to look after, and I could go flying without the 30-minute drive to Orange Airport. Sweet!

About the same time all this was happening, there was a very significant move to allow ex-military aircraft to fly in Australia. Previously, only aircraft that had been civil-certified were able to fly in private hands, and the vast majority of military aircraft didn't have civil certification. They didn't need it. That meant that the wonderful array of military aircraft left over at the end of WW2 had no value other than as scrap metal. Within a few years, within Australia, many hundreds of perfectly good fighters and bombers from the RAAF and USAAF, some brand new, were either cut up for scrap, melted down, or buried where they stood.

The list included Spitfires (by the hundred), F4U Corsairs, Kittyhawks, B-24s, Mosquitos, Beaufighters, Wirraways, Ansons, even Mustangs. Most types were rendered extinct, and only a few types were left with one or two survivors, usually saved by farmers wanting hydraulic bits and pieces, or to make a chicken coup from the fuselages. I only wished that I'd had the wherewithal to grab a few Spitfires and Kittyhawks during the late 1940s and early 1950s, before the smelters claimed them. I'd be a rich man now!

Anyway, I'm getting ahead of the story. During the 1970s a group of aircraft enthusiasts approached the Civil Aviation Authority to create a new category for limited use of ex-military aircraft by civilians. The primary purpose was to display them to the public at airshows and other special events. Probably thinking that it would lead to a few derelict airframes being restored by aircraft nuts, the CAA came up with regulation ANR 108A. There were quite stringent limitations on the origin of aircraft it covered, and how these restored aircraft could be used, but for the first time in Australia, civilians COULD own and operate some really interesting aeroplanes.

Word spread quickly amongst the small community of military aviation enthusiasts, that this new regulation was coming. At that same time, the RNZAF decided to retire its fleet of venerable North American AT-6 Harvard training aircraft. The reader might remember that we sprog pilots had no great love for the Wirraway, but the more refined US-built Harvard was a really great aeroplane.

The day I read that the RNZAF Harvards were up for disposal, I began chasing contacts in New Zealand. Alas, I was already too late. Collectors around the world had picked the eyes out of the RNZAF offering. All that was left were a few parts that nobody wanted. I cursed my luck. Then in September 1979 I received a trunk call, (cell phones hadn't yet been invented), from New Zealand.

'Hello Mr Richards, it's Murray here from the Historical Society here in Auckland. How are you today?

I'd had no idea who the guy was, but I did know that every second NZ male had the first name of Murray.

'Er, fine thanks Murray. It's Rick by the way. Where did you say you were from?'

'The Aviation Historical Society. It's in Auckland. I'm the president. I got your name and number from RNZAF disposals. They tell me that you were after a Harvard, but just missed out.'

'Yes, Murray. That's true. Why, has one become available? Has a purchaser pulled out?'

'Er, not exactly. What we do have is an instructional airframe. It has been used to train apprentice engineers on the innards of a Harvard. It has no prop, no engine or engine cowls, and there are a few internal bits missing. The good news is that this airframe has been in a building for many years, and hasn't been corroding out in the weather, like some of the flyers have. Would you be interested?'

'Well, Murray, I could be. I guess it depends a bit on just how much you want for it?'

'Rick, to be frank, nobody here is interested in it, as several complete aircraft are going to stay in New Zealand. We're just keen to get it off our hands. What would you say to $4,000, and we'll arrange freight to Sydney?'

And that is how I acquired my own Harvard.

NZ1007 arrived in Sydney as deck cargo aboard a cargo ship. She was a 1942 model, and she sat on her wheels, but the outer wing sections came separately. She looked a bit forlorn, with a blank firewall where the engine and all its ancillaries should have been. Nevertheless, we had the fuselage and the wings trucked to the farm on a low loader, and so NZ1007 took up residence alongside WWC (the 337), in my new hangar. I began collecting parts immediately. The Pratt & Whitney R1340 engine came from the USA, the prop from the Zimbabwean Air Force, and lesser bits from the UK and USA. Under the supervision of one of my engineers from Tiger Aerial Services, who'd retired to the orange district, (luckily for me), I began to overhaul parts and reassemble the old warbird.

In 1980 regulation ANR108A was at last promulgated, and Australia's warbird industry took off running. Instead of a few derelict airframes being restored, as the CAA expected, ex-military aircraft from all over the world began to appear. Very soon the NZ Harvards were flying here, and they were followed by CJ6 trainers from China, Mig fighters from Poland, Sea Furies from Iraq, and so on. Before too many years passed, Australian audiences could watch a variety of exotic aircraft from WW2 through to the Cold War era being displayed in the air.

My NZ1007 took a bit longer. It emerged from the hangar, pristine, in 1987, registered as VH-HAR. She more than fulfilled my expectations. Demanding enough to make a good flight satisfying, but for a pilot with my level of experience, a delight to fly. Just sitting in its no-nonsense cockpit took me back years. I revelled in its military looks, feel, and even smell. Over the following decade, Ellie and I travelled to all the mainland states in Hotel Alpha Romeo, meeting fellow enthusiasts and simply enjoying a freedom that is hard to describe. Life could not have been better.

∗∗∗

Trouble has a habit of finding one, no matter how hard you try to avoid it. In my case, I thought I was just about immune from any problems, but I was brought down to earth with a thud one morning in 1992. I was about to turn 70, sitting contentedly in our sunroom with a cup of coffee, when an early morning call came, I answered, expecting it to be from one of the boys wanting to wish me a happy birthday. Instead, it was Frank Burns, our local police sergeant.

'Hello Rick, I'm sorry to bother you on this fine spring morning, but I have some news that I should pass on to you. As you know, Phil Doak has been in gaol in Sydney for the last five years. You'll recall that we didn't catch up with him until 1987, ten years after he blew up your house. He's now been released from gaol, and he's turned up at his mother's. She's a very old lady now, and has no control over him. We're concerned that he is going to cause trouble in the district, and, as he has expressed a desire to get even with you, you could be his first target.'

The very last thing I wanted was another run in with my ex step-brother. But worse was yet to come. I had another call from Frank a week later.

'Rick, I know that you had a few problems over the years with your neighbour, old Bert McLaren. Well, Bert was an old bastard, and not too many people in the district mourned his passing. Now his son William owns the place, and he's a lot worse.'

'Yes, Frank,' I interrupted, 'We've had niggling issues with Bert for as long as I can remember, and I had a run in with William on the school bus when I was a kid. He's never forgotten it. I also know that since Bert died and William's been running their place, he's been making a few more enemies along the way.'

'Yeah, I'm afraid so. He's been a bully all his life, and now that he runs the biggest property around, he thinks that he's king shit!'

I laughed. 'Frank, I keep out of his way, and I think he knows better than to start trouble with us. I reckon he's just a bag of wind in reality.'

'Rick, I hope you're right. There are two things you should know. Apparently, William is a fan of American western movies. He's taken to wearing a Texan-style hat, elastic-sided boots, and a six-gun.'

'A six-gun? You mean a Colt revolver?'

'Yeah, that's right. It's only a .22 calibre, not a .45 thank God, and he can only wear it on his own property. It's illegal outside. But, he has a short fuse, and so I'd be a bit wary of ever getting into a confrontation with him.'

'Okay Frank, I appreciate the warning. I've got no intention of crossing paths with William again.'

'Now the second thing you should know, Rick, is that your old mate Phil Doak has landed a job at McLaren's, and from what I'm told, he and William are now like peas in a pod. I worry that they'll feed off each other, and we might all be in for some shenanigans. I thought I should warn you.'

***

Weeks went by, nothing untoward happened around town, and I began to think that Phil had probably learned his lesson, and would stick to the straight and narrow in future. I couldn't see what harm the unlikely pairing of William and Phil could do to me, either. Then strange things began to happen, things that reminded me of the niggling problems Dad and I had had with Bert McLaren decades earlier.

We checked our water troughs every day to make sure the stock always had water. We found one trough with a jammed ball cock, so that no water flowed in. The trough itself had been drained, and as it was a hot December day, the sheep in that paddock were milling about, looking for water. Some were obviously distressed already. It was a simple fix, but if we hadn't checked that day, we could have had losses overnight.

A gate was opened the following night, allowing stock to get into a wheat paddock, just days before we were due to harvest it. In those few hours in the paddock, the sheep trampled enough of the crop that our yield of grain was well down on expectations. For several nights running, either odd gates were left open, or the fences along the main road were cut, allowing stock to wander out onto the road.

Initially I'd thought that Brian, Max, or myself were getting forgetful, but forgetful people don't accidentally cut fences.

It dawned on me that perhaps Phil and probably William had begun a campaign of harassment. We began a nightly patrol with good torches, at odd hours so that no intruder could predict our movements. Not once did we find any intruder, but for some weeks, the incidents ceased.

Like most farmers, we had a letterbox that was a 4-gallon drum mounted on a post. A slot was cut on the roadside end, and a hole big enough to put your hand in on the farm side. Whoever went past the letterbox after midday would collect the mail. Ellie did exactly that one Monday afternoon, and leaped back in fright. Some bastard had caught an eastern brown snake, broken its back with a stick so that it was unable to move, and had placed it in our letterbox. Ell was very lucky not to have been bitten by the deadly reptile.

That was the last straw. I killed the unfortunate creature, put it in a sack, and drove to the McLaren farm. It was knock-off time and both William and Phil were standing with a couple of farm hands outside their massive machinery shed. Phil looked typically dishevelled, and I couldn't help but wonder how he'd ever landed a job with anybody. William had put on a lot of weight since I'd last seen him, and most of it was in a beer gut hanging over his wide belt and holstered Colt revolver. That and the outsized Texan hat with its curled-up brim made him look ridiculous. I would have laughed if I hadn't been so angry.

I walked up to the group, and all turned towards me. Not a word was spoken. I dumped the still-writhing reptile at William's feet. I turned and walked back to my car. As I opened the door I called out, 'Enough is enough, boys. You've had your fun. The next one who tries a trick like this might find out what it's like to have a shotgun shoved up his arse!'

***

Every farmer needs a gun, in case of feral dogs attacking stock, or sometimes having to put down injured animals. We had Dad's ex-army Lee Enfield .303, and Max, always a good shot, had had plenty of opportunity to improve his marksmanship in the army. I'd had a .22 rifle as a kid, and the RAAF had taught me how to use other firearms. So, after these odd incidents started, I'd gone into Orange and bought an FN-Browning 12-gauge semi-automatic shotgun. It had a 5-shot magazine, and I bought for it a selection of cartridges, including some with size 10 "bird shot" pellets. I also bought a powerful 12v spotlight that worked off a small motorcycle battery we could carry.

That night Max (Snr) and I reinstated our nightly foot patrol, taking particular interest in our boundary with the McLaren farm. Nothing untoward happened for a couple of weeks. On the third Monday after my visit to McLaren's farm, Max and I left our patrol until midnight. We first covered the boundary fence, then checked out the paddocks along the road. It was now two in the morning, and we'd had enough off stumbling around in the dark. About to quit for the night, Max said 'Let's do one more stroll along the boundary. I've got a funny feeling that tonight's the night.'

We heard some nervous bleating, and it sounded like it was coming from our side of the fence. Max saw a flash from a torch, and so we approached quietly. Although the night was very dark, we soon surmised that the neighbours were in the process of rounding up some of our sheep, to herd them through a cut in our shared fence. We could just make out five individuals. We got ourselves into position, half way between them and the cut fence, and I turned on the spotlight, catching William in the centre of the powerful beam.

Blinded, he hesitated momentarily, then wheeled around and drew his revolver. I'm not sure if he really intended to hit one of us, but the puny pops of the .22 were not at all intimidating for anyone who'd been under fire in WW2. Neither Max nor I even flinched. Beside me, Max calmly shouldered the .303, held steady aim for about two seconds, then expertly blew the torch that was in William's left hand to smithereens. The boom of the heavy rifle echoed around and rolled through the hills behind us. Our five opponents were frozen, open mouthed, and silent. Then Max reloaded. The click-clack of opening the chamber to eject the spent cartridge and pick up a new round as he slammed the bolt home broke the silence. It was a chilling noise to someone at the wrong end of a .303 rifle.

As one, five men bolted towards the cut in the fence in abject terror. William dropped his beloved six-gun along the way. The four others dropped their torches. We had positioned ourselves so that in turn they presented their backsides to us, at a range of about 25 yards. I had five beautiful targets, and five shotgun shells in the Browning's magazine. I didn't miss one. When the echoes of the five shots had died, we could hear high-pitched squeals, and a couple of heavy thuds as the intruders ran head first into obstacles they now couldn't see.

After picking up William's abandoned gun, and making a hasty repair to the fence, we went back home, where Ellie was waiting in high anxiety. She hadn't heard William's shots, but like everyone else within a couple of miles, she had heard our replies. To Max and me the whole incident suddenly seemed hilarious, and we had great difficulty in relaying events between howls of mirth.

'Just picture the McLaren kitchen right now,' I cried. 'Five rough blokes, pants around their ankles, waiting in turn to have shotgun pellets picked out of their arses.'

Max chortled 'Who do you reckon got it worse, the blokes who copped the pellets, or the poor sod who has to pick them out?'

***

The following day Max and I took William's Colt to our workshop, heated the barrel cherry-red, then bent it into a neat U-turn. Later, on my way into town to report the incident to Sergeant Burns, I dropped the modified Colt into McLaren's letterbox.

I omitted some minor detail in my report, that being that Max had shot a torch out of William's hand, and that I'd peppered their backsides with birdshot. I knew I was pretty safe, as I was quite sure William and his cronies would not make a complaint, not wanting to admit to being bettered in that way.

Stock theft is a pretty serious offence, and Frank Burns was quick to inspect the crime scene. It didn't take a forensic genius to see what had gone on. The fence had been cut, and William's men had dropped their tools and torches on our side of it in their haste to escape. William and Phil were charged and convicted, but with my agreement, received suspended sentences. William also had to surrender his permit to carry a handgun. I figured that with jail terms hanging over their heads, they'd behave themselves in future. I think it did have that effect on Phil. He'd already had five years in gaol, and wasn't keen to go back. He disappeared entirely from our lives as soon as his court case was over.

I put the whole matter behind me, as I thought commonsense would tell William to forget his dented pride, and concentrate on running his farm. Ellie kept telling me that Phil and William where different fish altogether, and she feared that one day William would again seek revenge.

Peace did settle over the valley, and as time passed, the serious side of our fight faded in our memories. Somehow word got around about the birdshot wounds, and the story became part of local folklore. I even heard that behind his back, William was now known as "birdshot Bill." Perhaps he did get wind of the nickname, because on the odd occasions we crossed paths in town, he let me know that as far as he was concerned, bygones were certainly not bygones.

✳✳✳

In the spring of 1992, I was asked to take my beautiful Harvard to an airshow at Scone. It was a two-day event that was well advertised, so I guess it was common knowledge that I'd be away for the entire weekend. I left Ellie, Max, and Brian to round up the sheep in preparation for the shearing that was to begin on Monday.

The airshow, a biennial event, was busy as usual, and on Saturday was packed with members of the public. My afternoon slot was for a 5-minute solo aerobatic routine. On the Sunday morning briefing the weatherman predicted that a front, approaching from the south, would arrive about midday, and it would bring strong winds followed by heavy rain. The officials running the show made some hasty changes, which were announced at the 8am briefing.

'Gentlemen, if the forecast is accurate, we'll have to close the airshow at midday. To give the paying public something for their money, we are going to begin the show at 9 o'clock instead of 10, and will move all the headline acts into that first three hours. If we can go past noon, the support acts will fill in then. We suggest that as you complete your displays, you might consider heading home, weather permitting. Rick, would you mind opening the show for us?'

That suited me just fine, because I'd then be able to help with the round up at home later. I took off, did the usual loops, rolls, and steep turns, and at five minutes past nine, I made my final fast pass down the runway. I then pulled up, climbed to 6500 feet, and set course for home.

The part of the Great Dividing Range just south west of Scone is high and rugged, but once I was passed the peaks I relaxed and enjoyed the easy trip. I stayed at 6500 feet until about fifteen minutes out from my airfield paddock, made the appropriate radio calls, eased off power, and began the descent. At five hundred feet above the threshold, I turned base, dropped gear and flaps, and pulled the power right back.

At that moment, just half a mile off to my left, I spotted something very strange. A mob of our sheep were being herded towards the shearing shed yards. I could see our dogs working around the flock, and I could see Ellie on horseback. What was unsettling was that I could also see a stranger on a motorbike, rapidly approaching Ellie from the rear. It didn't look right.

In a few quick movements I applied power, pulled HAR out of its descent, and raised both flaps and undercarriage. As airspeed built up, I racked the machine into a steep turn, and aimed at the motorbike rider. I couldn't be certain, but in my gut I knew who it was: William bloody McLaren.

Suddenly Ellie's horse sprang from a canter into a gallop. I could see why: McLaren was shooting at her. I could see puffs of smoke as he bore down on her. He must have obtained another pistol, and this time it was not just a .22 calibre. This time he meant business, and both Max and Steve were too far away to intervene. But I wasn't. If ag pilots are good at anything, it is judging their height above the ground. I pushed the throttle and pitch levers all the way forward, and made a curving dive on McLaren, levelling out just behind the speeding motorbike. My aim was to take his head off. I was playing for keeps this time.

McLaren's Yamaha dirt bike was fast, but HAR was much faster. The roar of its angry P&W 1340 was also much louder than the bike's screaming engine. He suddenly heard it, glanced behind, and instantly realized that he was about to be taken apart by a propellor that was rotating at 2200 RPM. He swerved, lost control, and both bike and rider tumbled end over end in a tight embrace. As I pulled up steeply, I looked back to see that the bike was in pieces, and William lay still. He had broken his neck.

The inquest absolved me of all blame. He had apparently

shown signs of mental disturbance, his farm was in financial trouble through mismanagement, and according to one of his trusted stockmen, he blamed all his troubles on me. The loaded .45 Colt revolver, three shots gone, indicated that William meant to kill someone that day.

∗∗∗

Six months later the McLaren property was sold to a syndicate from Sydney, and on my recommendation, they appointed Brian Stubbs as their new manager. I had to find a new guy, but it was worth it. Brian would serve them well, as he had us, and he had earned his promotion. Now the whole valley could run in harmony. It had taken a long time to achieve that, but nobody appreciated the result any more than Ellie and I did.

Our combined farms prospered. Our boys had their own families by now, and both had settled in Sydney, just over three hours' drive on the improving roads. We added a bunkhouse to accommodate everyone, and enjoyed getting both Richards and Hetherington families together during the boys' regular visits.

In 1994 Mrs H passed away peacefully, aged 96. Max was bereft, but a year later met an old school friend who had married, moved away, then returned to Molong when her husband died. Max and Sheila were married in 1996, both aged 74.

At that time of my life, many told me it was time to hang up my flying helmet. I disagreed. Instead, I decided it was time for me to convert to jets. I'd done the research, and discovered that after the breakup of the Soviet Union in 1991, desperate for US dollars, some ex Soviet states were selling off military hardware. Included were a number of Aero Vodochody L-39 two-seat advanced jet trainer / light attack jets, and the prices were hard to believe. For as little as US$50,000, you could buy an aircraft that new, had cost the Soviets many millions. The L-39 was also a brilliant aircraft: it was well designed, well built, and it looked fast even when standing still.

I chose carefully, picking a 1985 model that had only 1,200 hours total time, and a brand new engine. It cost US$90,000. It was shipped to Sydney, trucked to Bathurst, and assembled there, as my strip was way too short for the jet. It cost another A$120,000 to have the aircraft fitted with modern western radios and instruments, including GPS, assembled, and stripped to bare metal for repainting. We repainted it into a genuine Soviet air force scheme, complete with a red star each side of the tail.

Conversion to jets took me a few hours under the capable instruction of a friend of mine who was a Qantas captain and keen warbird enthusiast. Jets are a bit different to prop-driven aircraft, but I revelled in the new experience. So, if you are out on the western plains of NSW and you hear a jet high above, probably looping and rolling around the cumulus clouds, look up. If it's a sleek jet with a red star on its tail, give it a wave, because it could be Ellie and me.

ABOUT THE AUTHOR

Jeff Muller is well known in the Australian aviation world. He has served as a director for the Aircraft Owners and Pilots Association, the Australian Warbirds Association, and the Historical Aircraft Restoration Society. He is a member of the Gliding Federation of Australia.

Jeff and wife Liz have owned and operated six aircraft, from a racing class glider, to an ex-Soviet jet.

For many years Jeff has flown warbird aircraft like the Harvard, Zero replica, and L-39 jet in airshows in Queensland, NSW, and Victoria.

His first novel, *The 36th Eagle*, was published in 2022.

He is a retired scientist, and has lived in the beautiful Hills District of Sydney for many years.